DEATH AT THE WEDDING FEAST

A John Rawlings Novel

Deryn Lake

This first world edition published 2011
in Great Britain and in the USA by
SEVERN HOUSE PUBLISHERS LTD of
9–15 High Street, Sutton, Surrey, England, SM1 1DF.
Trade paperback edition first published
in Great Britain and the USA 2012 by
SEVERN HOUSE PUBLISHERS LTD.

British Library Cataloguing in Publication Data

Lake, Deryn.
  Death at the wedding feast. – (A John Rawlings mystery)
  1. Rawlings, John (Fictitious character) – Fiction.
  2. Pharmacists – England – Fiction. 3. Great Britain –
  History – 18th century – Fiction. 4. Detective and mystery
  stories.
  I. Title II. Series
  823.9'14-dc22

ISBN-13: 978-0-7278-8086-4 (cased)
ISBN-13: 978-1-84751-384-7 (trade paper)

Typeset by Palimpsest Book Production Ltd.,
Falkirk, Stirlingshire, Scotland.

In memory of my grandparents
Wilhelm Friedrich Walter Koehling and Petrea Charlotte Koehling,
with my love.

One

It was a delicious moment. In fact probably the most delicious moment of his life. And then John Rawlings, with an impish sideways grin, remembered a particularly special occasion in his misspent youth – an incident involving Sukie, his master's kitchen maid – and decided that this was the second most delicious. Be that as it may, nothing could take away from his present triumph. He had at last, after many years of experimenting with water, finally succeeded in carbonating it. The bottle he was holding up to the light and peering at contained sparkling bubbles.

After his father had moved to Kensington John had set up a rather large piece of equipment in his home in Nassau Street. Barrels and vats, boxes and a handwheel, to say nothing of a mass of pipes joining one piece of machinery to another, now dominated the room at the back formerly used for cleaning boots and Sir Gabriel's shoes, together with the knife cleaning area. Sir Gabriel's best pair, worn on special occasions only, had glittering pinchbeck heels; however footwear more ordinary, with shining buckles and bright rosettes, sufficed the great old man for everyday wear.

It had taken John Rawlings, apothecary of Shug Lane, Piccadilly, some years to perfect his bid to get water to sparkle like the heart of a fountain. But now, judging by the bottle he held at eye level, he had finally succeeded. It bubbled, it fizzed, it glinted and gleamed. It was everything he had ever hoped for. Before he allowed himself a wild cheer of joy the Apothecary went to his log book and entered the date.

'19th February, the Year of our Lord 1768, today I succeeded in Carbonating Water.'

Then he let out a whoop of joy and executed a few nimble flights of foot before rushing into the main house holding the bottle on high. Unfortunately there was not a soul in sight to share his celebration. In fact the Apothecary felt a decided shiver at the emptiness of the place. Disconsolately, he went into the library and sat down. But a few seconds later he leapt to his feet again and rushed into the hall.

A footman came hurrying up. 'Are you going out, Mr Rawlings?'

'I'm thinking about it. At what time is Miss Rose expected back?'

'Miss Rose is taking tea with Miss Thomas and should be returning at about three o'clock.'

As Miss Rose and Miss Thomas were aged six and seven respectively John gave a crooked smile. 'I see. Well, would you be kind enough to tell her that I have gone to see Sir John Fielding but will be back in time to say goodnight to her.'

'Very good, Sir. Will you be walking or shall I get you a chair?'

'The walk will do me good, I believe.'

So saying, John Rawlings left the house in Nassau Street and strolled through the crowded and noisesome ways towards that tall, thin house in Bow Street where Sir John Fielding held court daily. Tucked in an inner pocket of his greatcoat was a bottle of that saucy, bubbling liquid whose secret he had finally found.

As he walked, John thought. Thought back to his early life and the time he and his mother had begged on the streets of London until kind Fate had brought them into the path of Sir Gabriel Kent. Quite literally because his coach had run them down. But oh what goodness, what gentleness John had felt when Sir Gabriel himself had lifted them up and taken them back to his house. Later, much later, when he had taught her to appreciate the finer things of life, Sir Gabriel had married John's mother. But their happiness had been all too brief for Phyllida Kent had died giving birth to his daughter and all Sir Gabriel's love and affection had transferred itself to John.

Avoiding a group of beaux, walking along and chattering, swinging their great sticks and elevated on heels of a somewhat alarming height, the Apothecary thought of himself when he had been younger and was grateful that he had never been as silly and empty-headed as the mincing little gang he had just passed. Mark you, he had not led an exemplary life, far from it. His love affair with the actress Coralie Clive had caused quite a scandal in its day, not to mention a few other little peccadillos gathered on the way. But then he had reformed at the time of his marriage, only for his sweet Emilia to be snatched away from him and for him to be left – a desirable young widower – in charge of bringing up his daughter, Rose.

Not that that, he thought as he swung into Long Acre, had seemed to stem the ladies' interest. But the Apothecary, being such a contrary creature and by nature loving that which always seems a little unobtainable, had declared his passion for a totally unsuitable female. A woman older than he was, a woman titled in her own right, a woman of decided views and wayward beliefs. In other words the beautiful and capricious Marchesa Elizabeth di Lorenzi.

The very idea of her stopped the Apothecary dead in his tracks. Pulling out his fob watch he stared at the date which ran inside the minute hand in a small but clearly marked ring, enclosing, in their turn, a blaze of stars, a moon and an exceedingly grumpy-looking sun.

'My God,' whispered the Apothecary, under his breath, 'she's due very soon. I must get to Exeter as soon as possible.'

For the fact of the matter was that he had left the Marchesa well and truly pregnant, getting very large and moving much more slowly than usual about her great house. But for an hour or two he must devote his thoughts to Sir John Fielding, the blind magistrate, the powerhouse who brought law and order to the city of London as best he could. Patting the bottle of sparkling water that nestled in his pocket, John made his way to the Public Office in Bow Street.

Being somewhat late in arriving, John was surprised to hear the sound of loud laughing coming from the courthouse. Pushing his way through the crowd of members of the *beau monde*, who had made it the height of fashion to see criminals brought to justice, he found a seat in the second row of the gallery and peered to see what was causing the merriment.

Standing at the bar, pertly dressed and with a fashionable hat tipped over one eye, was a soncy lass standing all of five feet tall and most attractively rounded, her mass of blonde hair cascading down in ringlets from beneath the brim. She had obviously said something to Sir John – who sat in a high chair at the far end, the space between being occupied by John's friend Joe Jago, who sat at a writing-desk, bewigged and with a snow-white cravat at his throat, at the shorter end of the bar also facing the prisoner. He was grinning broadly, the Apothecary could see.

'Well, Sir John,' the young woman was saying, 'he was handsome like, though not as well set-up as yourself, Sir.'

The magistrate, clearly in a good mood, retorted, 'I hardly think that that is the point at issue, Miss West. You are charged with visiting the Covent Garden theatre and there relieving a gentleman of the contents of his pockets. What have you to say to that?'

'I say that I might have pushed against the gentleman – accidental like – but take something from him? Why, Sir John, I'd as soon jump from a cliff.'

So saying she curtsied to the gallery as if she had been making a great speech. They whistled and catcalled back at her – John included – forcing the magistrate to call for silence.

'Miss West,' he said severely, though John knowing him as he did, could not help but notice a slight rumble of laughter beneath the ferocious tone, 'would you be so good as to turn out your pockets.'

Miss West curtsied again, this time in the direction of the magistrate who obviously could not see and had to lean forward to hear what it was Joe Jago whispered to him. He smiled to himself as he heard the words and the Apothecary, observing, thought the Blind Beak might have a soft spot for his naughty defendant.

From the back of the court Beak Runner Smallwood stepped forward.

'Is the arresting officer present?' boomed Sir John.

'Here, Sir,' Smallwood replied.

'And the complainant?'

'Here, Sir,' answered a smartly dressed gentleman who had been sitting on the end of the front row of spectators.

'Now, Miss West,' said Sir John deeply, 'your pockets, if you please.'

These particular articles of clothing were carried underneath the skirt and Miss West drew them out with a glimpse of garter and bare thigh which she allowed to remain on display for a few seconds before lowering her dress once more. A terrific whistle rose from the gallery and Sir John banged his gavel.

'Silence!' he roared, but the *beau monde* were in no mood to be hushed and continued to murmur softly one to the other.

Aware that she now had the full attention of everyone present, Miss West slowly fished in her pocket and drew out a guinea, some silver and, finally, a white carnelian stone.

'That's mine,' called Mr Wilson, the complainant.

Miss West flounced her skirt prettily and exclaimed, 'Why no, Sir. I think you must be mistaken. That stone has been in my possession for the last three months.'

Mr Wilson went very red and turned to the magistrate. 'I swear to you, Sir John, that that is my carnelian.'

Fielding's black ribbon, concealing the useless eyes that were beneath it, turned in Wilson's direction. 'You have a witness here who can swear to that?'

'No, Sir, but I can bring along such a person tomorrow. The lapidary who cut it and would know it anywhere.'

'That should prove excellent.' The blind gaze turned towards the saucy Miss West who was blowing kisses to the gallery. 'You must spend a night in the cells, Miss West. The rest of your case will continue tomorrow morning.'

'Oh I don't mind at all, Sir John,' she chirruped. 'They're nice and clean compared with some others I could mention. Besides, you're treated like a human being there.'

'Thank you for the kind words,' answered the magistrate, a definite smile on his humorous mouth. 'Take her below, Smallwood.'

And with a bob of her perky hat Miss West disappeared from their view.

There was one more case to listen to. A low personage in the gallery at the Theatre Royal, Drury Lane, had actually stood up and made water on the crowd below. Orange peel and rotten fruit theatregoers were used to, but this was going too far. He was knocked to the ground by two burly patrons and handed into the custody of Runner Raven, who happened to be on duty in the theatre that night. His case was now coming up before the Blind Beak, who dealt with him sharply.

'What you did was disgusting and I can only conclude that you were drunk at the time. But that is no excuse. I sentence you to hard labour in Newgate. Your term to last one year. And you are to serve the full twelve month of it. Now get him out of my presence.'

He banged his gavel hard and nodded at Joe who stood up and said, 'The court rises.'

There was the usual pandemonium as the *beau monde* tried to get out but Sir John and his assistants had already left by a door leading them to the stairs that led to the private apartments, while the shackled prisoners behind were taken – with many moans and groans – to the cells below.

John thought that the pretty Miss West was not going to have such a comfortable night of it as she had envisaged.

As he climbed the winding staircase he thought that he would be a rich man if he had been awarded a guinea for every time he had clambered up them, and he also thought of the powerful person he was to meet at the top. For Sir John Fielding, whom he had known for so many years and in so many different circumstances, was a force to strike fear into the breast of even the most hardened criminal. From outside the door to the salon on the first floor he could hear the sound of laughter and his heart lifted in his chest. Knocking politely, he heard the magistrate's voice call out, 'Come in,' and, doing so, John entered a den of comfort.

It was a bitter February with a cheerless world outside, but within the Blind Beak's living room there was a scene of great jolliness. Joe Jago, wig removed so that his bright red curls shone in the firelight, was helping Sir John to remove his shoes and put on a pair of comfortable old slippers. They were laughing together like the great friends they were. Joe, seeing a movement in the doorway, looked round and winked and John, signalling with his hands, asked him not to tell the Blind Beak that he was there. Thus he had a moment or two to quietly watch the legendary magistrate.

Though the great man looked older he was in fact still only forty-seven years of age. For once he had removed the black ribbon hiding his eyes which, half-open as they were, showed themselves as being of a greenish-blue. His wig, however, of long flowing white curls was still on his head, surrounding his handsome features and giving him a gentle look, very different from his demeanour in court where villains quailed before him.

Bodily, Sir John was starting to put on a little weight. Probably, John thought, because of sitting all day in the court-room and getting little exercise. But for all that he still presented a fine figure, standing well over six feet and with impressive shoulders and a strong chest. Even though he knew the magistrate could not see him John bowed, a habit of his the origins of which were lost in the mists of time.

'Good evening, Sir John,' he said.

The magistrate jumped a little and it took him a second or so to place the voice. Then he said, 'Mr Rawlings, what a wonderful surprise. What brings you here on this bleak February afternoon?'

'Sir, I wanted to share with you my triumph. I have finally succeeded in carbonating water.'

Joe Jago, having finished putting on the Blind Beak's slippers, rose to his full height and seized John's hand which he pumped up and down with great vigour. 'Oh well done, Sir. Well done. I know you have been working on this project for some years.'

'It seems like all my life. But, Joe, I've done it! I've put *joie de vivre* into water. Look.' And John produced from his greatcoat pocket a bottle and held it up to the light of the candles which were just being lit by an unobtrusive manservant.

'By Jove, Sir. It sparkles like diamonds.'

'You're right, Joe. That's a true description.'

And putting his arms round the clerk, the Apothecary danced a small jig of triumph. The Blind Beak meanwhile had taken the bottle from Jago's hand and was feeling it carefully with his long and finely shaped fingers.

'These are one of the few moments when I wish that I could see,' he said, and sounded so sad that John bounded to his side.

'But you shall be the first to taste it, Sir.'

'Will I? Do you promise me that?'

'Only I have done so before you, I swear.'

'Then fetch three glasses, Miller, and we'll drink to Mr Rawlings's famous brew.'

'Very good, Sir,' and the manservant left the room.

Because the downstairs floor of the Bow Street house was entirely taken up with the Public Office – the courtroom being built in the grounds of the house next door – the layout of the premises was somewhat unusual. Sir John's parlour was on the first floor – and very comfortable he had made it too – with the kitchen quarters on the same level. The family rooms and living areas were on the floor above, the bedrooms above these. And way at the top of the house were the rooms where the servants slept. Small wonder, then, that Number Four, Bow Street towered above its neighbours.

The manservant returned with the glasses and John poured a measure into each. Handing the first to the Blind Beak, he and Jago stood respectfully awaiting his opinion. The magistrate raised the glass to his lips, which he then smacked together with appreciation.

'By God, Sir, you're made a delicious brew here. I'll warrant this will sell well to the public.'

It was Joe's turn. He quaffed the lot. 'I'll second that, Mr Rawlings. You have produced something quite delicious.'

John looked at them both seriously. 'You really think so?'

'Indeed we do,' the magistrate answered, speaking for them both.

The Apothecary frowned. 'I had not thought of actually *selling* it.'

'But you must,' insisted Sir John. 'It is unique – at the moment. Take an advertisement out in the *Morning Post*. Say that bottles of the liquid are available from Two, Nassau Street. Do, Mr Rawlings, I beg of you.'

'Well, I . . .'

'Come on, Mr Rawlings,' said Joe, holding out his glass for a refill, 'get in first before some other rascal does so.'

John laughed. 'How can I refuse? I shall go and see my

father and take him a bottle – and get his opinion at the same time.'

'And give my kind regards to the great old man.'

'And mine too,' added Joe, and once more drained his glass.

Two

Arriving in Kensington on the following morning, driven by his personal coachman – Irish Tom – and travelling in the coach with his monogrammed initials on the side, now grown a little the worse for wear, John, having disembarked, made his way briskly to his father's residence in Church Lane, walking up the pathway that ran between the High Street and the gravel pits. His father had moved to the country in 1758, nearly ten years previously, and had now reached the great age of eighty-six. Yet the years had laid their hand upon him kindly; his golden eyes still gleamed with full cognition of all that was taking place, his voice was firm and strong with none of the quavering tones of the very elderly, his hearing, though fading, was still sharp enough. Let in by a footman, John stood in the doorway of the library and gazed upon the old man, glasses perched upon nose, avidly reading the newspaper, a cup of coffee standing on a small table at his side.

It was true that age had not faded Sir Gabriel and yet there was an air of fragility about him. He had never been overweight but these days there was a new thinness, a new angularity to his features. His hands, John noticed before he spoke, had a rustling quality about them as they turned the leaves of his beloved newspaper.

'Hello, Sir. How are you on this fine day?'

Sir Gabriel looked up in a gleam of gold. 'John, my boy, I never heard you come in.'

'I was on tiptoe,' John lied, and hurried forward to stop his father rising and to give him the huge kiss that the good old man merited.

'Well, now, this is an unexpected pleasure. It must be at least two weeks since I last saw you.'

It was nearer three but the Apothecary did not correct him. 'You are looking well, Father. Are you continuing to take the physick I made for you?'

'Of course I am, my dear. Otherwise I should not be in such fine health.' Despite John's protestations he stood up and walked, stiffly but for all that with an excellent carriage of his shoulders, to where stood a sherry decanter and a selection of glasses.

'Now, Father, you should let me do that.'

Sir Gabriel turned on him an amused smile. 'My good child, the more you try to remove tasks from me the more senile I shall become. Let me, I beg you, continue to do anything of which I am still capable as long as my poor wits will allow.'

John immediately felt contrite. How many times in the past had he lectured the families of those growing older to let the elderly continue in their small duties as long as flesh would allow? And now here he was trying to remove his own father's from him. He accepted the sherry and waited quietly until Sir Gabriel was seated once more before he said anything further.

'Sir, I have brought you a present.'

The grand old man sipped his sherry and raised a shapely white brow. 'Oh? And what might that be?'

'This,' said John, and produced a bottle of carbonated water from his pocket.

Sir Gabriel looked at him. 'My dear, you've done it. You've succeeded in getting the bubbles in.'

'I have indeed – and not before time either. Do you know I went to see Sir John Fielding – who presents his highest compliments to you, as does Joe Jago – and they both insisted that I should market the stuff. In other words bottle it and sell it to the public at large.'

His father rose once more and fetched himself a clean glass. 'Pour some for me, my boy.'

John did so and his father quaffed deeply, then looked up with obvious surprise. 'I never thought to admit that I actually enjoyed the taste of water, but I can truly say that this is excellent. I shall have some more.' And he held out his glass for a refill.

The Apothecary smiled broadly. Sir Gabriel had always had a preference for fine wines and the very best champagne, and now here he was asking for more water. This was praise of the highest order.

'So what do you think I should do about selling it?' he asked.

'You must indeed comply with what the Blind Beak suggests. Remember that he has one of the highest intellects in the land, and I personally would follow his advice without question.'

'But there is a problem, Sir.'

'And what is that?'

'Elizabeth is due to deliver her child shortly and I promised to return to Devon to be with her. If I am to set this up as a business I shall need an able assistant.'

Sir Gabriel stroked his chin thoughtfully. 'Indeed you will and I fear that I am a trifle old for such an adventure.'

John suppressed a smile.

'What about young Dawkins?'

'But he is married now and lives in Chelsea.'

'Yes, and to that lovely girl Octavia. Do they have any offspring yet?'

'Not that I've heard.'

'Well that is beside the point at the moment. Why don't you contact him and ask him if he would like to come back and work for you?'

'I could try, I suppose.'

'My son, unless you try nothing will ever get done. If he says no he might suggest a friend of his. Who knows?'

'Father, you're right. I leave for Devon in five days' time. I shall go and see him tomorrow. In fact it would be easier to travel from here. May I stay the night with you?'

'And what of Rose? Will she be safe?'

'She has a whole household at her command. I am sure she will manage just for one night.'

'Then nothing would give me greater pleasure than to have your company for the evening. Perhaps after we have dined we might have a game of cards.'

'But you nearly always win, Sir.'

'Perhaps tonight, my dear, your luck will change.'

It was feeling very cheerful that John made his way to Chelsea next morning. Normally he would have gone by water, enjoying the experience of the river's flow and watching the wildlife that teemed along its banks. But today he felt that Irish Tom should earn his wages and consequently set out in his coach. The best route was along Chelsea Road and Tom took this, passing the fields and outbuildings of Avery Farm, to say nothing of the pretty farmhouse nestling comfortably amongst its barns. Beyond the next outcrop of trees there was a junction of tracks and Tom bore right, avoiding the stretch of water crossed by Chelsea Bridge. This waterway was fed by the Thames and the bridge was little more than a wooden structure, hardly fit for a coach to venture on. Passing down Strumbelo, then Jews Row, Tom finally turned into Francklins Row and drew the coach to a halt outside a very smart apothecary's shop. Nicholas Dawkins and Octavia had obviously done very well for themselves.

Nick's surprise on seeing his old master enter the shop was profound. His pale features flushed bright red, his large eyes widened and he almost cut his finger on the suppository-making machine.

'Mr Rawlings! What a pleasure to see you. Come in, come in.'

He went to a door behind the counter, opened it and called up, 'Octavia, Octavia. Can you come down? Mr Rawlings has arrived to see us.'

'I'll be there in a moment,' answered a distant voice.

'I think you'll find Octavia somewhat changed,' said Nicholas, his eyes very twinkly.

John guessed at once that she was pregnant, then immediately thought of Elizabeth. He must journey to her next week at the latest. He loved her too much to let her face what was bound to be a difficult labour on her own.

The door flew open and there stood the girl with eyes the colour of blackberries, still as ravishingly pretty as when the Apothecary had first seen her. And, as he had thought, she was in the early stages of expectant motherhood and this only served to make her look more attractive than ever. She pulled a wry face at John and laid her hand on her stomach.

'As you will see, Sir, I am now two people.'

He went to her and whirled her round. 'And if I may say so, Madam, it becomes you enormously.'

'Enormous being a most suitable word, Mr Rawlings.' Octavia burst out laughing. 'Oh, how very good it is to see you again. And how is your dear father?'

'Spry and as fit as his age will allow.'

'That is all I wanted to hear.'

'And he sends his fondest love to you both. You wait till I tell him your news. He will be as thrilled as I am by it.'

'The talk is all of babies round here,' Octavia said delight-edly. 'Nick and I think it must be the freshness of the air.'

John smiled, thinking to himself that the air in Devonshire was not doing too badly either. But Octavia was still prattling.

'You must stay to dinner. Say you will. And Irish Tom can dine in the kitchen. It will be just like old times.'

The Apothecary looked pleased. 'I should be delighted. As long as I am not interrupting anything.'

'Then it is agreed.'

And Octavia hurried back through the door and towards the kitchens to speak to the cook.

It was indeed like old times. John was placed opposite his former apprentice while Octavia sat at the head of the table, her honoured guest on her right. In this position the Apothecary was able to study Nick, going back in his mind to when he had first seen him in Bow Street, taken in by the kind-heartedness of Mr Fielding, as the Magistrate had been in those days. The boy had been nothing much more than a starveling; tall, eyes the colour of a Thames barge sail, limping, yet with an indefinable air about him. They had called him the Muscovite because of his proven Russian heritage. And John, knowing that he was being manipulated but rather enjoying the feeling, had agreed to take on this not very desirable boy as his apprentice.

Just before they had sat down to eat he had given Nick and Octavia a bottle of his carbonated water to try and they had both uttered cries of delight on tasting it.

'This is just the sort of thing that would sell well at Ranelagh Gardens,' she had exclaimed.

'Which brings me to an interesting point which I shall tell

you while we dine,' John had answered. And now he said, 'Our old friend Sir John Fielding thinks I should sell my bottled water to the public. Thinks I should take out an advertisement in the newspapers to that effect.'

'And so you should, Sir,' Nicholas answered.

'But there lies the difficulty, Nick. Without giving up my apothecary's shop, without changing my life completely, I could not manage it. If this business is to be run then it must be run well. Indeed I was half hoping that I could persuade you to come back to Nassau Street and do it for me. But now, seeing how happy and settled you are here, I realize that would not do at all.'

'I would gladly take on sales direct to Ranelagh Gardens,' Nick answered earnestly. 'But return to London I could not do. Octavia and I are happy in the country and want our child born in this pleasant place. You do understand?'

John nodded. 'Of course I do. It would be a lot to ask of anyone.'

Octavia spoke into the silence. 'I might know someone.'

Both men turned to look at her.

'Who?' asked Nick.

Ignoring him, Octavia turned to John. 'This would be an entirely suitable person to run your business and I think make a success of it. I feel certain of that or I would not be recommending them.'

'Who the devil is it, Octavia? Why are you being so mysterious?' asked her husband.

The blackberry eyes twinkled. 'Because, gentlemen, I speak of a woman.'

'A woman?' said John, flabbergasted.

'Yes, Sir. I am talking about a certain Mrs Jacquetta Fortune.'

There was a long silence broken by the Apothecary, who said, 'At least she has a lovely name. Can you tell me more about her?'

'Gladly. I meet her on my morning walks which I take as part of my daily exercise. She is young, pretty and of good family but, alas, Lieutenant Fortune died at sea and now she is living most frugally. She takes in sewing to make ends meet.'

'But how does this equip her to run a developing business? A business that might grow very big?'

'Because, my dear John, before she married Jacquetta used to run her father's business for him.'

'Then why isn't she . . .'

'Wealthy? A sad tale but a true one. Her father owned a shipping company – that is how she met Lieutenant Fortune, a sailor on one of his ships. The old man trusted her completely with all aspects of his affairs but when she told him that she wanted to marry – and to whom – he fair had apoplexy. He offered her all kinds of inducements to continue and she agreed – but as a married woman. To get to the point, she gave up all for love. Her father cut her out of his will and she received the bag. And then her husband was killed!'

'A calamitous story indeed.'

Two blackberry eyes were regarding him seriously and a pretty white hand laid itself on his arm. 'John, say that you will at least meet her. I beg of you to give her a chance.'

Nick spoke up. 'I can endorse what Octavia has just told you, Mr Rawlings. Jacquetta is truly an orphan of misfortune. But she has not been broken by it. She is like a sail before the wind in her determination to survive.'

John paused, considering, then said, 'You must understand that if I agree to meet her there is no guarantee that I will employ her. I might not think she would be capable of running such an enterprise as mine. Or I might just not like her.'

Octavia opened her mouth to speak but Nick rushed in and said, 'That would be completely understood, Mr Rawlings. We shall arrange the meeting tomorrow morning if that would be suitable for you. Now, would you care to spend the night with us?'

'Thank you but no. I must return to Sir Gabriel. Though still very fit he is ageing and I know that he worries about me. I'll get Irish Tom to earn his keep, though I thank you for the offer.'

Octavia picked up her glass. 'Then I'll propose a toast. To dear John – you see I have got out of the habit of calling you Mr Rawlings . . .'

The Apothecary laughed.

'And the fervent hope that he takes to Jacquetta Fortune.'

'I'll drink to that,' added Nick. 'Here's to Mr . . .' He corrected himself. 'John,' he said.

Three

To say that she was slender would have been understating the case. The fact was that Mrs Jacquetta Fortune was very thin. Tragically so. The Apothecary could see at once the signs of food deprivation and suffering that recent times had brought on her. Yet there was a subdued loveliness about her; buried in her pinched and tragic face was a raw beauty that might one day bloom again. But this was most certainly not the day. She stood before the Apothecary like a ghost, dressed in a threadbare silver gown and a hat that had once been pink but which was now so faded that its colour had become indeterminate. Small wonder, he thought, that the kindly Octavia had taken the woman under her wing.

John sat silently, regarding Jacquetta. She reminded him vividly of a silver birch tree, from the colour of her hair downwards − for what hair he could see peeping beneath the brim of her hat was that glorious shade of blonde that looked touched by frost in certain lights, while her eyes were the soft green of spring. As for her body, encased in its silvery gown, it was sparse and inclined toward tallness. In other words, had Jacquetta been given a decent diet on which to exist and had not fate been against her at every turn, she could have been a charming and rather delightful woman. Every instinct in the Apothecary told him to give her the job on trial and see how it turned out.

He cleared his throat and broke the silence. 'You do realize, Mrs Fortune, that the work I have described to you will require a great deal of effort. There will be the placing of the advertisements, the bottling of the water − the secret of which I will entrust to my apprentice Gideon Purle − the bookkeeping regarding the orders and who has how many bottles delivered and to where, to say nothing of the banking of the money and the starting of a new account.'

She spoke for the first time. 'And where will you be while this happens, Mr Rawlings?'

'I have to go to Devon. I have some urgent business to attend to down there.'

How he had the face to say it and not blush he could hardly understand himself. But this was not the moment to go into the details of his private life, particularly with a total stranger. Thinking, despite himself, about newborn babies, he said, 'Do you have any children, Mrs Fortune?'

The poor woman looked even sadder. 'I lost a daughter, alas. Poor little girl, she lived only four hours and then she died. It was so tragic. My sweet little Justina . . .' A tear trickled out of one verdant eye and ran down her cheek. 'My husband never saw her,' she continued. 'By the time he returned from his duties she was gone, buried, a tiny grass mound in the churchyard.'

'I think you have been very brave in the face of your adversities,' said John.

'Do you?' she answered. And suddenly a smile came that was like sunshine lighting the Arctic wastes.

'Yes, I do. Now, can I get you another bun?'

They were sitting in the Chelsea Bun House, a small shop that was besieged on Good Fridays by thousands of Londoners demanding their Hot Cross Buns. But today all was quiet and John had thought it a reasonable place in which to conduct an interview. Really, he knew well, he should have done it in Nassau Street, sitting formally behind his desk. But to expect the wretched widow to find enough money to travel to London would have been too much to expect. So in his usual manner he had put her at her ease – as far as that were possible – by buying her coffee and a bun and looking sympathetic.

She answered his question. 'Yes, I would rather. Are you having one?'

John, who had been turning sideways before a mirror recently and wondering if that were just the tiniest bulge appearing over his stomach, knew that he should answer no, but to keep her company he nodded. 'Perhaps half, if you could help me out with the rest.'

Mrs Fortune ate slowly but heartily and after another cup of coffee seemed somewhat restored. She sighed and leant against the back of her chair.

'Mr Rawlings,' she stated, in as firm a voice as she could manage, 'I promise you that I can run your new business and make it a success. I was in sole charge of my father's company and had staff working under me, you know.'

'But in that case could you not undertake a business of your own? A milliner or a mantua maker or something of that sort?'

'Money makes the mare to go, Mr Rawlings. I could not raise the capital to start such an enterprise. My father cut me out because I loved Lawrence Fortune – and I did love him, oh so much – and he, poor soul, left me naught but a little accumulation of back pay. I am afraid that I have fallen on truly hard times.'

The Apothecary drained his cup to give him a moment to think. Should he give this pale shadow of a person a chance? But if he did not could he ever forgive himself? And then into his mind crept an image of Rose nodding her rose-red curls and saying, 'Oh come on, Papa.'

John put down his cup and turned to his companion. 'Very well, Mrs Fortune, I will give you a three-month trial period. Starting as soon as you can make arrangements to move into Nassau Street. I take it you have no objection to that? You shall have your own apartments and can eat with the family. The salary will be two guineas a month which will grow if the business is successful. How does that suit?'

Her breathing quickened and her eyes dilated, and one poor thin hand flew to her breast. 'I . . . I . . . don't know what to say.'

'Then say nothing,' John answered briskly, and went to the counter to pay the bill. He had long experience of women bordering on hysteria and knew that one of the most effective ways of treating them was to leave them alone. When he looked round he saw that Jacquetta had recovered her equilibrium.

She rose to her feet and dropped him a slightly stiff curtsey. 'I thank you from the bottom of my heart, Sir. I promise you that I will turn the carbonated water of John Rawlings into something famous.'

John smiled his crooked smile. 'That would be rather splendid. But I do not ask for that. Merely make a small profit and I will be satisfied. Now, will a month's salary in advance be suitable?'

A little colour came into her cheeks. 'More than somewhat. I was going to have to borrow the money from Nick Dawkins to move what pieces of furniture I have.'

'Well, that won't be necessary now, will it. And that concludes our business, I think. I shall send my coachman to you tomorrow with two guineas and you may use his services for the rest of that day. But now I must bid you adieu. I have a great deal to do before I leave for Devon.'

She curtseyed again, this time more deeply. 'Thank you for trusting me, Mr Rawlings.'

John gave a swirling bow and said, 'My pleasure, Mrs Fortune.' And he walked off towards his coach thinking that he was probably the biggest fool in the universe.

A brief call on Sir Gabriel on his way home, whose plea to stay the night John had to decline with much sadness, and he returned to Nassau Street to find his daughter within and anxiously awaiting his arrival. She had grown quite tall and was a striking looking child, with a marvellous complexion and that glory of rosy curls about her head. She was to be seven in April and John had arranged to send her to Madame de Cygne's Academy for Young Ladies situated in the country area of Kensington Gore. He had thought the air healthy and pure and had particularly liked the school's teaching of the French language, Madame de Cygne being of that nationality and very keen on instilling the correct pronunciation into her pupils. As well as French, of course, the girls were to learn English, with correct orthography, together with geography, embroidery and needlework, dancing, music, deportment and carriage, and basic mathematics. In fact as full and interesting a syllabus as any parent could wish for. John realized that the teaching of herbs and their various properties would have to be left to him in the holiday times. But the school also taught religious instruction, a subject that John was glad he would not have to impart to his child as he had not fully made up his mind on the matter.

They went into the library where a coal and wood fire had

been lit against the chilly evening and Rose climbed on to his
lap, putting her arms round his neck. But instead of snuggling
into his shoulder she held him at arm's length and stared into
his eyes. They were very beautiful eyes, which seemed to reflect
different shades of blue according to her mood. Tonight they
were vivid, the deep, rich colour of a Mediterranean sky.

'Father, I think you might be in danger,' she said directly.

He stared at her, quite shocked despite his casual expression.
'Why is that?'

'It's hard to say, really. But I keep getting this impression
of you being attacked. Do you have to go to Devon without
me?'

'My darling, you may come if you wish. But I really think
it is better if you do not. Mrs Elizabeth is about to give birth
to a baby brother or sister for you and there won't be a great
deal of time to devote to you. Besides, I have a woman moving
in in a few days' time. She is to run my new business for me.
I would be grateful if you could be here to look after her.'

Rose was silent for a while and then she said, 'All right, I'll
stay if it would please you. But Papa, be careful. In my head
I see danger coming.'

'From whom?'

'A horrible old woman in a brown dress and bonnet. Oh,
she's such an evil old creature.'

And quite unexpectedly the great eyes filled with tears and
she turned her head into the Apothecary's shoulder and wept
bitterly.

John cuddled her close to him, but his brain could not help
but take in what Rose had just said. He knew the child was
psychic, had known it ever since their eyes had first met and
she had smiled at him. And now he took her warning seriously, thinking as he did so that an old woman in a brown
ensemble with a bonnet to match was going to stick out like
a mason's maund to an apothecary. He muttered into her ear,
'I swear I'll look out for the old beast and give her a culp if
I should see her.'

Rose smiled through her tears. 'Promise?'

'Yes, I promise.'

'And can I visit the new baby quickly please?'

'I will arrange for Sir Gabriel to bring you down as soon as possible.'

She slid off his lap and looked at him, reminding him of a flower that had just been caught in a shower of rain.

'Come here,' he said very gently. She did so and he wiped the tears from her face with his handkerchief. 'Don't worry,' he whispered. 'Papa is used to taking care of himself. I promise not to let that old woman hurt me.'

Rose's eyes became motionless and staring. 'When you see her, lie flat,' she said quietly.

John could not help but grin at the thought of prostrating himself at the feet of every woman wearing brown that he was in future to meet.

His daughter reacted in a totally childish manner. 'You're laughing at me. I shall never tell you anything that I see again.' And with a loud stamp of her foot she ran from the room and pounded up the stairs.

John stared after her, shaking his head. He would obviously have to be more careful in future when his daughter warned him psychically of something.

Two days later Jacquetta Fortune, sitting with the carter who brought her few sad pieces of furniture, arrived at Two, Nassau Street. John, receiving her, was only glad that Sir Gabriel now lived in Kensington and was therefore unable to see the fragments of a married home carried in. On the ground floor he had cleared out Emilia's parlour, leaving in the harpsichord as it occurred to him that Jacquetta might care to play. Upstairs he had, in company with Rose's maid, revitalized one of the guest bedrooms, tactfully removing the bed as he felt quite sure that Mrs Fortune would be bringing her marriage bed with her.

He was not mistaken. The very first thing carried in by a sweating carter and a small-sized boy who looked as if he hadn't eaten for a week was the bed. They lugged it upstairs, Jacquetta following behind like a moth. But she exclaimed in delight when she saw the room and the pretty curtains that the maid had rescued from somewhere in the depths of the house.

'Oh, Mr Rawlings,' she said. 'How delightfully you have prepared it for me.'

'I merely ran an eye over the proceedings. You have Emily to thank for this.'

'Emily?'

'Rose's maid.' He changed the subject, thinking how wan she looked. 'Would you like a little something to eat? A pre-dinner entrée perhaps?'

'Thank you. I am rather famished.'

'Then come downstairs, do. I'll get the servants to prepare something. Besides you have to meet Rose.'

He offered her his arm, but his enquiry as to the where-abouts of his daughter was met with a servant's crisp reply that she was playing in the garden and was not coming in until five. John's banging on the French doors elicited no reply, and he was just about to step outside to fetch the naughty child in when Mrs Fortune stopped him.

'Oh, Mr Rawlings, leave her in peace, I beg you. Can't you remember how down in the dumps you felt when interrupted in a game? She is surely wrapped up warmly and is no doubt enjoying herself enormously.'

He looked at Jacquetta closely, once more taking in her thinness and general pale manner. 'Very well, as you suggest,' he answered, and gave her a little half-bow.

But he knew that Rose's curiosity would be aroused and, sure enough, after five minutes or so a little face appeared at the window, peering in. Playing the game, John ignored it, at the same time whispering to Mrs Fortune, 'My daughter has arrived and is studying you. Be so good as not to notice.'

She smiled that sudden-sunlight smile of hers, and John wished for the briefest of brief seconds that he was not involved with Elizabeth di Lorenzi, had never met her in fact, and that he could spend the rest of his days bringing Jacquetta Fortune back to the woman that she must once have been.

At that moment there came two simultaneous knocks, one on the outside of the French doors, the other on the entrance to the study. John admitted the study visitor first and discovered Gideon Purle, hat in hand and looking terribly smart, standing there.

The young man had grown even taller and these days stood well over six feet. His face had changed too, losing that boyish chubbiness and now dominated by a pair of lively eyes that darted hither and thither so brightly that one was left with the impression of flashes of colour shooting round the room. He was twenty years old and would be leaving his apprenticeship in the next couple of years. John sighed, suddenly feeling that he was getting on in years. He had had two apprentices in his career. But what men they had both grown into: the hulking, attractive young creature who had just entered the room, and the pale, limping but alive with character Nicholas Dawkins. John felt a huge burst of pride.

There came another knock at the French doors and Mrs Fortune, at a nod from John, went to let her in. The little girl, slightly nervous for once, stood eyeing them all without saying a word. Eventually, though, she approached the Apothecary and slipped her hand into one of his.

'Mrs Fortune,' he said gravely, 'may I introduce my daughter, Rose Rawlings?'

Jacquetta stared at her a moment before dropping a deep curtsey. 'The pleasure is entirely mine, Miss Rawlings.'

Remembering her manners, Rose did her best curtsey back and said, 'No, no, Madam. It is mine, I assure you.'

Four

Mrs Fortune had finally removed her hat and John could see at breakfast the next morning that her hair was very much as he had imagined it would be, the colour of shining silver-gilt. The meal done, she and Gideon immediately got to work and spent the rest of the time in conference, ordering bottles and ledgers and the million other sundries that apparently were needed to start a business. Young Mr Purle was obviously very taken by the fact that his master had, once again, done the unusual and appointed a woman for the task. And the Apothecary could not help but smile to himself at the obvious enjoyment his apprentice got from Jacquetta's company. He, meanwhile, had returned to the quiet of Shug Lane, removing himself from all the hurly-burly and excitement.

John had decided that on his next extended trip to Devon he would leave Gideon in sole charge of the shop, and considering this made him think of getting a new and young apprentice, someone that the older one could order about. He had accordingly written to several schoolmasters asking them to recommend any leavers who might be interested in becoming an apothecary and one answer in particular had caught his attention.

> Master Robin Hazell might be just to Your Suiting, Sir. He has a Carefree Disposition but Studies Assiduously Everything to do with the Nature of Herbs etc. He is leaving School on the twenty-third day of February – Easter being so Early – and I can Send Him Direct to You should You so Desire it.

The Apothecary had replied by return post that he did so desire and awaited the arrival of Master Hazell at two o'clock on the 25th. Unfortunately this was the time when the shop suddenly became thronged with customers, all wanting attention and wanting it quickly, and John worked so hard that he noticed nobody enter, and finally, feeling flat as a flounder, collapsed on to a chair behind the counter when the rush was over.

'Please, Sir, but would you be Mr Rawlings?' asked a small voice from the corner.

John jumped up, smoothing down his long apron, and peered in the direction of the sound. Wondering whether he needed spectacles, John narrowed his eyes but could see no one there. Then he felt a tug on his apron strings and wheeled round to behold a very small boy who was standing behind him.

'And who might you be?' he said rather crossly.

'I'm Robin Hazell, Sir. We 'ad an appointment – or so I fawt.'

'But you can't be sixteen,' John answered, staring down at him.

'I am, Sir, honest. It's just that I'm small, like me mother was.' The boy, who reached just above John's waist, looked suddenly forlorn. 'Am I too short, then?'

'For what?' answered the Apothecary, slightly irritated.

'To become your apprentice, Sir.' The boy's lower lip trembled and his eyes looked large with tears, though none as yet had trickled down his cheeks.

John suddenly felt profoundly sorry for the little chap. 'Shall we go into the compounding room and there have a cup of tea?' he asked in a much gentler tone.

'I would like that very much, Sir.' And a small hand crept into the Apothecary's as they walked together to the back of the shop.

There was absolutely no way that this boy could be much more than twelve, John thought, and wondered what particular kind of trick was being played upon him.

'Now, sit down,' he said kindly, 'and tell me all about yourself.'

Robin – if Robin it actually was – started on some long tale about finishing at school and being recommended by his headmaster to which John listened, not believing a word he was hearing. Finally, the child stopped talking and looked at the Apothecary with boot-button eyes.

'Well, Sir?' he asked.

John's mouth twitched. 'You're a good actor, I'll grant you that.'

'What do you mean, Sir?'

'I mean that I don't believe a thing you've just said to me. In other words, you're not telling the truth, my boy.'

The child opened his mouth to reply but at that moment the door of the shop shot open and another boy whirled in, panting and gasping for breath.

'Mr Rawlings?' he managed.

'Yes,' said John, going to meet him.

The newcomer held out his hand. 'I'm Robin Hazell, Sir. And I apologize for the lateness of my arrival but I've just been robbed in the street.'

Behind him the Apothecary heard a subdued squeal and, turning round, saw the little chap preparing to run. Gently but firmly John put his hand on the child's shoulder, thus pinioning him where he was. He turned back to the true Robin Hazell, thinking how well the name suited him, for the boy looked like autumn personified. His hair gleamed in an amber aureole, while his eyes, shining and honest-looking, were like glasses of light sherry. At the moment his freckled skin was bright red with a mixture of annoyance and exertion, but when it resumed its natural hue it was obvious that this young man was the handsomest of creatures. Inwardly the Apothecary sighed, thinking how all his apprentices were interesting and attractive people. Once again he felt slightly old.

'And there,' said Robin, catching a glimpse of the urchin standing at John's heel, 'is the little jackanapes who did it.'

The Apothecary decided to teach the young miscreant a lesson. 'You devilish dog, Sir. How dare you come in here with your fancy tales, wasting my time and putting Master Hazell into a fine how-dee-do? Explain yourself immediately.'

He sat down, standing the scrap in front of him and putting a hand on each shoulder. But instead of speaking the little boy wept, loudly and noisily, until John was obliged to produce a handkerchief and dry his face. He glanced up at Robin and saw that he, too, was quite moved by the sight.

'Don't be too hard on him, Sir,' Robin whispered into John's ear – and at that moment the Apothecary knew for sure that he was going to take young Master Hazell as his apprentice. The urchin continued to howl until the Apothecary boomed, 'Be silent! Enough of this caterwauling. Now just tell me your story and I will sit here and listen – and so will Master Hazell.'

He motioned the older boy to take a seat and eventually the little chap said in a voice, punctuated by sobs, 'I don't know who me parents are, honest, Sir. I was abandoned at the door of Coram's when I was a babe. But me mother left a bracelet in me box, so she must have been someone special.'

John's heart bled for him. The great man Thomas Coram had founded the home for abandoned and deserted children – who had quite literally littered the streets of London – in 1745. Hogarth and Handel had both become governors and Handel had allowed performances of 'Messiah' to take place in aid of the institution. The trouble was that there had been more children than there had been room for, so that a balloting system had come into being. Knowing this, mothers had left their babies in bundles and boxes near the gates of the orphanage and, often, they had put a keepsake in with the child. John had seen a few of them and it had moved him to tears. A button, a brooch, a lock of hair; how wretched the girls must have been to give up their children in this sad and melancholy situation.

He looked at the unhappy, skinny, snotty, tiny boy standing before him and said very seriously, 'Yes, she must.'

'Anyway, when I was eight I had to leave and go to work and they got me a job as a kitchen boy in a big house. But the head footman beat me – and the cook – so I runs away and steals the papers from Master Hazell, wot was bulging out of 'is pocket, and I thought I would come here first, seeing that I've always been interested in herbs and the like. But it didn't work, like nothing ever does and . . .'

The child collapsed into tears once more.

The Apothecary ignored them and asked, 'Can you read and write?'

'Oh yes, Sir,' the boy snivelled. 'They taught us all that at

Coram's. That's how I knew about the headmaster and to come here and all.'

'How old are you? And I want the truth this time.'

'Nearly twelve, Sir.'

John turned to Robin, who had been watching all this with red cheeks and an extremely sad expression.

'What shall I do with him, Master Hazell?'

'You can't turn him out on the streets, Sir. It wouldn't be right.'

'No.'

John looked thoughtful and the boy, sensing hope, gazed at him, suddenly bright-eyed.

'Tell me,' said the Apothecary, still not smiling. 'Is it your custom to thieve?'

The boy looked startled, his weepy eyes opening wide. 'No, Sir, honest, I never done it before. I was desperate.'

'I believe him, Sir,' interrupted Robin. 'I mean to say you only have to look at him. He's thoroughly wretched.'

'I tend to agree,' said John, still keeping up his act of extreme severity, though, head averted from the child, he winked one vivid eye at Master Hazell. He turned back to the boy. 'What is your name?'

'Frederick, Sir. After the King's father.'

At last a grin spread over John's features as he thought of this highly unlikely pair of people. Frederick, so anxious to please, grinned toothily in reply, but the anxiety showed through the smile and the Apothecary knew that he was going to make a fool of himself once again.

'All right,' he said sternly. 'I am going to give you a chance, Fred. I may call you that, mayn't I?'

Fred nodded, his expression hovering between hope and despair.

'I am going to offer you the job of general factotum in this establishment. No, don't say a word until I have explained. In the apartment upstairs live some law students who need someone to clean up and look after them. Also, I shall need someone to assist Master Hazell with the general keeping of good order in this establishment. Now, if so much as a leaf goes missing from one of the herbs, if the students complain that their money is short, then out you go and no two ways about it. Do you understand?'

'Oh yes, Sir. Oh thank you, Sir. You've saved my life, Sir. Honest you have.'

John rearranged his features in an effort to look stern again but had to give up. Fred was staring at him with such an honest look that, once more, the Apothecary felt his heart melt.

However, he spoke seriously. 'You will be answerable to my chief apprentice, Mr Purle. He will report your behaviour direct to me and I shall ask him for regular bulletins. Now, Fred, there is a very small bedroom in the attic, above the lawyers' rooms. You may sleep there. As for food, you shall eat with the other apprentices and build yourself up.'

Fred opened his mouth to speak but John had already addressed himself to the red-headed youth who was now waiting anxiously.

'Master Hazell,' he said, 'you can go home and tell your father to contact me. If you would still like the position I will be most delighted to have you as my new apprentice.'

Later that evening John sat in the library thinking that he must be losing his reason. About to go away, on the brink of fatherhood, he had taken three new people into his life, all of whom – with the exception of Factotum Fred – would hold positions that, with varying degrees of responsibility, could make or break what he now realized was going to be the biggest commercial venture of his life. Could skinny Jacquetta Fortune really take charge of a business empire? Could Gideon Purle, still not yet qualified, be trusted to run a shop and bottle more water in his spare time? Had he made the right decision about appointing Robin Hazell as his new apprentice?

The Apothecary gave a wry smile. The only one about whom he had no doubts was poor, wretched Fred. For if the little chap turned out to be a regular thief then John would have no hesitation in turning him out. If, however, Fred decided to be as honest a man as any, then he could stay and make good. Maybe even become a future apprentice.

John caught himself up. He would be thirty-seven on his next birthday; forty was staring him in the face. He wished, suddenly, that his father still lived with him. Or, indeed, that Elizabeth had agreed to marry him so that he might have someone with whom to share his worries. He poured himself another sherry and opened his book, but could not concentrate on reading.

Then the door opened and Rose, in night attire, stood there.

'Good evening, Papa.'

'Rose!' he exclaimed. 'What are you doing out of bed?'

'I just felt that I wanted to hug you.'

'Then come here, little bundle, and do so.'

She climbed on to his knee and he stroked her spirals of red hair.

'Couldn't you sleep?'

'I woke up and felt you were sad.'

'True, I was feeling a bit melancholy. I thought I was getting old.'

'But we're all doing that. Even your baby . . .' She stopped speaking very suddenly and gazed into space. Then she let out a delightful giggle. '. . . is getting older every minute.'

'What was the laughing about?'

'Nothing.' She clutched her hands together in childish glee.

'Something amused you.'

She shook her head, her eyes twinkling. 'It's a secret.'

'So you're not going to tell me?'

'No.'

John shook his head with a smile and dropped a kiss on the top of her head. 'I suggest you go off to bed, young lady.'

'Walk with me. It's a trifle frightening on the stairs.'

'Very well. Let's both carry candles and then we'll scare the hobgoblins away.'

Hand in hand they climbed the staircase and John tucked her into bed, and left one of the candles in her room as an extra night light. The house was quiet and he realized that Jacquetta Fortune had also retired for the night. While Gideon, no doubt, was sleeping the sleep of sheer exhaustion in the attic above.

Tomorrow, thought John, I must leave for Devon and whatever fate has in store for me next. Hoping that all would be well in his absence, the Apothecary retired to the library to try to read some more of his book.

Five

John rose early the next morning, even before daylight, so that he lingered for a moment by his window watching as the sky lightened to the colour of a seal's pelt. It was going to be a raw day for his travels, he thought miserably, and called downstairs for some really hot water to wash and shave in. Half an hour later he was dressed and his clothes packed in a small trunk which he would be able to handle without help. Naturally he had wanted to take more garments and make a show, but practicality had triumphed over pretentiousness and the Apothecary had reluctantly packed only a few fashionable rigs.

When he descended the stairs for his favourite meal, John found to his astonishment that Jacquetta and Gideon were already seated at table and had started to eat. They both looked up in some surprise.

Gideon rose. 'We knew you were going early but had no idea exactly when, Sir. Forgive me for not eating with the servants but Mrs Fortune and I have a great deal to discuss.'

'Of course. I think you should waive that rule, Gideon. I am delighted to see you both up and about at this hour.'

It was five-thirty and John could not help but be pleased that the people in charge of his new business should be taking it so seriously. He turned to Jacquetta Fortune. 'I hope these hours aren't going to prove too much for you.'

She laughed. 'Because I am thin, do you mean? Don't worry, Mr Rawlings, I shall soon put on weight with portions like this served up to me every day.'

'Excellent. That's what I like to hear.'

And John cut himself a large helping of ham and devoured it hungrily.

He had asked Irish Tom to come round with the coach at six fifteen and so, between mouthfuls, explained to Gideon all about Fred and his deception, then how the real Robin Hazell had rushed in and the truth had been revealed.

'So you have ended up with *two* boys, Sir?' his apprentice exclaimed.

'Yes, and I think they will both be useful. Now, Gideon, when Robin returns with his father and indentures are to be drawn up I want you to oversee everything up to the point where my signature is required. Explain to them that I will be back in four weeks but tell the boy that he can start work immediately. If he is agreeable then make the very best of him. I think he is level-headed and industrious. He should be extremely helpful to you during my absence. As for the other child I want you to watch him like a hawk. If his thieving habits return then turn him out and no questions asked. But if he does his duties well then reward him by raising his wages to a shilling a week.'

'Surely that is a little overgenerous, Sir.'

'A little, perhaps. But I believe the lad has potential and I want you to encourage that if possible.'

'I shall do as you ask, Mr Rawlings.'

'And I,' chimed in Jacquetta, 'shall launch your business with some attack, I promise you.'

'Then,' said John, hastily swallowing a pickled herring, 'I shall go away content.'

It was his intention to get a flying coach to Devon. These were faster and more comfortable than the stage but cost a good deal more. However, money was not the point at issue, it was the fact of actually obtaining a place in one. The system was to get four passengers to share the cost, but if only three persons were interested then the fare would automatically rise. John's fear that the places would already be taken was allayed by the fact that two postilions were standing by a rather highly polished vehicle drawn up by a sign which read, 'The Exeter Fast Coach for the Safe and Reliable Conveyance of Passengers. Fare 5d a mile. Two stops for Dining. Horses changed regular.' The cost was exorbitant but time was of the essence. Bidding farewell to Irish Tom, John booked himself a place and got inside.

Staring out of the window he thought back to the last time he had made this journey, that time travelling on the public stage, and all the terrible events which had followed. But he threw off the memories. He was going to Devon to await the birth of his second child and see Elizabeth through what would undoubtedly be a difficult experience for a woman of her age. John set his jaw, then was immediately diverted by the entrance of a pretty woman of about thirty-five. She smiled, bowed her head in acknowledgement and went to sit at the back. But a few moments later she gave up her seat when a bashful young man, hand-in-hand with an equally bashful girl, entered and enquired if this was the post chaise to Exeter. They were so obviously madly in love and probably newly married as the female had not a chaperone in sight, that to have kept them apart would have been cruel beyond belief.

'Do take my seat,' she said to the man, who bowed then banged his head on the coach's ceiling. She moved over to John, with a great deal of clambering. 'May I sit next to you, Sir?'

'It will be my pleasure,' he answered politely.

As she sat down one of the postilions put his head through the window. 'Well, we've a full complement, ladies and gents, so we'll be off. Ready, Rob?'

'Aye.'

It was a four-horse team pulling a fairly light weight, and so they made good time, especially as the coach was built to literally fly across the countryside, its high back wheels eating up the miles. A glance behind him told the Apothecary that the young couple were locked in a deep embrace, while the woman sitting beside him was reading a novel as best she could with the jolting and swaying. He closed his eyes and when he woke up it was to find that they had covered the thirty miles or so between the Gloucester Coffee House and Bagshot and were briefly stopping to change the horses.

He bowed his head to his fellow passenger. 'I'm so sorry, I indulged in a little snooze. I hope my snoring did not keep you awake.'

She laughed. 'It was a light, pleasant buzz. Allow me to be so forward as to introduce myself. I am Lettice James, a resident of Exeter where my husband is employed as a merchant.'

'I am delighted to make your acquaintance, Ma'am. I am John Rawlings, an apothecary of Shug Lane, Piccadilly, London.'

'And what are you doing travelling to Exeter, Mr Rawlings, if I may make so bold?'

John felt he could hardly say that he was travelling to see his mistress who was about to give birth to their child, so muttered something about visiting friends.

Mrs James nodded. 'Anyone I might know? I am quite a socialite in my quiet way.'

The Apothecary felt truly uncomfortable and could think of no answer except the truth. 'Lady Elizabeth di Lorenzi – or the Marchesa if you prefer it.'

'I don't really. I prefer English titles. Lady Elizabeth, now let me see. She has not been seen at any social events for the last . . .' She ticked them off on her fingers. '. . . five months or so. Tell me, is she unwell? Are you visiting her in a professional capacity?'

John hesitated, wondering what to reply. Eventually he said, 'No, just as a friend.'

'Then you will know the reason why she has been absent, surely.'

The Apothecary stared into her face and realized that she was not as attractive as he had first thought. There was a certain hardness about her eyebrows and her lips were thinner than they had initially appeared. He mentally put her down as Exeter's queen of gossip.

'I think she has been busy with her numerous business interests,' he answered.

'Business interests?' said Mrs James, all aflutter at some juicy piece of new information.

'Indeed. Her late husband, you know. He left her vast estates in Italy and many and varied companies. Export and import. Wine, lace – you know the sort of thing.' He waved a hand vaguely.

'Really?' Lettice's eyes were round with delight at learning some new facts. 'I had not realized that the Lady Elizabeth is a business woman.'

'Oh yes,' answered John expansively, 'she also travels a great deal. Did you not know that?'

Lettice lowered her eyes. 'Well, yes. Of course. But Lady Elizabeth is very discreet. She does not boast of her dealings.' She cleared her throat. 'Has she been abroad recently?'

'I believe so,' John answered vaguely. 'But I am not privy to all her movements.'

'Well, do send her my very best wishes and my earnest hope that she will be gracing our little social gatherings once more.'

'I will certainly pass on your kind thoughts. And now if you will excuse me I shall take a breath of air.'

He hurried out of the coach and went to the boghouse, conveniently situated beside the inn, only to find Lettice James waiting outside. She blushed and passed within while John returned to the conveyance, only to see the young couple still locked in an embrace. Thinking about the first flush of youth, John took his seat and with the return of the Exeter gossip they were off once more.

The route taken by the flying coach was not the usual one. In order to speed things up, the carriage passed through Bagshot, then on to Basingstoke and a great push through to Salisbury, where they stopped overnight and had a late dinner.

John found himself seated at a large trencher table with another two loads of passengers, recently arrived. Lettice, whom he had rather come to mistrust, was sitting some distance away. As for the young couple, they bolted their food and then retired upstairs, accompanied by a good deal of giggling. John could only hope that they did not have a creaking bed or those within earshot would have a disturbed night of it.

The next morning saw them leave Salisbury at seven o'clock. Lettice looked tired and yawned greatly, whispering to John that, just as he had thought, she had had a room next door to the honeymooners and as a result had had hardly a wink of sleep. The young people themselves, appearing much the worse for wear, climbed on to the back seat and instantly fell asleep. John, who had been forced to share a room with a nifty little tailor from Woodyeats, who slept silently as a cat which he rather resembled, felt in fine fettle. Fortunately for him the inquisitive Mrs James dozed off at once and so the Apothecary, with a great stirring of his heart which he always felt in the beautiful countryside through which he was now passing, was free to gaze through the large front window at the scenery.

They stopped once more at Dorchester, where they dined, and then pushed on through Honiton to Exeter where they arrived as the dusk of evening was just casting a shadow over the land. John, as courtesy demanded, saw Mrs James into a waiting hackney carriage, doffed his hat to the two youngsters who were plunging into The Half Moon with alacrity, and turned in the direction of the livery stables that he had used before.

Wary as he was of riding, he did not like the look of a vast chestnut stallion that was led out for him, clomping over the cobblestones and baring its teeth as soon as it saw him.

'Have you got nothing a bit smaller?' he asked nervously.

'Sorry, Sir, but this be the last beast left. Night's falling and all the horses are hired. Strawberry's all right as long as you let him know who's master.'

'Oh God,' the Apothecary muttered, and gamely put his foot in the stirrup which, even with the mounting block, was a very long way up. Finally, with much heaving of his backside from the stable lads, he was seated. At which the horse took off, furiously going out of the yard, and down the street as if all the devils from hell were after it.

'Whoa,' shouted John and pulled hard on the creature's reins, at which it slowed its pace a little – but not a lot.

So it was with great speed that John left the city behind and started to traverse the countryside outside. With every step the animal took he felt that he would be thrown.

'Stop that! Behave yourself! Slow down, you fiend,' he shouted at various intervals. But Strawberry took no notice whatsoever and continued to plunge onwards as if its life depended on it. The Apothecary had a vision of himself shooting over the animal's head and landing in a ditch, and even while he was trying to control the horse his hat flew away and he was left with his cinnamon curls flying into a tangled whirl like those of a rain-soaked scarecrow. And finally that which he had been dreading throughout the whole terrible ordeal happened. A fox, startled by the sound of approach, bolted from its lair right at Strawberry's feet. The stallion came to a dead stop and John whizzed over its head and on to the ground below, where he landed in a boggy piece of earth. Looking up dazedly he saw that Strawberry had turned and was bolting back to Exeter like a racehorse.

'Damn your eyes!' he shouted at its retreating rear end. The horse whinnied and tossed its head to show how much it cared and continued on its journey at breakneck speed.

Slowly and gingerly the Apothecary got to his feet, relieved to find that nothing was broken. Looking round him he discovered that he had reached the bottom of the hill on the top of which stood Elizabeth's house. Walking carefully and somewhat painfully with no light to guide him except that of a new moon, John made his way upwards. He fell over six times during the journey, once landing in what he could only think was a dried-out cow pat. By this time he had acquired a hole in the knee of his breeches and his stockings were filthy and torn. And all the while the lights in Elizabeth's home taunted him, never seeming to draw nearer however hard he tried to reach them. At long last he reached the main gates and rang the bell on the lodgekeeper's cottage.

He stood, panting in the darkness, while he heard two big bolts being drawn back and the eventual creak as the door opened. The lodgekeeper stood there, lantern raised on high. John stood rooted to the spot as he stared down the barrel of a blunderbuss.

'Don't shoot, Harrison, for the love of God. It's me, John Rawlings.'

'Get away you varmint. You tatterdemalion. Be off with you.'

'Harrison, please. It really is me. I was thrown by my horse and I've had to walk here.'

The lantern was thrust right into his face so that John was forced to screw up his eyes, squinting at the brightness.

'Stap me, if it *ain't* you. I'd never have recognized you, Sir. You look like a tramp.'

'Thank you,' John answered with what little patience he could muster.

'You'd best come in, Sir, and have a bit of a wash before

you goes to the big house. Mind you, Lady Elizabeth ain't there.'

'She's not? Where is she then? Do you know?'

'She went off in the carriage to see Lady Sidmouth and she hasn't returned, Sir.'

'How long ago was this?'

'Three days, Sir.'

'Oh, hare and hounds, I haven't missed another one,' John said to himself.

'We don't know, Sir. We ain't had no word.'

'I'd better go there straight away.'

'Wash yourself first, Sir. They'll not let you in else.'

John looked at his reflection in a small mirror and allowed himself a shriek of horror at the sight he presented. Then he set to in an old tin bowl and kettle full of hot water, stripping off until he had managed somehow to remove the top layer of dirt. He surveyed his clothes as he put them back on. There was no help for it. He would have to go to the big house and change into something that he had left behind on his previous visit, his trunk being left in Exeter to be brought the next day by a man with a cart.

Plodding up the drive with Harrison lighting his way, John suddenly felt exhausted. Every step he took hurt and by the time he reached the grandeur of Withycombe House, the Marchesa's great and stately dwelling, he felt fit to faint. The head footman took one look at him and immediately ordered him to bed.

'But Lady Elizabeth . . .'

'Sir,' said the footman firmly, ''twill make no difference if you go tonight or not. Anxious as we all are for Milady's welfare there is nothing you can do about it at this hour of the night. Now go to bed, Sir, and you will arise fresh and well in the morning.'

'Will you wake me at six?'

'You will be woken at seven, Sir, if you've no violent objection – and there's an end to it.'

Too tired to argue, John slowly climbed the great staircase and made his way to the guest suite, glad that someone else had made the decision for him.

Six

To John's horror when he opened the clothes press on the following morning, he discovered that he had left only two ensembles behind in Devon. One was a perfectly ghastly affair in a violent shade of lime green with violet embroidery – a colour combination that could have come off had it not been for the vivid hue of the lime. It had been created by a tailor in Exeter and the Apothecary felt he only had himself to blame for the purchase. The second was the divine outfit he had had made for Lady Sidmouth's ball, crimson satin decorated with silver butterflies, with a straight-cut short waistcoat also made of silver. This too had been made locally, though by a different craftsman. The decision was to choose which to wear.

Eventually John chose the lime, thinking it preferable to look like a piece of fruit than a complete dandiprat, one who tries to be something that he was actually not. Very conscious of his vivid apparel he covered all with his long travelling coat – from which the servants had obligingly scraped off the mud – and set forth for Lady Sidmouth's lovely home, perched high on the cliffs overlooking Sidmouth Bay. John suddenly found that he was sweating profusely – bathed in it, in fact – at the thought that Elizabeth might be dead. She was very old indeed to be a mother and it came to him that her body might have been too tired for the rigours of childbirth. Then it occurred to him that the child might be dead as well and he would be going to a house draped in darkest mourning. He prepared his face as he rang the bell and thus was looking extremely stern when a footman answered the door.

'Good morning, Sir.'

'Good morning. I have come to call on the Lady Elizabeth di Lorenzi.'

'Very good, Sir. Step inside. I will fetch Lady Sidmouth.'

The man seemed cheerful enough and John felt his spirits begin to rise. He was ushered into a small parlour and then his hostess came in, bustling like a harvest mouse, her strange face with its tiny mouth as jolly as he had ever seen it.

'Elizabeth . . .?' he said.

'Asleep and not to be disturbed,' she answered promptly.

'And has she . . .'

'Oh yes, indeed, my dear John. Come upstairs and meet your . . . No, I shall hold you in suspense a moment or two longer. Shall we go?'

Feeling that he was running the gauntlet of emotion, John found that his legs were trembling as he followed Lady Sidmouth's comfortable form up to the first floor. 'Have I a son or a daughter?' he asked, his voice sounding strange even to his own ears.

She glanced over her shoulder. 'Wait and see.'

They entered a small corridor and went straight to the end where Lady Sidmouth threw open a door to permit a beautiful view of the pounding sea. But it was not to the sea that John's eyes were drawn. Instead he saw to his amazement that a strange man was inside, holding a small baby in his arms and examining it carefully. Before John could utter, Lady Sidmouth made the introduction.

'Dr Hunter, allow me to present to you Mr John Rawlings, an apothecary of London.'

Where one moment John had stood askance wondering what was going on, now he bowed deeply. 'Dr Hunter, the honour is entirely mine. Your name is spoken of with ringing tones throughout the medical profession.'

For he was standing in the presence of one of the most eminent men of his day, physician extraordinary to Queen Charlotte and the man who had brought obstetrics out of the domain of the midwife and into the general stream of medical practice. John bowed a second time. It was the greatest respect he could pay. Still not knowing what sex the child was that Dr Hunter was holding, he said, 'Is it a boy or a girl, Sir? I really would like to know.'

William Hunter grinned widely. 'He is a boy – and so is the other one.'

John's mouth fell open. 'What?'

'Yes Sir, Lady Elizabeth was delivered of twins by Caesarean section. I performed the operation myself and now she is stitched up neat as you please.'

The Apothecary was released from his trance and rushed to look at both his sons. Hunter handed him the child he had been holding and John lifted the other one up from his cot. Two pairs of eyes regarded him solemnly, neither smiling nor frowning, simply looking at him as they might any other individual. With neither of them did he have the experience he had had with Rose. That great yet indefinable feeling that they had always known one another.

'I take it you are the father, Sir?' asked William in his gentle Scots accent.

John looked up. 'Yes, Sir, I must admit I am.'

'Well, you've a handful to look after then.'

The Apothecary pulled a wry face. 'I don't know about that, Sir. It all depends on Lady Elizabeth.'

Lady Sidmouth said firmly, 'I do not feel the nursery is a suitable place for such a conversation, gentlemen. You may continue it downstairs. Now put the twins down, John. They need their sleep.'

There was no arguing with the woman; she was the kind who would order the Queen's physician about and he would meekly obey, as he now did. But John turned in the doorway and suddenly rushed back to the two cribs standing side-by-side. The twins had indeed fallen asleep, their long dark lashes standing out against the fresh white pillowcases which cradled their heads. They were both black-haired – like their mother – but John thought he could see something of himself about their faces. But whoever they resembled, one fact stood out plainly – they were identical.

John leant over swiftly and kissed each baby on its downy cheek. 'Hello, my son,' he said to one after the other, then he straightened up and joined Lady Sidmouth and the doctor as they made their way downstairs.

During the conversation over a glass of sherry, when he could speak to Dr William Hunter frankly – Lady Sidmouth having bustled off somewhere – John was told the entire story of Elizabeth's travail. It seemed that she had gone to take tea with

Lady Sidmouth and the mysterious dark waters of the womb had ruptured, at which her hostess had ordered her to bed and refused to let her travel another step.

'But how did you come into it, Sir? Are you of Lady Sidmouth's acquaintance?'

'No, but my brother is.'

'John Hunter, the renowned surgeon?'

'The same. He has a small country estate not far away – it was left to him by our uncle and John often asks me down for a short break in my routine. Well, a servant of Lady Sidmouth's arrived at his house and explained the situation. Said that the labour was growing difficult, the midwife suspecting there might be a breach presentation. Naturally, I attended at once, and after an examination believed there could well be twins. So, somewhat reluctantly I might add but in view of the mother's age, I performed a Caesarian and out came your two little boys. But I stitched Lady Elizabeth's abdomen back with the greatest care, Mr Rawlings, I can assure you of that.'

'How has she taken all this? Will she really recover?'

Dr Hunter took a small sip of sherry and allowed himself a smile. 'She is one of the strongest women I have ever come across, Sir. She has a body like steel caused by years of riding and exercise. She is not milk and sugar like many women today but more red wine and spice. We must wait to see if any infection sets in and then I think we can safely say that she will survive.'

'If you have no objection I would like to give her a decoction of Feverfew.'

'You have some on you?'

'No, but I can ride to Exeter tomorrow and have a mixture made up.'

For the first time since their meeting Dr Hunter looked slightly superior. 'If you think that it might do good, then by all means do so. It will do no harm at any rate.'

John said nothing, thinking that it was to Dr Hunter's skill and kindness that he owed the birth of his sons and the safe delivery of Elizabeth. His sons! The words suddenly struck him and he felt a broad smile cross his face. Those two angelic beings upstairs were his progeny, his blood, his bone.

William Hunter saw him smile and said, 'I am sure that you are very happy with the outcome.'

'I am indeed, Dr Hunter. And it is all thanks to you. I think you probably saved Elizabeth's life – as well as that of my boys.'

Again he grinned. Even saying 'my boys' gave him pleasure.

'Well, puerperal fever will appear tomorrow if it is going to appear at all. But be assured, Mr Rawlings, I washed my hands thoroughly in soap and water before I started to operate.'

John knew that many doctors thought this an unnecessary precaution but it was one in which he fervently believed, having been taught by his old Master, Mr Purefoy, that in the future this would be the coming thing.

Lady Sidmouth popped her head around the door. 'Elizabeth is awake and is asking for you, Mr Rawlings.'

He stood up, bowed to Dr Hunter and followed her upstairs to a room opposite the nursery. Opening the door, he thought he had never seen a more beautiful sight. The Marchesa sat propped against the pillows in a large bed, very modern, and obviously imported from France where the fashion was just gaining ground. Gone were the tester and the carved wooden poles supporting it. In its place was a large curving bedhead made of walnut adorned with floral garlands, draped ribbons, scrolling waves and acanthus leaves. Against all this splendour, pale, with her long black hair loose about the shoulders of her white nightgown, sat Elizabeth herself.

John bowed so low that his hair swept the floor, then knelt beside the bed and took one of her long tapering hands in his.

'Oh my darling,' was all he could think of saying.

She looked at him and though he could see the lines of fatigue around her eyes, they still had the same sparkle in their depths.

'What on earth are you wearing?' she said.

John put his head on the counterpane and laughed. And in the laughter tears came until he was sobbing uncontrollably with joy at the successful birth of his gorgeous twin boys and the safe delivery of that most wonderful creature, the Marchesa di Lorenzi, clearly very much alive and no worse that he could see for the experience.

There was a knock on the door and two maids came in, each carrying a baby in her arms.

'Your sons, Milady,' said the older girl and bobbed a curtsey.

John stood up and took the two bundles from them, then he held them out to their mother. 'We made these,' he said.

She grinned at him and then put the babies to her breasts.

'You're feeding them yourself,' he said, delighted.

'Of course,' she answered. 'I read the paper by Carl Linnaeus and that convinced me it was by far the best way. Besides, it will slim my figure and I intend to go riding again soon.'

'You are a miraculous being,' he said in amazement, watching his two sons taking milk contentedly.

'And you,' she answered, 'though closely resembling an over-sized lime, are a genuinely nice man. Now be off with you. Leave me in peace with my sons.'

'Any ideas on names?' asked John from the doorway.

'I thought perhaps Jasper and James. Do you like those?'

The Apothecary repeated them under his breath, looked at the two tiny boys, then said, 'I can't think of anything nicer.'

Lady Sidmouth would not hear of him going back to Elizabeth's mansion that night, and so he not only was invited to dine with them but offered a small guest room into the bargain. He had wanted to see Elizabeth again but was told that she slept once more, but he was allowed another quick peek at his sons before they were put down for the night.

Observing them closely he noticed that even at this early age they were totally the same. Both dark-haired, their eyes still baby-blue, they nonetheless had noses that were destined to be strong and lips that were going to be passionate. At least that is what John told himself fondly as he observed their tiny little hands, kissed their minute feet and tickled them under their wobbly infant chins. So he was in the first throes of delightful fatherhood as he made his way downstairs, only to be halted by the sound of muffled giggling. He turned to see who it was and cast his eyes on two young women he had met before, namely Lady Sidmouth's daughter Felicity and her cousin, Miranda Tremayne. Knowing that he was the object of their derision, presumably because of the hideous colour of his clothes, John gave them a florid bow.

'Good evening, ladies. I trust I find you well.'

They bobbed brief curtsies that suggested he was hardly worth the courtesy. Then Miranda spoke.

'Good evening, Mr Rawlings. I have remembered the name correctly, have I not? La, what a flutter with the house full of babies. How do you like your little bast— I mean your sons?'

'I like them very well,' John answered evenly.

Miranda continued, 'We were saying how well Lady Elizabeth looks despite her ordeal. We think it is nothing short of a miracle at her age.'

She had made this kind of remark once before, at Lady Sidmouth's summer ball to be precise, and John felt his fury grow. 'Elizabeth is a remarkable woman,' he said, 'and has been through many ordeals to become the person she is today.'

There was another muffled giggle and he realized that his answer could have been taken two ways.

'But one thing,' he continued firmly, 'that one could never say about the Marchesa is that she is shallow. She is like steel compared with many of the drooping lilies that one sees around one. Would you not agree?'

There was silence, then Felicity said, 'Shall we go down to dinner?'

'After you, ladies,' said John, and felt that he had just won that round.

During the night he was awoken by the sound of crying, and for a moment thought he had gone back in time and that it was Rose who wanted him. Then he came to his senses and was just about to get out of bed when he heard footsteps in the corridor and realized that maids had already picked the infants up and were at this very moment carrying them in to their mother. He thought of Elizabeth being woken up by two hungry boys and decided that as soon as she was on her own he would creep into her room and tell her how much he loved her.

He lay awake listening for the sound of the maids returning the boys to the nursery. Eventually he heard them, then the house grew silent and still once more. Softly John got out of bed and walked across the corridor to where Elizabeth lay sleeping. Her black hair was spread across the pillow like a fantastic web, shot with silver where the moon peeped in through the vents in the curtains. Walking quietly, John went to the window and drew them apart a little. Far below him the sea churned and leapt, and the Apothecary spared a thought for the many poor devils spending the night on the treacherous waves. Then he pulled the curtains closed and turned back to the bed.

A great surge of emotion filled him as he looked down at the woman who had so courageously undergone the mighty experience of giving birth. Then he bent and gently kissed her on the cheek before snuggling in beside her and – oh so gently – taking her in his arms and falling asleep.

Seven

As dawn came creeping over the River Exe John kissed Elizabeth, who still slept deeply, and then went back to his own room where he enjoyed a couple of hours of perfect, dreamless sleep before the smell of distant cooking woke him up. Ringing for hot water, he washed, shaved and dressed in his terrible lime green suit then went down to the breakfast room. It was empty except for Lady Sidmouth who, as usual, was doing her busy bee act.

'Ah John,' she said, raising her quizzer to her heavily-lidded dark brown eye the better to observe him. 'You look well and rested – but the colour of that suit is enough to put one off one's food. Would you kindly remove the jacket?'

John did so and, helping himself to a substantial amount from the servers placed on the sideboard, sat down in his violet waistcoat and prepared to tuck in. But the fork was only half-way to his mouth when the door opened and Miranda Tremayne, eyes downcast and looking excessively prim, entered and sat down.

Lady Sidmouth said, 'There have been some interesting changes since you were last here, John.'

'Oh really? And what might they be?'

Miranda spoke up, eyes still not raised. 'I have become betrothed, Mr Rawlings, and indeed am due to be married in June.'

'How very delightful. And who is the lucky bridegroom?'

Lady Sidmouth interrupted. 'Miranda has done very well for herself. She is to marry the Earl of St Austell and will go to live in his grand house in Cornwall.'

'What a good match,' John murmured politely.

Miranda looked up and straight at the Apothecary and he noticed that her eyes were shuttered, all her secret thoughts hidden from the world. 'The Earl is a very gracious man and I care for him greatly,' she said, just a fraction defiantly.

'What Miranda is trying to say,' Lady Sidmouth put in, 'is that she doesn't give a toss for the fact that he is fifty-two years her senior; in fact she snaps her fingers at it. She says she loves the man and there's an end to it.'

'I am so pleased to hear it,' John answered politely. 'Tell me, where did you meet him?'

'He is one of society's doyens in Cornwall. It was at a hunting assembly at Lord Austell's home that I was presented by my cousin Robin. They ride to stag on Exmoor, you know.'

'Yes, I did know,' John muttered.

'Well, he was so handsome and debonair – as only an older man can be – that I fell in love with him at first sight.'

'How nice!'

'And of course his wife had died just a few months previously after many years of being an invalid. Poor darling, I don't know how he coped with all those weeks when he tended her lovingly.'

'He had a nurse to help him,' put in Lady Sidmouth with a touch of acerbity.

Miranda's eyes dropped once more. 'Yes, of course.'

John thought most unkindly about the enormous wealth to be gained and the huge estate and all that went with it – fawning servants, splendid food, great occasions at which the beautiful Miranda would be belle-of-the-ball – and wondered that anyone could be taken in by her duplicity. He caught the canny eye of Lady Sidmouth and just for a moment read the same sentiments there.

The door opened and Milady's youngest daughter, Felicity, walked in. Though not exactly good looking she had improved during the few months that John had not seen her and was nowadays carrying herself with more dignity and poise. Having obtained her breakfast and seated herself at the large table, she turned to John.

'The twins are really sweet. I popped in and looked at them before I came down. How much longer are they staying?' She turned to her mother.

'That rather depends on Dr Hunter. He will call and examine the Lady Elizabeth today. It will be on his pronouncement that we will await.'

'I am sure that the Marchesa will be anxious to return home and get into a routine with Jasper and James as soon as possible. Notwithstanding the generosity of your hospitality, Lady Sidmouth.'

'Nonsense, I'd have done the same for any of my friends. Not that my other friends are as likely to get into the identical sort of mischief as Lady Elizabeth, I might add.'

John laughed while the two girls tittered into their teacups.

'Well, we owe you a million thanks, none the less. But you will soon need to clear the place of guests if you are preparing a big wedding. I take it it's going to be celebrated here?'

'Indeed it is,' Lady Sidmouth answered cheerfully. 'The ceremony will be conducted in St Swithin's Church nearby and the breakfast will be held at the bride's home, which is this house.'

'I cannot think of a more beautiful setting,' said John, meaning it. 'Are you having many guests?'

'The world and his wife,' said Lady Sidmouth before Miranda interrupted, 'Beg pardon, Cousin.'

The older woman inclined her head and Miranda went on, 'Montague's family is quite large. He has an unmarried granddaughter who is dying to find a husband. Then he has two grandsons, Viscount Falmouth and Lord George. They are the children of Montague's son, who died when they were all quite young. They all hate me because they think I might present Montague with another baby and they wouldn't like that at all.'

'Why?' asked John. 'The oldest boy is bound to inherit everything, isn't he?'

'Yes, unless he dies of course.'

The Apothecary's mobile eyebrows rose in surprise. 'Surely he is not sickly?'

'Not he,' chimed in Felicity, 'he's as fit as a pudding for a friar's mouth. And he's a clever devil too, always striding round with a book in his hand. All in all I think he's a crimping fellow.'

'There's no need to be rude,' Miranda retorted. 'I know he's not handsome but he's — clever and kind.'

'Kind be blowed. If he would just remove his beastly spectacles it might improve his looks.'

'Well, he's going to be my step-grandson so I won't hear another word.' Miranda giggled. 'Though secretly I rather agree with you.'

Lady Sidmouth opened her mouth to protest but John forestalled her. 'And what about the younger brother? What's he like?'

Again Felicity spoke before Miranda had a chance to answer. 'He's a handsome thing. As unlike his brother as chalk is to cheese. He's tall, dark, never wears a wig and his hair reaches his collar. He's a regular dashing blade and doesn't he just know it.'

John smiled. The word-picture had completely conjured up the man. He wondered vaguely if Felicity ought to write.

'Well,' Miranda said, somewhat defensively, 'the grandson may be handsome but the grandfather is by far the most debonair.'

'I can't wait to meet him,' stated John, his voice free of expression.

'Well, you shall,' said Miranda, smiling sweetly. 'We are giving an assembly a few nights before the wedding. You must come – and the Lady Elizabeth, if she is sufficiently recovered.'

'I am quite sure she will be,' John answered. 'And I thank you.'

Lady Sidmouth spoke up. 'You must both come to the wedding – and dear old Sir Clovelly Lovell. He is quite one of my favourite people.'

'And mine too,' said the Apothecary.

'Well, I shall be sending out the invitations shortly. And you are all three added to my list.'

'Excellent,' said John, and paid serious attention to his breakfast.

Dr Hunter proclaiming himself well pleased with the healing process of Elizabeth's scar, she and John left the glorious house on the cliff-tops exactly five days later. There was much to-do about their leaving. First Elizabeth was handed into her coach, then one baby followed, howling his head off and not enjoying this change in his routine. He was put into the arms of a nurserymaid who immediately calmed him by rocking him, somewhat wildly, from side to side. Another coach was pulled up behind the first and John got into this, was briefly handed the baby, before a second nurserymaid followed. This second child – was it Jasper or James, John wondered? – slept peacefully through the whole ordeal and did not wake until they reached Elizabeth's home, when he opened his eyes and gave a great yawn.

'Which child is this?' John asked Elizabeth anxiously.

She peered into his face. 'Why, this is James. He has less hair than Jasper. Besides Jasper is the noisier of the two. If anyone is going to cry it will be Jasper.'

'May I hold them a minute?'

'Of course you can.'

With a bundle in each arm, John sat down in the Blue Salon and stared at both his sons' faces intently. He could never have imagined in a thousand years that Elizabeth would give birth to twins. And then he remembered Rose, his first-born child, recently giggling and saying words to the effect of wait and see. She had known, the pretty minx, with her wonderful ability to envisage future events, exactly what was going to happen.

His thoughts switched from his two sons, who were awake but thankfully quiet, to his daughter. Would she love them, he wondered, or might she be jealous of these two rivals for her father's affection? But then he knew that with her generous, warm heart she would love them as much as he was starting to, would play with them and teach them all the wonderments of the world so that they would grow up as fine a person as she was going to be. He suddenly glowed with happiness, looking down at the little scraps who were looking back at him, and feeling a tremendous sense of well-being and affection. A true family man.

He heard a noise behind him and looked over his shoulder. The two maids, presumably hastily appointed by Elizabeth after she had given birth, were bearing down on him.

'I'll take Master Justin, if you please, Sir.'

'And I'll take Master James.'

Somewhat reluctantly he handed the twins over and watched them being swept up the grand staircase to their apartments on the first floor. Before following them he sat a moment and imagined Sir Gabriel's and Rose's faces when his letter arrived. He had written it the day after he had shown up at Lady Sidmouth's and knew that it must have been delivered to Kensington by now. No doubt Sir Gabriel would send for champagne and allow Rose a thimbleful. Then they would clink their drinking vessels and toast the newborn. How sad that neither of them would be able to see the boys for some while.

He went up the stairs rather slowly, thinking of this, and made his way to Elizabeth's room where he knocked on the door.

'Come in,' she called.

She had changed from her travelling dress and was sitting *déshabillé* at her dressing table, brushing her long black hair.

'Ah,' she said, 'how timely. You may do this for me.'

'A pleasure, Milady.'

He looked at her reflection and saw that though the birth had weakened her she was now recovering and some of the old fire was returning to her. He thought of Dr Hunter's description of her – red wine and spice – and realized yet again what a rare creature she was.

'Do you remember the first time we met?' he asked.

'Very clearly. I can recall fighting you in the fog.'

'I was thinking more of when we came back to this house.'

In the mirror he saw her smile up at him and then turn to look at him. 'I can remember that. I said I longed to kiss you. And that is what I want now. If it is no trouble, Mr Rawlings.'

'Never a difficulty as far as you are concerned, Madam.'

And he bent his head to her upturned face and kissed her full on the lips while one hand reached down inside the open robe she was wearing to caress her lovely neck and shoulders.

They went to bed but did not make love, for John knew how bad for her this would be. But for all that they gently played and embraced until Elizabeth finally fell asleep. Then the Apothecary rose quietly and tiptoed along the corridor until he reached his own room. His trunk had arrived long since and some clothes had been sent up to him at Lady Sidmouth's so that he had been able to abandon the ghastly green and was now soberly attired in Venetian blue. Looking in the clothes press he determined to go to Exeter on the morrow and see a tailor. And also to renew his acquaintance with Sir Clovelly Lovell and try to glean some more information on that soon-to-be-married fellow, the elderly Earl of St Austell.

Eight

'The trouble with old St Austell,' said Sir Clovelly Lovell, thoughtfully nibbling with sharp little teeth upon a sweetmeat, 'is that he won't act his age. Still thinks he's a helluva fellow. Can't – or will not – accept the fact that he's seventy-two.'

'Good gracious!' exclaimed John, who was sitting opposite him, toying with a glass of sherry. 'I hadn't realized that he was quite that old.'

'In his younger days he was the very devil of a rake. And with respect to Mr Hogarth, St Austell's progress was from woman to woman. Just couldn't get enough of 'em. Different one every night – that is, when he wasn't on the ran-tan.'

'He was a heavy drinker?' asked John.

'He was everything you can imagine,' said Sir Clovelly with weight, and allowed his words to sink in.

The Apothecary was frankly bemused. His mental picture of Lord St Austell had been one of an old man in love with a girl a quarter of his age, probably a frail old being whose last declining years were going to be spent happily while she ran around him. But a different portrait was emerging, that of a raging-bull young man   large limbed and ready with his fists – who would grow into something quite cruel in his declining years.

'What does he look like?'

'A giant of a fellow, though somewhat stooped these days I fear. He had a shock of long hair, now white, on the top of which he would slap a wig which never sat right on his head. His eyes are a brilliant blue. The sort of eyes which one could imagine as belonging to the Devil – or am I being fanciful? He has strong features, with a great roman nose in the middle of his face, and a large mouth full of gnashing white teeth. These are now false, alas, and somewhat more subdued than once they were. I remember him biting some young man in a tavern brawl and the poor chap was scarred for life.'

'He sounds a thoroughly nasty piece of work.'

'He has mellowed as we all do with the onset of age. Uses a stick to support himself and has grown somewhat hard of hearing. But he's still got a violent temper so I hope his poor bride does not step out of line.'

If ever there was a young woman more likely to misbehave than Miranda Tremayne, John would like to see her. A cold shudder clutched his spine and he shivered involuntarily.

It was noon and a raw March day, with a chill wind blowing from the river and echoing down the streets of Exeter. Against its cold Sir Clovelly had had fires lit in every room, so within his house in The Close it was warm and welcoming. John, who had taken Elizabeth's small carriage into town, had called upon the tailor who had made his scarlet suit and had then gone on to visit Sir Clovelly, that sweet little man whose passion was eating. He had put on weight even since John had last seen him and now resembled a tub, in fact he was almost as broad as he was long. But his jolly face with its many chins and his merry little eyes all a-twinkle welcomed his guest, so that John was pleased to sit down with one of his dear friends and partake of a midday repast, at which John picked. Sir Clovelly, on the other hand, dug in with much enjoyment and smacking of the lips.

'So old Montague's getting married again,' he said between mouthfuls.

'Yes. Do you know the bride-to-be?'

'A cousin of Lady Sidmouth did you say?'

'Child of a cousin I would imagine.' John leant forward. 'She's a bit of a handful in my opinion. Rather a rude little madam.'

'Old St Austell will soon cure her of that. He won't stand for any nonsense.'

'But surely at his age . . .'

'Don't you believe it. He'll take his cane to her if necessary.'

John sat nonplussed. 'Well, the situation is not as I read it at all. I thought she would be marrying some compliant old fool who would sit in the corner chumbling his gums while she went out and about as she pleased – and with whom she pleased.'

Sir Clovelly shook his head. 'Well, unless St Austell has plunged downhill in the last few weeks I would suggest, my dear John, that you have got that entirely wrong. Montague will guard her like a lion and no doubt about it.'

That said, Sir Clovelly dived on to a plate of red blancmanges made with port and began to attack them earnestly.

On his way home John called in at the apothecary's shop to cancel his order for Feverfew and replace it with Marsh Mallow. He asked to be sold some roots and seeds which he intended to boil in wine to help Elizabeth's supply of milk and to ensure that her breasts did not become lumpy or swollen. He had just been handed the packet by the apothecary who, by now, he knew quite well, when the door of the shop opened in a hurry and a young and flustered woman came in. Seeing John, she backed to the other end of the counter and pretended to study what was on display. The apothecary approached her.

'Can I be of assistance, Madam?'

She shot a look at John and muttered something in an undertone.

'I'm sorry, Madam, I didn't quite catch that.'

'I wish to have something to bring on my courses,' she whispered.

John immediately guessed the situation. The woman's monthly moon flow was late and she feared she might be pregnant. He had one or two remedies for such an occurrence in his own shop but this was Exeter and he wondered what the other apothecary was going to do.

His answer came at once. 'If you would like to step through into my compounding room we can discuss the matter in private.'

'Certainly,' she replied, but at that moment her reticule came undone and the contents spilled over the floor of the shop.

'Allow me,' said John, and helped her to retrieve the contents.

It was only as he was leaving the shop that he found a card case with some newly printed cards inside it. 'Lady Imogen Beauvoir', he read, before hastily placing the cards back in their holder. He retraced his steps and looked round but Lady Imogen was still ensconced in the compounding room. John left the card case on the counter in a place where she was bound to see it and went on his way.

He had always loved Exeter, loved its back streets and alleyways and now he found his feet heading towards the river, bustling with life and activity. But as he went towards the West Gate he saw the tavern The Blackamore's Head and felt that he had to go in there and have a jug of ale for old time's sake.

He sat at a table, feet stuck out in front of him, listening to the voices with their soft Devon burr speaking all around him. And then one voice rose above all the others, strident and compelling, a voice that had his full attention, though his negligent position at the table altered not at all.

'I demand that you repeat that,' it said.

The other person gave a laugh and answered, 'Indeed I won't, Sir. I insist that you forget and forgive.'

There was the sudden sound of a chair scraping back and the louder voice shouted, 'Damn you, Sir, you said something I cannot forgive. You insulted my sister and you'll take it back or pay for it.'

This was followed by the noise of a hearty punch and then a groan, then the sound of someone else rising and a fist crunching. John rose to get a better view.

Two handsome young bucks were going at each other hell-for-leather. The taller of the pair was dressed in the very latest fashion with a short, high waistcoat and tight trousers which left very little to the imagination. His coat he had cast to one side. The other fighter was smaller and more genial-looking. He was not so fashionably dressed, wearing a longer waistcoat which had seen better days and a somewhat tired coat which was hampering his return blows.

A circle of men had formed round them shouting encouragement and remarks like 'Hit him, George' and 'That's the spirit, Freddy'. They were clearly known to one and all and the Apothecary stood by fascinated, watching them punching the lights out of one another. And then the landlord stepped in. He had changed since John had last visited the tavern and this new licensee was a massive chap, built like a bull and with a neck that emphasized the point. He came round majestically from his side of the bar and stepped in-between the two scrappers, seizing each by the collar and raising them off their feet.

'Enough!' he roared. He even sounded like a bull. He shook them both violently and then banged their heads together. 'You'll have to continue this in the street. I'll have no more fisticuffs in this establishment.'

And with that he threw the couple out, single-handedly, and so hard that they both landed on their backs on the cobbles. John, convinced that they were going to need his services, followed them. The jollier fellow was scrambling to his feet, bleeding profusely from his eye and lip.

'Please allow me,' said John, 'but I think you will need a stitch or two in that. Let me escort you to the apothecary's shop.'

'Thank you but no,' replied the other, giving a small bow. 'My father is a physician and I live only a step from here. I'll make my own way – but thanks for your kindness.'

'No, you won't,' growled the taller man, getting to his feet. 'We'll finish this here and now, Freddy Warwick.'

'I wouldn't advise it,' the Apothecary interceded. 'Brawling in a public street is highly frowned upon these days.'

'I wouldn't agree with you at all about that,' drawled the other man, 'Exeter on a Saturday night is no place for those of a delicate constitution.'

'None the less,' John answered, 'I think you two should stop. You are both wounded badly, and in my opinion as an apothecary both of you require medical attention. Urgently.'

The taller man looked belligerent, despite the fact that his nose was pouring blood. 'Apologize, you cur,' he said to Freddy.

'I apologize for everything,' the young man replied with a certain cold dignity, and turning on his heel walked quickly away, applying a handkerchief to his bloody eye.

'Well, you have your apology,' John remarked, 'and now I think it would be best if you sought some help.'

'That man is an absolute dandiprat,' growled the other, staring at Freddy's departing back. 'But you can escort me to an apothecary's if you wish. By the way, my name is George Beauvoir.'

Suddenly everything made sense. He had to be the brother

of Lady Imogen who had been so upset in the very shop to which they were now making their way. And Freddy – whom John rather liked – had perhaps hinted that she was pregnant and got a damaged eye for his pains.

'Lord George?' asked the Apothecary.

'The very same. And what's your name, Sir?'

'John Rawlings of Shug Lane, Piccadilly, London.'

'Should I be impressed?' asked George.

'Very,' John replied succinctly.

They made their way along towards High Street, but his lordship was bleeding so badly that John decided they should go to the first apothecary they came across. Sure enough, after they had proceeded just a very few yards, they saw a small shop with the familiar jars in the window and John hurried his patient inside.

The apothecary's apprentice came out to see them and immediately called his master from the compounding room.

'Now what have you been doing, Lord George?' the elderly man asked him. 'I shall have to tell your brother of you.'

'Don't you dare,' said George, and his voice was semi-serious.

'I was merely being jocular. I am hardly likely to see him,' the apothecary answered with a hint of acerbity. 'I do not move in such exalted circles. The new apothecary on High Street has taken most of my custom and I fear that nowadays I am called upon for little except mopping up after fights and handing out the pills which are in much demand.'

'What would they be?' asked John, interested.

'Oh, the usual thing: tablets for gout – they are a favourite – a cure for the clap, my best seller. And, of course, boiled Pennyroyal for helping young women who . . .'

'Quite, quite,' interrupted John, 'I am an apothecary myself. And, believe me, the demands for physics are exactly the same in London as they are here. Now, what's to do with this poor fellow?'

'Get him lying flat for a start. Then apply bruised leaves of Fluellein to that nose of his.'

Together they got George down to the floor and put the application on to his nostrils. Throughout this procedure his lordship kept complaining loudly and uttering vague threats but the two apothecaries ignored him and started a counter conversation about the use and effectiveness of various plants.

During all this John was able to whisper, 'Who is this brother that you spoke of earlier?'

'Viscount Falmouth. Their grandfather is the Earl of St Austell. He's about to remarry – since when every young woman in the place has been throwing herself at the Viscount, the Earl being off the market, so to speak.'

'With any success?'

'None at all. He's a bookish chap and seems in no hurry to tie himself down.'

'Wise man.'

There was a squeal from the floor. 'What are you two muttering about? I've been trying to tell you for the last five minutes that my nose has stopped bleeding.'

'Remain where you are for another five. Then I will give you an infusion of Blueberries to take home and apply frequently. You'd best keep your nose under a bandage for the rest of this night.'

'Dammit, man. I wanted to go out this evening.'

The older apothecary looked down at the figure on the floor. 'It is entirely up to you, of course, but I would suggest a quiet few hours of complete rest. You have no wish to start the flow of blood once more.'

From his place on the floor George muttered evilly. 'Curse that little wretch Freddy Warwick. I'll have it out with him, I swear it.'

John spoke up. 'I think it would be best, Lord George, if you gave up this unfortunate habit of having things out with Freddy. You may have thumped him but he thumped you equally hard in return. If you carry on you will lose your handsome features, you can be sure of it.'

George turned on him a malignant glance. 'I didn't ask for your opinion.'

'No, but I gave it,' John answered, and turning his head to one side winked at the elderly apothecary who gave him a toothy grin in return.

Nine

At dinner that afternoon John shouted down the length of the great table, 'What do you know of the Earl of St Austell?'

'Not a great deal. He was a contemporary of my father's, a little younger perhaps. Why?' came the answer from the Marchesa.

'I discussed him with Sir Clovelly today. It seems he had a fierce reputation when he was younger.'

'Why the sudden interest in the man?'

'Sweetheart, have I forgotten to tell you? Miranda Tremayne – that nasty little girl – is going to marry him.'

'What? But she's young enough to be his granddaughter.'

'Easily. Though that doesn't deter our Miranda. She's looking like a creamed cat and more than a little pleased with herself.'

'For once I feel robbed of speech. But of course I can see the attraction. He has a huge estate in Cornwall and is as rich as Croesus, so they say.'

'And will eventually die, leaving our Miranda a very wealthy widow indeed. Let it be hoped that his temper sweetens with age.'

Elizabeth looked thoughtful and took a sip of wine. 'I'm not so sure about that.'

'About what?'

'St Austell growing more and more gentle. He was a vicious and rather cruel young man, I believe, and I think he will just get nastier and nastier as time passes.'

'You and Sir Clovelly may be quite right. We shall just have to wait and see.' John cleared his throat. 'My dear, there is something I want to ask you.'

'And what is that?'

'I wish to return to London for a brief visit. First of all I want to see Sir Gabriel and Rose. Secondly I wish to discover how Mrs Fortune is proceeding with running my new business.

And lastly I want to check on my new lads and see how they are getting on, particularly Fred the Factotum.'

The Marchesa pealed with laughter; a lovely, bubbly sound. 'How long will you be gone for?'

'About a month. Then I will return so that we can be in time to attend the wedding.'

'Oh, so we are going to be invited, are we?'

'That is what Lady Sidmouth told me. She is also inviting Sir Clovelly Lovell.'

'It should be greatly piquant to see Miranda acting the innocent – and going like a lamb to the slaughter.'

For a moment the acoustics in the great dining room seemed to go out of kilter and the Marchesa's voice was distorted, as if it were echoing down a tunnel. For no reason the Apothecary felt afraid.

'John, what is the matter? You've suddenly gone very white.'

He drained his wine glass to get control of himself. ''Twas nothing. A moment's lapse, that's all.'

There was silence and then Elizabeth said, 'Why don't you bring Rose back with you? I am sure she would love to see the boys.'

John dropped his napkin, rose from his seat, and walked the length of the table. 'Madam, I loved you,' he answered, 'but now I love you more than ever. May I accept the invitation on my daughter's behalf?'

'Very gladly, Sir,' she answered, and regardless of the footmen who stood at the back of the room, kissed him on the lips.

Two days later John caught the flying coach and had a very jolly time of it indeed, his fellow passengers being three young bachelors going to London to celebrate the betrothal of one of them. When they heard of his recent triumph in the realms of fatherhood they cheered wildly and insisted on wetting the heads of the two babies in every stop they made. Consequently the Apothecary arrived at the Gloucester Hotel and Coffee House feeling much the worse for wear and caught a hackney to Nassau Street in something of a grumpy mood. This was not alleviated by his reception, which proved to be minimal, all of the upstairs staff being busy running errands for Mrs Jacquetta Fortune who seemed to have taken control of the entire place. On catching a glimpse of him coming through the front door she dropped him a brief curtsey.

'Oh, Mr Rawlings, how very good to see you home. We were not expecting you, as you have probably noticed. My dear Sir, the business has taken off like a thing deranged. Orders are coming in daily for the carbonated water. The whole enterprise is going to be a great success, I can assure you.'

'Well, I am delighted to hear it. I shall no doubt be needing extra cash as I am now the father of twin boys.'

Jacquetta's eyes opened wide. 'How wonderful, Sir. Please accept my heartiest congratulations. What are their names, may I ask?'

'Jasper and James. They are the sweetest little devils and absolutely identical. One day you must meet them.'

'Will they be coming to London?'

'I don't know,' John answered, and suddenly felt inexplicably annoyed with Elizabeth for her aversion to the capital and her refusal to so much as visit it. To take his mind off these feelings he decided to make his way to his shop in Shug Lane. Once there he alighted from his coach and sent Irish Tom back home. Not knowing quite what to expect, he sauntered over the threshold.

Within the place gleamed; every wooden surface shone like a mirror; every jar glinted its vivid contents. Even as he stood surveying the scene John could see Fred's back bent as he dusted a low-placed box of pills. He was suddenly reminded of the child's namesake, Fred the mudlark, that ridiculously healthy child who had lived in an upturned boat on the banks of the River Thames. In many ways they were so alike, both undersized, both cheerful – and both with a habit of acquiring things that were not rightfully theirs.

'Well, well,' John said admiringly, 'you've certainly made a good job of the shop. Is Master Purle pleased with you?'

Fred straightened up, somewhat startled. 'Oh hello, Sir. We wasn't expecting you back so soon.'

Gideon appeared from the compounding room, looking every inch the apothecary in his long apron, his curling hair tied back in a neat bow. John cast his mind back to when he had first taken him on as an apprentice and marvelled at the change. The Apothecary had signed on someone totally lacking in flair; now Gideon had become a young man more than capable of running the shop in Shug Lane and entering that most noble of professions. And how handsome he had grown. A veritable sight for sore eyes.

'Fred,' said Gideon, 'go into the compounding room and help Master Robin with chopping up the herbs. There's a good lad.'

'Right ho, Sir.'

The diminutive figure disappeared obediently, and John turned to Gideon. 'How has he been behaving?'

'Impeccably. I cannot fault him. And, strange to tell, he has formed a good friendship with Robin.'

'And he? How is he turning out?'

'Excellent, Sir. The boy is genuinely interested. He is far more alert and alive than I was at his age.'

'You were a late developer, Gideon.'

The young man flushed, colouring from his neck up to his bright hair. 'I suppose I was.'

John smiled at him to show there was no ill feeling and at that moment the door of the shop rang, then opened, accompanied by a young man who walked towards them, his nose buried deep in a book.

'Good morning, Sir. How can we help you?' said Gideon, just as John was opening his mouth to ask the same question.

'Eh? What? Oh sorry.' The young man closed the book with a snap and looked about him with a vague expression on his face. 'Ah yes. Of course. Something for my grandpapa.'

John took over. 'What did you have in mind, Sir?'

The young man looked at him. 'Do you know, I'm not sure. Can't think what it was he wanted.'

He opened the book again and read a few lines as if this would refresh his memory. John glanced at the pages sideways and saw that they were full of mathematical equations. He cleared his throat and the young man looked up and fixed him with a vague expression.

'What?'

'I did not speak, Sir,' said John pointedly. 'You were trying to remember what it is your relative required.'

'Was I? Oh yes.'

This conversation was getting nowhere and Gideon intervened.

'Would it be something for gout?'

The young man looked doubtful. 'No, I don't think so. Ah yes, it is coming back to me now.'

'Thank goodness for that,' said John.

'It is for . . .' He lowered his voice to a whisper. '. . . potency. He is getting . . .' He now began to speak so softly that the Apothecary was forced to cup his ear. '. . . married again. He wishes to perform his marital duties vigorously. You understand?'

He said these last words with such a great deal of embarrassment that John almost felt sorry for him. He became very professional.

'How old is the gentleman concerned?'

'Seventy-two.'

'A good old trooper then,' was out of John's mouth before he could curb the words. 'Now, Sir, I have some strengthening physick of my own composition which is considered invaluable by many elderly gentlemen. And in your grandfather's case I would recommend rubbing oil of Jessamine into the appropriate part three times a day.'

The young man looked vague. 'You mean . . .?' He pointed downwards.

'Yes,' said John firmly, 'that is exactly where I do mean. Now, is there anything further I can help you with?'

'Yes . . . I mean no. Thank you kindly. How much do I owe you?'

'Three shillings and six pence.'

'Oh. Yes. Of course.'

The young man took the package that Gideon had wrapped up for him and paid the money. Then he raised his hat – and bumped straight into the door post on the way out.

Ten

The next morning John ordered the coach to be brought round at seven o'clock. Irish Tom eventually turned up at half past, swearing like an old sailor, saying that one of the horses had cast a shoe and that he had had to take him round to the farrier. The Apothecary, still recovering from his riotous journey to London and the rather odd day that followed, said nothing but climbed aboard and fell fast asleep.

They reached Kensington in record time, or so it seemed to him – the horse appearing to have a new sense of *joie de vivre* for having had its hoof attended to and inspiring its fellow – and interrupted Sir Gabriel sitting at the breakfast table reading a copy of *The Gentleman's Magazine* while Rose perched quietly nearby, drawing a picture in a copy book. They looked up as John entered the room unannounced and both gave him a smile before his daughter rushed into his arms. How sweet she smelled and, as always, John was vividly reminded of his late wife, Emilia, whom Rose resembled in so many ways.

'My dear child,' said Sir Gabriel, who sat in a long gown and turban with jewelled slippers upon his feet. 'We did not expect you quite so early.'

'I am sorry, Papa. It was just that I was anxious to see you both.'

'How are your sons?' asked Rose and looked at him with eyes twinkling.

'You little devil,' John answered, chucking her under the chin, 'you knew very well that they were going to be twins, didn't you? How did you do that?'

'I get pictures inside my head sometimes.' She lowered her voice. 'But don't talk about it because it upsets Grandpa.'

John crouched down so that he was level with her eyes. 'Does it? Then we won't mention it in his presence.' He stood up again.

'What are their names, Papa?'

'Did I forget to write that?'

'You most certainly did, my boy.' This from Sir Gabriel. 'What are you calling them?'

'Jasper and James. They are truly identical, Sir. I think you will really love them.'

'I wish I could see them.'

And there was a wistful sound in the old man's voice. John stared at him and saw that the years were beginning to sit heavily on Sir Gabriel's shoulders.

'Come with me, both of you,' he said impulsively. 'I shall be returning to Devon in the next few days. Please regard this as a holiday and keep me company, do.'

'But the Marchesa,' said his father, 'we cannot intrude on her hospitality.'

'She invited you both,' lied John. 'And if she should find it too much to cope with there are plenty of places in Exeter where you might stay. Please come with me, Pa. I really want you to see my sons.'

'Yes, Grandpapa,' echoed Rose. 'You know you will enjoy it.'

Sir Gabriel folded the magazine and laid it on the table, putting his spectacles beside them. Then he sat in silence before announcing, 'By Jove, I will come with you. As I remember it the Lady Elizabeth plays a damned good hand at whist. I shall enjoy seeing her once more. When do we leave?'

John went up and hugged him, then planted a kiss on his cheek. 'Father, you have made me totally happy. The journey would not have been complete without you.'

'And me,' said Rose quietly.

'And you, darling girl,' said John, lifting her up to his shoulder height.

And let it just be hoped and prayed for that Elizabeth will be in agreement, he thought to himself.

Three days later they left London. Irish Tom, pleased as punch to be driving to Devon once more, took the coach and the pair of horses out along the route used by the stages and some of the flying chaises. John had considered that the other means of trans-port would prove too much for the two vastly differing ages that were to accompany him. So the journey took somewhat longer

than usual as Tom kept his team throughout, resting them overnight. Sir Gabriel, with great spirit, enjoyed the journey almost
as much as Rose, peering out of the window and exclaiming at
the various objects of interest they passed. The fourth member
of the party, a nursery maid belonging to Rose, sat beside Irish
Tom, much to the enjoyment of both of them.

Deciding that tact was by far the best option, the Apothecary
left his father and daughter settled comfortably in an inn in
Exeter and took the high road to Elizabeth's house while daylight
still held. Once arrived, he sent Irish Tom to the kitchens and
announced himself at the front door. A footman answered.

'Come in, Mr Rawlings, Sir. The Lady Elizabeth is dining
at the moment with the Lady Felicity Sidmouth and the
Honourable Miranda Tremayne. Should I announce you?'

'Yes, if you would.'

The footman knocked on the dining room door and another
footman answered. There was a deal of whispering and then
the Apothecary was announced in ringing tones. Elizabeth
swept to her feet in a rustle of taffeta.

'My dear, I had not expected you back quite so soon. But
I am delighted to see you. Have you dined?' John shook his
head. 'Then pray join us. You know the other two, of course.'

He bowed to each female present very courteously, his most
graceful bow of all being saved for the Honourable Miranda
who regarded him with a glittering cat's eye.

'And how was London, Mr Rawlings?' she said, raising her
hand to her chin in a delicate gesture.

'The same,' he replied cheerfully. 'Still full of whores, beggars
and thieves. Not very different from anywhere else actually.'

'Oh fie,' Miranda answered, 'surely that could not be said
of Exeter?'

'I think it could be said of any metropolis in the world,'
John answered, taking his seat on the Marchesa's right.

'You have travelled widely?' asked Miranda, knowing full
well that he had never left the country.

'Unfortunately my Grand Tour was disturbed by the war
but I have met many people who have had experience of living
abroad. One in particular was Sir Francis Dashwood. You have
heard of him perhaps?'

'No,' said Miranda, lying.

'Well, I have,' put in Felicity. 'He's a notorious rake and ne'er-do-well, I believe.'

'Remember you are speaking of a peer of the realm,' Miranda rejoined sharply.

'I am only telling the truth.'

'Oh pooh,' said Miranda.

The two girls were glaring at one another, and to break the awkward silence that fell Elizabeth said, 'The twins are very well, John.'

He was profuse in his apologies. 'I am so sorry I didn't ask. But I thought somehow they would be. With a mother like you how could they be anything else?'

'How sweetly put,' said Miranda, dripping honey. 'Montague and I hope to have several children.'

'You'll be lucky,' Felicity answered spitefully.

'That's all you know.'

'Ladies, please,' said Elizabeth. 'I do not think the dinner table a suitable place for such a conversation. Let us reserve it for when we are in private.'

Miranda shot a look in John's direction and said, 'Of course. How remiss of me. Gentlemen present and all that.'

'Yes,' John answered. 'I am very much present and intend to remain so for some while. When are you getting married, Miss Tremayne?'

'In six weeks' time. The invitations are about to be sent out.'

'I shall look forward to receiving mine.' This from Elizabeth.

'Before then we are giving a betrothal party. Everyone will be there. You must come, Marchesa. And you too, Mr Rawlings.'

For the first time since the Apothecary had arrived, Miranda said something without a sarcastic undertone. Indeed she momentarily looked like an excited child as she glanced from one to the other, her eyes on fire with excitement.

'I must go to the manteau makers in Exeter,' Elizabeth said promptly. 'I have nothing to wear at all.'

John glanced at her, noting her figure, which was rapidly restoring itself to its pre-pregnancy suppleness. 'Well I have brought a great trunk packed with clothes for both day and night,' he said. 'I am sure something will be suitable.'

Elizabeth looked at him, smiling. 'So you've come in your own coach? In other words, Rose has accompanied you.'

'Yes,' he said, 'and also Sir Gabriel Kent, who is very old now and was so anxious to know the twins.'

'How lovely,' she answered. 'It will be a pleasure to see him again.' She smiled round at the others. 'You really must meet Rose, John's little girl. She is quite adorable.'

'Just like her father,' said Miranda, and once more her eyes were full of sarcasm.

After the two visitors had left, John and Elizabeth withdrew to the Blue Drawing Room for a few moments, then crept up to the nursery. The Apothecary felt as if his heart would shatter as he looked at the two small faces, fast asleep, so innocent, yet to learn the wicked ways of the weary world. 'Oh, how I am going to miss them as they grow older,' he said with a deep sigh. 'Elizabeth, could you not change your mind about coming to live in London?'

She laughed humourlessly. 'And give up this house and this glorious countryside? Never. But surely it would be easier for you to move to Devon?'

'In a way it would. But my life is in London. My shop is there and now my new business is taking off I would be loath to leave.'

'And there we have our situation in a nutshell. Both of us have our feet firmly planted in the place in which we feel comfortable. But why are you worried, John? You can come here regularly. You shall not miss the boys growing up.'

'I would rather be dead than do so. And what of you, sweetheart? Has the arrival of the twins filled the emptiness in your heart?'

She turned to him and he held her close, both arms round her, smelling the glorious scent which she carried with her everywhere, unique to her and her alone.

'Yes, it has. They are the gift of my middle years. They shall have everything that it is in my power to give them.'

'But you're not to spoil them.'

'That I will never do.'

And he knew it was true. She had too much fire, too much

strength to let her boys turn into idle wastrels. John's thoughts went briefly to the scrapping pair in The Blackamore's Head – George Beauvoir and Freddy Warwick – and thought what a couple of useless fellows they were, particularly George, whom the Apothecary considered to be extremely obnoxious.

Elizabeth misread his silence. 'You don't believe me, do you? I can assure you that I will keep them under control.'

Thinking of her first child, Frederico, and his terrible end, John decided that it was his duty to do all he could to assist in the bringing up of his twin sons. But the perfume of Elizabeth was in his nostrils and the delight of her was in his arms. So he did what any red-blooded man would do and kissed her warmly and lengthily, and temporarily forgot about everything else.

The next day Sir Gabriel and Rose moved into Withycombe House. The first thing Rose did was rush to the nursery where she discovered James and Jasper awake, looking at her with their blue eyes which were already turning to a somewhat darker shade.

'Oh, you two imps,' she said, as she leant over their cribs, 'how I love you and how I shall always love you, even if you go far away from me.'

'Why? Are they thinking of leaving the country?' asked Sir Gabriel, who had mounted the great staircase grandly with much use of his cane, which he had tied with two blue ribbons as a token of his esteem.

She turned to her grandfather and winked. 'Who knows?' she said, giving him her special smile.

Sir Gabriel did not believe in any such nonsense as second sight, but for all that he could not resist his granddaughter, whom he loved with all his heart. Now he put his hand in hers and let her lead him to the two cribs in which lay two identical babies. Sir Gabriel bent over them and one – he never knew which – stretched up a minute hand and pulled at his immense wig.

'Oh Jasper, how naughty,' said Rose. 'You must be more respectful to Grandfather.'

'How did you know that was Jasper?' Sir Gabriel asked, astonished.

'I didn't. But it worked, did it not?'

And they both watched as the tiny fingers disentangled themselves from the horsehair and returned to lie peacefully on the blanket.

Sir Gabriel shook his head. 'What fine, fine boys. I never imagined such a thing possible.'

'Why was that, Grandpapa?'

He looked a trifle embarrassed. 'These matters should not be discussed in front of little girls.'

'I see,' she said, and the very tone of her voice told him that she knew as much as he did about the whole affair.

John spoke from the doorway. 'For the first time the four most important people in my life are all together.'

Rose raised her finger to her lips. 'Hush, Father. Mrs Elizabeth would be most upset if she heard you.'

John glanced guiltily over his shoulder. 'Well, she's not in earshot. And you know perfectly well what I mean, Rose. It is a wonderful moment for me to see all my family in one room. So what do you think of them, Father?'

'I think they are strong, healthy lads and one day will do you great credit, John.'

'Shall we go downstairs and drink their health?'

'What a splendid idea. Lead the way.'

But after they had gone Rose sat on a nursery chair and started to croon a strange little lullaby and, unbelievably, the twins began to join in. Not crying but making small sounds to echo their sister's. Eventually, all three of them fell asleep, and that was how the nursery maid found them. The boys quite peaceful in their cots; Rose, red hair spiralling round her head, curled up in the chair, a smile on her face as she dreamed.

Eleven

A wonderful fortnight ensued, during which the Apothecary spent as much time as was possible with his daughter Rose. It was now high April and the weather typical of the season. Bright, cheerful but boisterous breezes blew amongst the trees, followed by vivid showers. The great house, which stood tall above the River Exe, had rain beating against the windows one minute and the next was full of brilliant sunshine, while rainbows arched high over the river.

John, very much aware that shortly after her birthday at the end of the month Rose would be going to boarding school, determined to make her his favourite companion for these last few weeks that they had together. So while Elizabeth was busy with the twins and Sir Gabriel snoozed in the afternoon sunshine he took her out walking or riding on her pony, while he struggled along beside her on one of Elizabeth's fiercesome mounts. Thus they many times came to the sea and it was then that John taught his daughter how to swim, she battling hard against the persuasive current, the Apothecary holding her securely round the waist but loosening his grip slightly on each occasion. One day when she was concentrating fiercely he let go altogether and she swam for about a yard before she realized that he was no longer holding her and began to flail. But from that time on it was a question of practice, and Rose soon mastered the technique and swam along beside him quite happily. She somehow seemed to ignore the cold, which John found quite piercing, though she emerged on to the beach chatter-toothed and shivering, her thin little body pale, her hair flaming in the sun.

Sir Gabriel meanwhile spent most of the day when awake playing with the twins – that is, when he was allowed into the nursery by the two fierce women who had control of the place. In this way he was rewarded by their first smile – James's a day before Jasper's – and rushed off to fetch Elizabeth to see, whirling through the house, leaning heavily on his great stick. She came back with him and James smiled again, a sight which reduced her to tears before she picked him up and made much of him, handing Sir Gabriel the other twin to hold on his lap, a fact which made the old man weep as well. So everyone was crying when John and Rose walked in, a situation which soon changed to general laughter and happiness for the entire family.

It was a slight surprise to the Apothecary, therefore, when Sir Gabriel said one evening, 'It is time I was getting back to Kensington, my boy.'

'Is it, Sir?' asked John, his svelte eyebrow rising. 'Why?'

'Fact is, I am being missed. I am frequently a card partner to Lady Bournemouth and she has written to me in quite anxious terms demanding to know when I am returning. Apparently she is playing with Lord Whatlington, a terrible old bore, and she is most persistent to have me back.'

John smiled, picturing this elderly card school and feeling terribly grateful that his father was still applying his mind to it and, moreover, was treasured by its other members. He found himself praying that Sir Gabriel would die in his sleep and not have to wait for death as he grew iller and iller, gaunt white face staring at him from between the sheets.

'So I thought I would ask Irish Tom to drive me back in two days' time.'

John stared at him. 'But who will go with you?'

'I shall travel alone, dear boy. What's wrong with that?'

'I don't like the thought of it. In fact I shall accompany you, Sir, if that is agreeable to you.'

'But you are needed here.'

'And I am needed in London as well. I just can't leave Jacquetta Fortune alone to cope with an ever-increasing business. Besides, I need to check on Gideon that he has got the formula correctly. I can't have second-rate water being sold under my name.'

'But what about the babies?'

'They will hardly miss me with all the care and attention they are getting. Anyway I shall only be away a fortnight or so. I have to come back here for various social events.'

'I suppose there is no chance of the Lady Elizabeth . . .'

'Marrying me? Not a hope in hell. That is the situation and I have long ago come to terms with it.'

'Poor John.'

'Poor me nothing, Father. The woman has borne my children, lets me use this grand house as if it were my own, lets me share her bed and her life. The one thing she does not want is to be tied down.'

'I somehow thought that being tied would have happened following the birth of twins,' Sir Gabriel answered drily.

'I don't think even that event could tame her spirit. She has already resumed riding and is becoming as beautiful as she was before. Or hadn't you noticed?'

'My dear boy, a woman is as old as she looks, a man is old when he doesn't look any more.'

John chuckled and accepted the mild rebuke with good grace.

The problem was what to do with Rose. John was all for leaving her behind in Devon, where she was always happy to be with Mrs Elizabeth – as she insisted on calling the Marchesa – and now she had the added excitement of twin brothers into the bargain. But when he questioned her, Rose had a strange answer for him.

'Father, I don't want you in any danger by yourself in London.'

'Rose, what possible danger could I get into?'

'Remember what I told you. There's a horrible old woman in a brown bonnet and you must lie flat when you see her. She is coming for you. I swear it.'

And one look at the child's eyes, distressed and wide with fear, told the Apothecary that she was having one of her strange moments of second sight. He took her in his arms to comfort her.

'Sweetheart, I promise you that I will lie flat, even if I have to prostrate myself in the street at the old woman's feet.'

The child giggled, unable to control herself because her father was pulling such terrible faces at her, contorting his features and making monkey grimaces. 'Oh stop it,' she said, pushing him away. 'I am serious. You will see.'

Rose was in that terrible state between laughter and tears, and eventually she wept as the only way of proving she was in earnest. John immediately stopped pulling faces and held her close, reassuring her that whatever evil was after him he would take adequate precautions to keep it at bay. Eventually she quietened down and asked how long he would be away.

'Two weeks at the most, darling. But I really rather need you to look after the boys for me.'

She nodded very seriously. 'They talk to me, you know.'

'How do they do that?'

'We have our own language. And we sing together too.'

The Apothecary asked no more, but within his heart he felt a warm glow at the thought of his twin boys in chorus with his strange, witchy little girl.

Going at a leisurely pace that he found rather irksome, John arrived in London three days later. First he took Sir Gabriel to Kensington, only to be met on the doorstep by a large woman, made larger by the huge hoops of her costume which flared out at least three feet on either side of her skirt. These were worn far less by the younger fashionable set, who regarded them as 'full dress', and had cast them aside in favour of side hoops. But this formidable dame clung to the fashions of yesteryear, and she also clung to Sir Gabriel's arm.

'Oh my dear, you are returned,' she gasped. 'Now at last we can have a decent card school.'

John's father was at his most elegant. He bowed low then kissed the lady's hand. 'My dear Lady Bournemouth,' he answered. 'How very nice to see you again. Did you not get my letter telling you I was returning?'

Her heavily rouged cheeks turned even pinker as she said, 'No, Sir Gabriel, I received none such.'

John shuffled his feet slightly and his father said, 'Madam, may I present my son to you?'

She fluttered, 'Oh certainly, Sir Gabriel. Please do.'

'Lady Bournemouth, it gives me extreme pleasure to introduce my heir, John Rawlings.'

The Apothecary bowed low, the epitome of politeness. 'Madam, I am most honoured to make your acquaintance.'

'The pleasure is entirely mine. Tell me, young Sir, do you play a fair hand at cards?'

'Reasonable, I suppose. Though nothing like as well as my father.'

'Well, I invite you round to my house this evening. It is one of my little soirées. I had posted an invitation to Sir Gabriel but, of course, he won't have seen that. But now I am here in person to ask you both to attend. Oh do say you'll come.'

As ever John felt a certain sympathy in the presence of the elderly, though he was sure that Lady Bournemouth would have been mortally wounded if she knew John thought of her as such.

'I really ought to get back to my house in London,' he answered somewhat lamely.

Her lower lip trembled. 'Oh what a shame! I had so hoped . . .' Her voice trailed away.

'Oh come along, John.' This from Sir Gabriel. 'What difference can one more evening make?'

And what indeed? So John made another elegant bow to Lady Bournemouth and said, 'Madam, my father has persuaded me. I shall be delighted to accept your invitation.'

Irish Tom, somewhat relieved to pass a night under Sir Gabriel's roof where he was very popular with the serving staff, got down John's trunk so that he could find a decent suit of night clothes, while Sir Gabriel went off to find himself something ravishing in black and silver.

Two hours later, dressed to the inch, the pair departed for Kensington Gore, to a house not far from the country seat of Sir John Fielding. Within, John found the decor rather ornate but was pleased that the company had an equal share of younger people to older. In fact he was glad now that he had let his better nature win and had accepted the invitation. The plan of the evening was to play cards, this to be followed by a cold supper and music. It was a delightful change, made all the more so by the fact that John was asked to partner Miss Cordelia Clarke, a great-niece of Lady Bournemouth's, visiting London from Exeter, by all the strange coincidences. The fact that she was very lovely to look at, with a great mass of red hair – very similar to that of Rose – and a delightful retroussé nose, made John's task even more pleasant.

'And tell me, Miss Clarke, where exactly do you live?'

She gave him a look from eyes the colour of purple pansies. 'Why Sidmouth, Mr Rawlings. Where I vow and swear I have seen you out walking. Though of course I must be mistaken.'

'Not at all,' he answered. 'I often visit Devon'

He should have added that he had a friend nearby – a very close friend – but some awful imp inside him made him cut the sentence short. But he needn't have bothered.

'Do you have friends down there?' Cordelia asked.

'Yes, several,' John answered. 'Lady Sidmouth is one of them.'

She clasped her hands together. 'Why, she and my mother are old acquaintances. But I am far better friends with her daughter.'

'Of course, Felicity. A charming girl. And do you know Miranda Tremayne?' he asked.

Cordelia gave him a rather dark look. 'Yes, indeed. Do you know her well?'

'Only casually. I have met her once or twice. Why do you ask?'

'Because I don't really take to her. There is something of a shifter about the girl.'

'Oh come now. I think she is merely jealous of other women and cannot resist a barbed remark if she can make one.'

Cordelia smiled. 'Well whatever the case, she doesn't like me.'

John should have been thoroughly ashamed of himself for playing the dandy, but he did so nonetheless. 'With your beauty, Madam, I am not at all surprised.'

Miss Clarke went a gorgeous shade of pink. 'Come now, Sir. I do declare you are flirting with me.'

John thought that he might be about to drift into deep water but saved himself by giving a small bow and saying, 'Forgive me. I have a habit of doing that in the company of lovely women.'

Thankfully at that moment Lady Bournemouth called everyone into cards and the Apothecary was saved from behaving reprehensibly. He played an even poorer hand than usual but glancing across the room saw that his father, spectacles clamped firmly upon the high bridge of his nose, was in fine form and scoring point after point. Love for the old fellow overwhelmed him and made him lose what little concentration he already had.

At last the ghastly game was over and everyone retired to the supper room. He was in some ways relieved to see that Miss Clarke had attracted the eye of another suitor – a superficial young fellow with a very small mouth – who was making much of her. She, still young and clearly inexperienced regarding the wicked ways of the world, kept glancing across at John who bowed and nodded and smiled.

'Who is that?' asked Sir Gabriel, pausing with a piece of cold salmon perched upon his fish fork heading towards his mouth.

'A great-niece of Lady Bournemouth's, I believe,' said John casually, hoping that he sounded more genuine to his father's ears than he did to his own.

'An extremely beautiful gal.'

'Yes, I suppose she is. Would you believe that she comes from Sidmouth?'

Sir Gabriel shot him an amused glance. 'Well, well, what a coincidence. Tell me, is she acquainted with Lady Elizabeth?'

'I'm afraid that our conversation did not touch upon the matter.'

'No, I'm quite sure it didn't,' answered his father, and turned his attention to the salmon.

They returned to Sir Gabriel's home fairly late and went immediately to bed. All around him the house was silent except for the ticking of the great clock that stood in the hallway, yet the Apothecary found himself lying awake, listening to the silence. For no reason at all he kept hearing Rose's voice telling him about the woman in the brown bonnet and how he was to lie flat when he saw her. It made no sense. In fact he would have dismissed it as an illusion had he not come across this sort of thing before. For his daughter was gifted in a way that he did not fully understand yet could not disregard.

When he finally dropped off to sleep he had a strange dream. He dreamt that he got out of bed and went downstairs to find that he was not in his father's house but instead in his own home in Nassau Street. He went into the living room and there were Sir Gabriel, years younger, and his mother, Phyllida, still alive and looking as beautiful as she had before death came for her. They were conversing fondly and John realized after he tried to speak to them that they could not see or hear him.

'Mother,' he called out, but she merely put her hand down and patted a large ginger cat which sat fatly upon a cushion beside her.

'Please look at me,' he shouted.

But she and Sir Gabriel continued to smile and gaze at each other till John thought it unseemly to stare at a couple who loved one another so much, and left the room and climbed back up the stairs and into bed, where he awoke next morning.

Twelve

He had promised Elizabeth that he would be away two weeks at the most, so felt that he would be rather overburdened with things to achieve in that short space of time. But such were Jacquetta's powers of organization that the Apothecary almost felt *de trop* when he sat down with her on the first morning of his return and went through a long list of figures. It seemed that this new sparkling mineral water was proving an enormous success. Vaux Hall had ordered a large quantity, as had Ranelagh Gardens, though this last piece of marketing had been achieved at the hands of Nicholas Dawkins, the Gardens' consultant apothecary. Mr Napthali Hart had ordered some for Marble Hall, which was to open in a month's time, and meanwhile was keeping a supply in store for his student dancers and fencers in Essex Street. But Mrs Fortune wished for a consultation about the bottles and called a meeting for that evening when Gideon Purle could join their company. John felt that it was the least he could do to ask his apprentice to dine with them, and duly broached the subject on arrival in his shop.

Gideon stood behind the counter in his long apron looking so terrifically assured that the Apothecary's heart sank. It would not be long now before the young man would apply to be made Free and the whole process would begin all over again.

'My dear chap, how are you?'

'I've never been better, Sir.'

John's heart sank even further as he thought that he would have to waive the fornication rule as he had done with Nicholas Dawkins several years ago. For one of the binding strictures of apprenticeship was that one would not have sexual relationships, which grew very awkward when the boys reached a certain age, as John Rawlings knew from personal experience!

'I hear that you and Mrs Fortune are going like hell-cats with sales of the water.'

Gideon blushed endearingly. 'They are indeed very good, Sir.'

'And tell me how the boys are shaping up. What about young Fred? Is he behaving himself?'

'He hero-worships Robin and has announced that he too would like to be an apothecary if only his reading and writing skills were better.'

'But surely they taught him those at the Foundling Hospital?'

'I think it was pretty basic stuff, Sir. Apparently his reading is well ahead of his writing.'

'Then we must give him some lessons. Everyone should be allowed to realize their potential.'

'Please don't look at me, Mr Rawlings. I am at full stretch with the shop and the business.'

'No, I wouldn't inflict that on you, Gideon. I'll have to send the child to a teacher of some sort. And talking of the business, can you come and dine with me today? Mrs Fortune has called a meeting for this evening to discuss the bottles.'

'Thank you, Sir. I knew about the meeting, of course.'

'You and she are fairly close these days, I take it?' John asked innocently.

'Yes, we are. Very. Only in a professional sense, of course,' Gideon added hastily.

'Naturally. I wouldn't have presumed anything else,' the Apothecary answered, and went into the compounding room, grinning.

They dined formally later that day. John, for once clad all in black, sat soberly at the head of the table looking at the beautiful woman that Jacquetta was turning into and thinking to himself that Gideon Purle was obviously and hopelessly in love with her. She, on the other hand, kept her thoughts and emotions very much to herself. Quite a shuttered and secretive person, John concluded. As she grew in confidence so she became more a woman of mystery. The Apothecary found her totally intriguing.

No sooner was dinner finished than the subject of bottles was raised.

'Just to put you in the picture, Mr Rawlings,' Jacquetta said, 'we were wondering what type of bottles should be used. We have so far been selling the water in containers which resembled those used for physick. This has the disadvantage of certain people thinking that they were literally taking their medicine.'

'I favoured stone bottles,' Gideon ventured. 'But Mrs Fortune could not decide. That's why we were waiting for your return.'

John paused. 'Well, we need something unusual. Something which echoes the contents.'

There was silence during which everybody thought, then John continued, 'Supposing we have two bottles; one stone and one glass. The stone being sold slightly cheaper.'

'But what about style, Sir?'

Jacquetta spoke. 'Why not have a square bottle with a slender neck rising from it, and the words "J. Rawlings, Nassau Street" etched on the front?'

'And it should be green to match your eyes,' said Gideon, then blushed so violently that he resembled nothing so much as a tomato.

John smiled and caught Jacquetta's glance, which remained blank, though a slight twitch of her eyebrow told him that she was highly amused. 'That, my dear Gideon, is a splendid idea,' he answered, partly to save his apprentice's discomfort. 'Green bottles it is. Now what do you think of having stone bottles as well?'

'A very good plan,' said Jacquetta. 'That means that the waters can be drunk by those not so well placed in society as others.'

'Which includes the majority of the population,' answered John, and so saying rose and poured three glasses of port from the decanter on a side table.

'Here's to the success of our enterprise,' he said, then turned to Jacquetta. 'And I would like to toast you, Mrs Fortune, for organizing the launch of the business so well. You truly are a woman of amazing skills.'

'Hear, hear,' muttered Gideon besottedly.

And this time Jacquetta smiled.

A week later and he was off, catching the same flying coach from the Gloucester Coffee House. But he, that most gregarious

of people, spent most of the journey in moody silence, realizing that he must make some plan for the future. The arrival
of the twins had sealed his fate, he could see that clearly.
Somehow or other he must impress on Elizabeth the importance of making a firm decision about what lay ahead.

Thirteen

Dressed in his lilac-bloom taffeta with a double breasted waistcoat in subtle rose-pink and silver, with breeches tight enough to take your breath away, John felt ready to take on the world as he carefully climbed into the carriage which was taking them to Sidmouth House for the grand rout to celebrate the betrothal of Miranda Tremayne to the Earl of St Austell. Beside him sat the Marchesa di Lorenzi, looking every inch the part, dressed in midnight blue, her hair swept high, a cascade of ribbons descending down one side of her face, accentuating the scar yet at the same time adding to her look of finely chiselled *hauteur*.

Yet despite her loveliness and despite his love for her, John could not help feeling that they were now both in a hopeless situation. Since the birth of the twins he had wanted nothing more than to live as a family unit. But this would mean giving up his shop in Shug Lane and moving to Exeter, against a formidable group of rivals – apothecaries who had spent many years building up their reputations and businesses and who would not welcome a newcomer on the scene. As for begging Elizabeth to move to London, he had given up on that score. She would point to her great house, her enormous estate, and say, with truth, that this was the place to bring up children; this was the place to let them breathe the fresh air of the Devon countryside; this was the place to teach them to ride and to swim. Mentally John shook his head. Elizabeth and he had reached a situation out of which there was no foreseeable way.

It was late April, and one of those exquisite evenings that the month could so breathtakingly produce. Everywhere, as the carriage moved forward, John could see the triumph of spring – that fresh, bright greenness of leaf and bud bursting through the dead wood of winter. Colour was coming back, crocuses were thrusting their way through one of the great lawns, while below them the sea was gentle and full of song. Just as they alighted from their coach the evening sun caught the edifice of Sidmouth House and bathed it in a luminescence like the inside of a seashell.

The receiving line that met them in the grand hall was headed by Lady Sidmouth herself, hideously gowned in puce, her small facial features swamped by a large feathered headdress. Next to her stood Miranda, clothed in pale blue with white lutestring decoration, a perfect example of blushing, maidenly modesty. With her eyes cast to the floor, she glanced up at each new arrival and lisped, 'Oh thank you,' as they announced their good wishes. And next to her stood the man himself – the Earl of St Austell, with his cruel raven's face and his long white hair, tied back in a scarlet ribbon, and his large imposing stature. John did not know exactly what he had been expecting but nothing on the lines of this. Sir Clovelly had given him some idea, had painted a word portrait, but this man exceeded everything that had been said about him. He was the picture of an absolute brute that age had in no way diminished. For one minute John felt a tremendous compassion for Miranda, before that was replaced by the thought that she had willingly chosen the man.

He caught Elizabeth's eye as they passed into the big saloon. 'What do you think?' he murmured.

'He's rotten to the core and doesn't give a damn who knows it.'

'But how old is he, for heaven's sake?'

'Seventy-two – and all set for another ten years at least.'

'Poor Miranda.'

'Poor Miranda indeed,' Elizabeth whispered back.

The saloon was filling up with people, several of whom John recognized. The first person on whom he set his gaze was Lettice James, the gossipy woman he had met on the stagecoach who had tried to pump him for information about Lady Elizabeth. Her eyes widened to twice their size when she saw them enter the room together. She came over, swift as a bird, literally trembling with excitement.

'My dear Lady Elizabeth, how are you? I have been so concerned. I was saying to this gentleman I met on the stage-coach – that was where it was, was it not, Sir? Anyway, I was saying to him that I had not seen you at all these past few months and was hoping you were not poorly.'

'Actually,' the Marchesa answered with a smile, 'I was pregnant.'

Lettice looked as though someone had hit her in the solar plexus. 'Oh, oh! I had not realized you had married again. Forgive me.'

'That's perfectly all right, my dear, because you see I haven't. You say you have already met John?'

A tiny nod came from the other woman.

'Well, he is the father. We had twin boys by the way.'

There was the sound of a strangulated gurgle and Lettice James became very pale.

'And now if you'll forgive me,' said Elizabeth sweetly, 'I see someone else that I know. Good day to you.'

And she swept on, John following behind like a little lap dog. Glancing over his shoulder he could see that the poor creature had been forced to sit down and that Felicity was leaning over her administering salts.

'Elizabeth, how can you be so forthright?' he reprimanded. 'The woman is in shock.'

She gave him a smile. 'Serves her right,' she said. 'She's the biggest gossip ever born and always knows everybody's business before they have even thought of it themselves.'

'Now, now,' he said. 'The quality of mercy is not strained.'

The Marchesa gave a humourless laugh. 'Indeed not. But it can come under a great deal of pressure.'

And John, remembering how her first child had died in the horrors of an opium den and how she had exacted punishment on those responsible, suddenly felt sorry for her and for a moment came near to understanding her overwhelming love for the twins and how she insisted on bringing them up single-handedly.

He felt Felicity at his elbow as the Marchesa wandered off.

'Good evening, Mr Rawlings. Is this not an elegant ensemble?'

'Very. But I know so few people. Perhaps you could tell me who one or two of them are.'

'Gladly.' Her eyes swivelled round the room. 'Well, there's Lord St Austell's younger grandson, George Beauvoir. Isn't he handsome? Mind you, they say he is a reckless blade. But he has a certain charm, would you not agree?'

'He's certainly of very good appearance. But does his character match his looks?'

'I shouldn't think so for a minute,' Felicity said – and gave rather a sorrowful little giggle.

John did not add that he had last seen George engaged in a tavern brawl with Freddy Warwick. 'And who's the young woman talking to him?'

'Oh that's Lady Imogen, his sister. She's a very sweet person – or at least so I am told.'

'Ah,' said John thoughtfully. He had recognized her on the instant. She was the woman he had seen in the apothecary's shop, the one he believed to be pregnant. And running his practised eye over her he thought that he could indeed see the first signs of a rounding. If he were correct then heaven help the girl. She would get no quarter from her grandfather and probably be sent away and her child handed to some wretched foster mother. Then she would come home to live a life of shame and misery and daily reminding of her terrible sin.

At that moment Lady Imogen looked directly at the Apothecary and he bowed courteously whilst she in return dropped the smallest curtsey imaginable. This led him to wonder if she were in fact conceited and full of the grandness of her station in life. He watched her say something to her brother who also looked in John's direction. The Apothecary could not resist it. He bowed, waved and grinned like a lunatic all at one and the same time. George glowered, then changed his mind and approached.

'How do, Mr Rawlings? That is your name, isn't it?'

'It is, and it please your lordship.'

George looked slightly surprised. 'Last time I saw you I was brawling in a tavern, I believe.'

'Knocking the living daylights out of one Freddy Warwick.'

'Never could abide the fellow. Yet he seems to shadow me. Trouble is that we both belong to the same social set so he has this awful habit of turning up wherever I am. See, there he is now. Talking to that fascinating woman with the scarred face. Dying to meet her but so far our paths have not crossed.'

John turned his head and saw Freddy deep in conversation with the Marchesa.

'She's the Lady Elizabeth di Lorenzi,' George continued. 'I
believe she married some damn Eyetie, hence the funny name.
D'you know, I've always been captivated by older women. By
God, I wouldn't mind going for a gallop with her, I can tell
you. I bet she'd give me the ride of my life.'

The Apothecary actually felt the colour leave his cheeks.
'Be very careful, Sir. You are speaking of my mistress.'

George turned on him a look of total surprise. 'Really?
Well, I'll be damned. By the way, who's your tailor?'

John was rendered utterly speechless by the incongruity of
the question and just stared at the fellow, who by now was
grinning like a cat.

'That's beside the point,' he said eventually.

'Oh, I wouldn't say that,' answered George, who was clearly
having the time of his life. 'His workmanship looks damned
good to me. I'll wager he dwells in London.'

'Yes, Sir, he does.'

'Damn fine. Well, I must be off. Got to pay my respects to
Sir Godfrey. *Au revoir.*'

And he sauntered away without a backward glance. John
was just about to rejoin the subject of the recent conversation
when he felt a small tug at his elbow and looked round to see
the beautiful Miss Cordelia Clarke regarding him.

'Oh Mr Rawlings, how nice to see you again. Is this not
an elegant gathering? And it is so wonderful to make your
acquaintance once more.'

John bowed very deep, then raised her small gloved hand
to his lips. 'The pleasure is entirely mine, Miss Clarke.'

She blushed divinely and John thought what a sweet and
attractive girl she was. And at that moment two people bore
down on him simultaneously: the formidable Lady Bournemouth,
clearly chaperoning Miss Clarke, and Elizabeth with a wary
look in her eye. John bowed again to them both.

'Oh do present me, Sir,' said Miss Clarke. 'I have admired
the Lady Elizabeth from afar for an age.'

Lady Bournemouth interrupted. 'My turn first, my child.
Mr Rawlings, pray introduce me to your companion. I saw
you together when you arrived.'

John turned to the Marchesa. 'Lady Elizabeth, allow me to

present Lady Bournemouth to you. She is held in very high regard by Sir Gabriel, with whom she plays cards.'

They bobbed curtsies at one another and the older woman said, 'How de doo? It is a pleasure to meet you, Lady Elizabeth. And now may I introduce you to my late sister's granddaughter? A very dear child. Cordelia Clarke.'

'I cannot think how we have not met before,' Elizabeth answered, giving a grand curtsey to Cordelia. 'What a lovely girl you truly are.'

Miss Clarke blushed becomingly once more. 'I am so thrilled to be presented at last, my Lady. I often ride past your house and look at it admiringly.'

'Well, next time you must come in, my dear.'

But this conversation got no further because at that moment Freddy Warwick joined the group, bowing magnificently to all the ladies in turn. Finally he stopped, fixed on John a look that besceched him not to say a word about the fight in the tavern, and said, 'How nice to see you again, Sir.'

Yet it was obvious, even at this stage, that Freddy had eyes only for Cordelia and had joined the group with the express purpose of talking to her. Having made his greetings to the other ladies he turned to the object of his desire.

'How nice to see you again, Miss Clarke. Did you enjoy your visit to London?'

'Oh yes, thank you, Mr Warwick. I met some most interesting people.'

'More interesting than the people one meets on the Exeter social scene I don't doubt.'

'Oh yes, far more.'

Her eyes were sparkling and she seemed full of fun – and John, regarding her, thought, young and innocent though she might be, she was quite enjoying putting this youthful admirer through a little bit of torture.

'But surely,' he replied with spirit, 'you did not attend anything as grand as this rout. I mean the betrothal of a peer of the realm is something to celebrate for sure.'

She drew his head down and whispered in his ear. He listened and then burst out laughing.

Lady Bournemouth drew herself up. 'Cordelia, whispering

in public is considered the height of ill manners. Were you at home I would send you to your room. Apologize to Lady Elizabeth and Mr Rawlings immediately.'

Miss Clarke dropped her eyes to hide the fact she was bubbling with mischief, and dropped a penitent curtsey. 'Please forgive me, Marchesa, Mr Rawlings – it's just that I have known Freddy for ever and a day. I'm sorry, I mean Mr Warwick.' Having said this she burst into a fit of giggling in which Freddy joined.

John was delighted. It seemed that this young couple had found the ability to laugh together, which was something he considered very important. Lady Bournemouth huffed angrily but saw the amusement in Elizabeth's expression and condescended to smile. So they were standing, a little group clearly enjoying themselves, when a shadow fell over them. Looking up, John saw the Earl and Miranda clearly waiting to be addressed.

In that moment, before a word was spoken, John regarded the elderly bridegroom-to-be and actually felt physically repelled. It was as if the man's soul had been dragged out, leaving a husk with cold blue-ice eyes with which to glare at the rest of mankind. And what eyes they were. It was like looking at an Arctic landscape and feeling the chilling gale blow, like gazing on a terrain where the sun never shone. Despite himself, John looked away.

St Austell stood there in silence, obviously considering himself too high up the social scale to start any kind of conversation. It was Elizabeth who saved the day. She swept a small curtsey, with much rustling of her gown, and said, 'We meet again, Lord St Austell. To remind you, I am Lord Exmoor's daughter. May I congratulate you on your forthcoming marriage. And you, Miranda, I wish you every happiness.'

St Austell stared at her and John could have sworn that a glimmer of salacity moved in the depths of those terrible eyes. Then he spoke.

The Apothecary had been expecting a deep boom but instead the voice rasped, almost painfully. 'How dee do, Lady Elizabeth? I trust you are keeping well. You may present your friends to me.'

Elizabeth did not meet John's eye as she introduced Lady

Bournemouth, who made much of curtseying to a peer of the realm, sweeping very low and then having some difficulty in rising again. Thankfully her great niece offered an arm and an embarrassing situation was avoided. John made a short bow and muttered his congratulations. On the one occasion he looked at the Earl it was to see the slightest of sneers upon his face.

Cordelia and young Freddy Warwick had obviously met the man before and all they had to do was to congratulate him and wish Miranda well, it being considered the height of bad manners to offer congratulations to the bride as if she had finally achieved her objective. This done, there was a short silence into which Miranda spoke.

'I can't tell you how happy I am,' she said gushingly, linking her arm through that of her future husband. 'Montague is so good to me. I dare not tell you or I think all you ladies will be jealous.'

Neither Elizabeth nor Cordelia smiled, but Lady Bournemouth let out a high-pitched titter. John caught Freddy's eye and they exchanged a glance. But George Beauvoir was making his way towards them at which young Mr Warwick, running his fingers over the back of Cordelia's hand in a gesture that no one was meant to see, made a hasty exit.

'Well, Grandpa, how are you doing?' George asked, bowing laconically as he did so.

'I am doing very well,' rasped the other.

'Surrounded by beautiful women as usual.'

'This is not the place for that sort of remark.'

'Sorry, Sir.' George paused, then said, 'Good God, here comes Falmouth. I thought he was still in town.'

John turned his head to see who they were regarding and scarcely recognized the figure that was coming towards him. Previously it had had its nose in a book and had appeared to be slightly subnormal, to say the least. Now it was wearing a well-tailored black taffeta suit and was striding along with a smile on its face; however, it still had the huge pair of glasses hiding the eyes.

'Ladies and gentlemen,' said St Austell in that grating rasp, 'may I introduce my elder grandson, Viscount Falmouth. He has just returned to us from the city of London.'

Lady Bournemouth contemplated another deep curtsey but, remembering the last occasion, thought better of it and gave a small bob.

John Rawlings bowed then stared at the fellow. 'I believe we have met before, Sir.'

'Have we?' asked Falmouth vaguely.

'Yes, Sir. You came into my shop in Shug Lane and I served you. Do you remember?'

'By Jove, yes I do. Well, how the devil are you?'

'I am very well indeed,' answered John – and gave a crooked smile.

Fourteen

Afterwards, when John was sipping a glass of champagne and standing alone, having wandered off to a window to gaze at the plunging sea below, he recalled that recent time in his shop in Shug Lane when Maurice, Viscount Falmouth, had come in, presenting himself as an absent-minded human being ordering strengthening potions for his poor old grandfather. How different he seemed today, alive and full of energy, though still clearly short-sighted. And, furthermore, could it really be true that the terrifying Earl needed aphrodisiacs, regardless of the fact he was in his seventy-third year? John knew that time could take its toll, but surely not from so fierce and vital a creature as St Austell. He had a sudden mental picture of the man crushing Miranda beneath him and despite the warmth of the day found himself shuddering.

A movement at his elbow brought his attention back to the present and he saw that Lady Sidmouth stood there, an oddly comic figure in her fine array.

'I saw you shake, my friend. May I ask what caused it?'

'I don't know, Madam. Perhaps a goose walked over my grave.'

And this remark made him think of that chilly warning given to him by his daughter, that strange little sprite who loved him so dearly. Looking round the room it seemed to John at that moment that the crowd gathered therein had somehow developed a sinister aspect. Everyone had a cruelty, a hardness about their features, even the Marchesa had become like a mask in a carnival, blank and uncaring.

Without thinking, John heard himself say, 'What is your opinion of the Earl?' a question he would never have dared ask directly had he not been in such a strange mood.

He felt Lady Sidmouth draw close. 'He is a monster,' she answered.

Startled, the Apothecary looked at her. 'Then why did you permit the marriage?'

She looked up at him from her half-closed eyes, and what he could see of her pupils were glazed and dull. 'I could do nothing to stop it. Miranda is merely a cousin. The poor girl's mother is dead and her father remarried to some uncaring wretch. She is twenty years old and she insisted that she had her way. Filled me up with some poppycock tale of being in love. With that ogre! But I think they deserve each other. The only thing that worries me is that he enjoys depths of depravity of which poor Miranda knows nothing.'

'Could you not tell her that?'

'I tried, believe me. I spoke to her more frankly than is common between guardian and ward but she would have none of it. Told me that I was mistaken and to say no more. Quite honestly, Mr Rawlings, I have had to give up arguing for the sake of my sanity and my daughter, Felicity.'

She let out a sudden suppressed sob and John instinctively put an arm round her shoulders. 'My dear Lady Sidmouth, you have clearly done your best and I am sorry that I said what I did. Miranda has always struck me as a self-willed girl and now, having made her bed, she can lie in it.'

'Which I believe she will with some enjoyment,' Lady Sidmouth answered sadly, and walked away with sloping shoulders.

Their conversation was at an end and John was on his way to rejoin Elizabeth when that extraordinary young man, Viscount Falmouth, bore down on him. John was about to make him a bow when Falmouth said, 'Don't bother with that, I beg you. It is I who should be bowing to you.'

Startled, the Apothecary replied, 'Why, my Lord?'

Falmouth gave him a good-natured grin and John saw that beneath his ugly glasses, beneath his rather other-worldly expression and his general air of bookishness, there lay a very handsome fellow indeed. His white wig enhanced his strong features and when one peered one could see a pair of dazzling green eyes, currently hidden by that unattractive pair of spectacles.

'Because I came in and asked for . . . well, you know.'

'For something to help your grandfather on his wedding night?' answered John directly. 'I should say – judging by his general demeanour – that he would need no such thing.'

Maurice Falmouth laughed. 'I think perhaps I was a little

previous with my request. I must admit that he looks hale and hearty enough to me now that I see him. You see, I was reading a book about an older man getting married again and failing miserably, if you understand my meaning, and that was what had me wandering into your shop and asking for your help.'

The Apothecary thought that it was a reasonable enough explanation for someone who had his nose in a novel most of the time, but had no chance to think anything more about it for at that moment George came bounding up, punching Maurice jovially on the shoulder.

'How did you enjoy London, you bugger?'

'Very well. It was dirty and smelly but of good cheer.'

'I'm glad to hear it. Did you manage to meet any rum duchesses?'

'That's more your style than mine.'

'I'll say,' answered George, rubbing his hands together.

'You want to watch where you tread,' Maurice said with meaning. 'Or you'll end up with something nasty.'

'Well, there's always a good apothecary to help me out.' And George slapped John so heartily on the back that he was winded for a full two minutes. Red in the face he gasped for air, a sight which seemed to highly amuse both Maurice and his brother.

No sooner had he recovered than John punched George hard, also in the back, saying, 'Oh yes, we can cure most things but not, I'm afraid, the great pox – from which the only way out is the powdering tub.'

'Not a pleasant idea,' said Maurice firmly. 'Well, it has been most delightful talking to you, Mr Rawlings. No doubt we shall meet again.'

'No doubt, my Lord.'

George bowed then sauntered off in the direction of Freddy Warwick who, seeing him coming, plunged into earnest conversation with the local vicar. After a few moments observing, George lost interest and went in search of a pretty girl. John finished his somewhat interrupted contemplation of the sea and went to rejoin the Marchesa.

★　　★　　★

Afterwards, riding home in the carriage, John said, 'You know I must take Rose back to London, sweetheart. She starts at her school next week.'

The Marchesa turned to look at him. 'Oh dear, I had quite forgotten about that. What a shame she must go. She is so sweet to have around the house and is very good with the twins. Do you know I have heard her sing to them and they join in with strange little cries. It is quite the most remarkable sound.'

'She must go and get an education, Elizabeth. I regret her departure as well but I would not like her growing up an ignoramus.'

'No more would I.'

'Madam . . .'

'Yes?'

'You wouldn't come as well, just for a short time? I would so like to show my sons to my friends in London.'

She turned to look out of the carriage window. 'I think they are too young to face the journey, don't you?'

A small clutch of hope departed from the Apothecary's heart. 'Perhaps at the moment. But one day in the future . . .' He left the statement hanging in the air.

Elizabeth placed her gloved hand over his and said quietly into the darkness, 'One day, John, it will all turn out as you wish.'

Fifteen

It was Rose's cries that woke John up. For a moment he wondered where he was, dreaming that he was still in Elizabeth's great house and that he was lying beside her. Then as he hastily struck a tinder and lit a candle, he saw that it was his bedroom in Nassau Street and remembered that he and his daughter had travelled back to London a few days before. The swift feeling of reassurance that he was back in town was instantly dissipated by the shouts of terror coming from her bedroom. Then as he leapt out of bed he heard another pair of feet running towards her door and flinging it open. Unable to gather his thoughts, John hurried to Rose.

Jacquetta Fortune was sitting on the bed holding his daughter in her arms but the child was looking toward the door and sobbing, 'Papa, Papa. Oh where is he? Is he safe?'

'I'm here, dearest girl,' he said from the doorway.

'Oh thank goodness you are alive! Oh Papa, I had such a terrible dream.'

Jacquetta released the child into his custody and stood up. John smiled at her and just for a moment thought how beautiful she looked with her lovely hair loose around her shoulders and that awful, frightening thinness disappearing and a shapely body starting to emerge. Then he turned his full attention to Rose.

He had never seen her so frightened; his spirited daughter, who was afraid of nothing, who had strange and rare abilities, whose very exuberance was a pleasure to behold, lay like a crumpled doll in his arms, her small frame raked with sobs.

'Shush, sweetheart. It was only a dream. It's all gone now. You're safe in your bed and I'm here with you. Tell me what it was that frightened you so much.'

She pressed close to him and he could feel her trembling. 'It was that wicked old brown woman. The one who wears

the big bonnet. She came in my dream and said she was going
to kill everyone. And you were there, Papa. I saw you.'

'Where? Where was this?'

'I'm not sure, that's the trouble. But there were a whole lot
of people all in one place. And then this terrible . . . Papa,
be sure to lie flat when you see her. It is vital that you do.'

'But why, darling? What is it you see about her?'

Rose wept again but this time with frustration. 'I don't
know, I don't know. It's just that something tells me you will
be safer lying down.'

'I swear I will go flat if ever I see this old apparition.'

'But you will see her, Papa. I am certain of it.'

'I promise you that I shall be on my guard,' replied John
solemnly.

She relaxed a little but remained in the protection of his
arms. 'Do you have to return to Devon, Pappy?'

'I do, my sweetheart. I promised Mrs Elizabeth and the
twins that I would return next month. So I am duty bound
to go.'

'I wish you didn't have to. I shall feel so far apart from you
when I am at school and you are miles away.'

'I promise to write often.'

Rose suddenly sat up and John could feel that her body had
gone rigid. 'She is waiting for you,' she said, and her voice
sounded tired and old.

The Apothecary was too wise to try and shake her out of
whatever vision she could see. 'Where?' he asked again.

'In Devon,' she answered, and fell back on to her pillows.

Two days later John escorted Rose to her new school. Irish
Tom had cleaned the coach till it shone and had retouched
the initials of its owner, gracefully entwined on the door. John,
going to inspect Tom's handiwork in Dolphin Yard, had walked
round the equipage with a look of great satisfaction.

'Is it to your liking, Sorrh?'

'You've done a grand job, Tom. It almost looks new.'

'Oh, it's taken a bit of punishment in its time, the old coach.
But I hope it will be grand enough for our Miss Rose to set
foot in.'

Sir Gabriel would have been irritated that a servant spoke in this familiar manner but John and Tom had built up a special and, in a way, very close relationship over the years and the Apothecary would have wondered what was wrong if the coachman had addressed him in any other way.

So with her newly bought trunk and a couple of hat boxes stowed on the top, John and his daughter set off down Gerrard Street, waved to by all the servants, the nursery maid in floods of tears, and by Jacquetta Fortune, who had come out of the office she had now established in the house in Nassau Street, to wave farewell. Gideon was, of course, at Shug Lane.

The destination was Kensington Gore but the carriage diverted to Sir Gabriel's residence so that he, too, might see his granddaughter into her first school. In a sea of stiff satin, black as always, the only colour being the white lining of his cloak and what one could glimpse of his shirt, Sir Gabriel emerged from his front door like the leader of fashion he had always been. Round his neck he had a bow at the centre of which glinted a diamond.

'Oh Grandpa, you do look fine,' Rose called excitedly through the window, then, as Tom lowered the step, hopped out and curtseyed as Sir Gabriel made his way within.

'Dear child,' said Sir Gabriel, fondling the strands of flame-coloured hair that shone beneath her new hat. 'I shall come and visit you often.'

'Yes, please do,' she answered.

John looked at her, thinking to himself that the effects of her terrible dream had completely gone. He wondered, in fact, when she was in that sort of state if she had no memory of it afterwards. For today she seemed radiantly happy, glad to be entering into the adult world, proud to be bowling along in the newly restored carriage with her handsome father and his imposing adopted parent, who was leaning on his great stick and looking out of the window from time to time.

But as they arrived at the school, amongst many other carriages and fine looking modes of transport, she suddenly turned pale. 'Oh, Pappy, will I be able to cope?' she asked anxiously.

John was about to answer when Sir Gabriel rose from his seat and got out of the carriage on to the step, holding out a hand for Rose to join him. It had occurred to John that over the years his father might have lost some of his ability to attract attention – a faculty that at one time had meant he could enter a room and stop the conversation – but not so. As he stood on the step, his great height raised even taller, his old-fashioned three storey wig with its cockaded hat atop glinting in the sunshine, he took Rose and motioned her in front of him so that she was in full view of the passing parade. Much to John's astonishment, Irish Tom let out a hearty cheer and a far tinier child than Rose stopped its howling and instead dropped a curtsey. Seeing this, several of the other children did the same.

'You see, my girl,' said Sir Gabriel, 'everything hinges on how one presents oneself. If you go in weeping and ashen-faced they will think you a sad creature from a wretched home and will treat you accordingly. But if you go in chin high and exude a confidence that perhaps inside one does not feel, then you will be treated with respect and as someone whose views are worth listening to. Now, child, let me lead you to your headmistress.'

Still within the carriage confines, John smiled. 'Go on, Rose,' he said. 'I will follow behind.'

So his daughter was led down a kind of ceremonial walk, with the parents and children falling back to allow Sir Gabriel – using his great stick to a nicety – to pass through. Thus they arrived at the feet of Madame de Cygne.

'*Bonjour, Madame. Votre école est magnifique, je crois.*' And he bowed low before her, then kissed her hand.

She was quite overcome, answered him in French and made much of Rose, whom Sir Gabriel introduced as his grand-daughter and eventual heir. Then John joined them, having walked slowly behind them, and the bowing and curtseying began all over again. Finally it was time for Rose to go inside.

She turned in the doorway and reached up to John for a last kiss. 'Be very careful in Devon,' she whispered.

'I will, I promise,' he whispered back.

Then he set her on her feet and she turned away and walked through the front door and into her new life.

★   ★   ★

Having spent the night with Sir Gabriel, John returned to town the next morning early and did a full day's work in his shop. After which, feeling in the mood for some fresh air, he went for a walk in St James's Park. Despite the evening being not yet truly warm there were a great many people about, those simply out to take the air, and those whose sole purpose in life was prostitution and picking pockets. A dismal child of about twelve approached him and offered him a short time in a back alley for two pennies. John gave her the money then ordered her away and told her to go to an apothecary's as the poor girl was covered with a most suspicious rash. She ran off and John continued his walk in peace.

A beau minced past in unfashionably high heels, somewhat worn down. On looking at him further one could see that he was genteelly shabby, a sad figure if he had not been such a ridiculous posturer. He turned his head as John approached, and raised his eye glasses which hung around his neck to peer. The Apothecary saw a face that must once have been handsome but was now raddled with dissolute living. There were cracks in the enamelled make-up and the huge eyes, heavily outlined with kohl, were heavy with bags beneath. John could see that the seam of his coat had split under the arm.

The man let out a little scream. 'Oh good gracious me! Zoonters, but I thought you were a pickpocket, Sir.' He stared at John closely, the eyeglasses reflecting the light. 'You are not one, are you?'

John smiled and made a small bow. 'No, Sir, I am not. But if you are so frightened of them why do you walk here?'

The beau's carmined lips parted in a smile. 'I am not afraid, Sir. No indeed I am not. And if a man cannot saunter along minding his business and enjoying his own company, then we are in a sorry plight indeed.'

Certain that if he agreed with him he would receive a lecture on the state of the nation, John smiled non-committally and would have passed him had it not been for the beau's arm blocking his way.

'Oh do chat a minute, Sir. It is so very pleasant to exchange news and views.'

John's heart sank slightly but out of common politeness he allowed himself to walk beside the beau who rattled off a load of nonsense in a high-pitched voice.

'. . . and as I was saying to Sir Rollo Golightly t'other day, one hardly dare leave one's home for fear of highwaymen. I mean, what indeed are we come to, that . . .'

John switched off his brain and allowed his thoughts to drift away, but was suddenly called back to reality by the mention of a familiar name.

'. . . of course, as I said to Lady Bournemouth—'

'Excuse me, but do you know her?'

The beau sounded slightly waspish. 'Of course I do. I am often invited to her place to play cards. Met a delightful girl while I was there, a Miss Cordelia Clarke. She invited me to stay at her home . . .'

'In Devon?'

'Precisely. But I wouldn't travel on the public stage or by post-chaise, come to that. One never knows what might be lurking behind the bushes, don't you know.'

This last remark struck John as funny and he felt his mouth starting to twitch into a grin.

'I am serious, my dear Sir. One takes one's life into one's hands when one steps abroad. I mean to say, anyone could be a pickpocket or a cutpurse, don't you know.'

'Then why are you walking along with me?' asked John mildly.

The beau shrieked with laughter, bending double and clutching his sides. John had a glimpse of his eyes, which he could now see were the colour of ginger spice, watering madly as he giggled away. 'Oh, my dear Sir, you're a regular rogue, so you are! Why, I haven't laughed so much since I last clipped the King's English!'

John decided that the man was very slightly mad and concluded that a rapid exit would be the order of the day. Pulling his watch from his waistcoat pocket, he said, 'Dearie me, is that the time? I promised to meet someone in ten minutes. I really must hurry along.'

The beau wiped his face with a lace handkerchief that had seen better days. 'It has been a great pleasure to talk to you,

Sir. I do hope my lack of decorum did not frighten you away. Alas I am given to such outbursts when something takes my fancy. Before we part, please remember me to Lady Bournemouth and Miss Cordelia Clarke if you should happen to see them.' At the mention of the last name the beau let out a deep sigh, clutched his heart and rolled a ginger eye.

John presumed from this that the fellow had a penchant for the young lady, thinking simultaneously that he was somewhat too old for her, and far too seedy. He nodded. 'Be sure that I will. What is your name, by the way?'

'Pendleton, Sir. Benedict Pendleton. And yours?'

'John Rawlings.'

And with this the two men bowed to one another and parted company.

Thinking that it was time he rewarded Jacquetta for the undoubted amount of hard work that she had put into launching the Rawlings brand of sparkling water, John invited her to accompany him to the Theatre Royal, Drury Lane, to see a revival of *The Parson's Wedding*, a play that in its heyday had made Samuel Pepys blush. Now she too, though laughing, had colour in her cheeks and John could not help but think it sailed a little close to the wind for a delicate female. However it had the desired effect of engaging the often rowdy audience who, instead of talking or throwing rotten fruit into the stalls below, guffawed heartily throughout.

Coming out into the chilly April night John decided it was too early to return home and instead took Mrs Fortune to a quiet tavern near Covent Garden and ordered a late supper. Having seated themselves and placed their order, she turned to him, looking at him with her clear eyes.

'Mr Rawlings, I would like to thank you for all you have done for me. I believe that you have quite literally saved my life.'

'Don't thank me, thank Octavia Dawkins. She is the person who recommended you, after all.'

'I am obviously aware of that. But you have been a very kind employer. Moreover you had sufficient faith in me to allow me to pursue my own way.'

'As a matter of fact I would like to be more involved in
the business in future. You see, I have been interested in the
properties of water ever since I can remember. Not,' John
added hastily, 'that I infer any criticism of your splendid
organization.'

'You are welcome to join Gideon and myself at any time,
Sir. You know that.'

Feeling that the conversation was drifting towards his
commitments in Devon and the difficulties that these were
already presenting him with, John changed the subject. 'I'm
glad that he has been of help to you. I must say he has developed really well. He used to be so clumsy, you know. I hardly
dared to let him loose in the shop.'

'He has certainly changed,' answered Jacquetta, and lowered
her eyes.

A pang ran through John, though of what kind he had no
idea himself. 'You are fond of him?' he found himself saying.

Mrs Fortune looked up again and directly at her employer.
There was no denying it. Her gentle green eyes held a look
of great tenderness. 'Yes, I am. Very.'

Why this should irritate John, Heaven alone knew – but
irritated he was. It was on the tip of his tongue to enquire
how far these feelings had led when he realized that it was
none of his damned business.

Instead he said, 'I am glad that the two of you get along so
well.'

Jacquetta smiled. 'Of course, I rather imagine that he has
fallen in love with me.'

'Of course he has,' John said loudly, then added, 'Who could
not?'

She gazed at him in great surprise. 'I don't quite understand
your meaning.'

The Apothecary was all apologies. 'Forgive me. It was silly
of me to say that. I really meant that for a woman as attractive
as you are you must be used to men fawning at your feet.'

She made a humourless gesture. 'Mr Rawlings, you know
as well as I that when you first met me I was a wreck of
humanity. It is the kindness of yourself at letting me live in
your beautiful home and enjoy your excellent food that has

brought about the changes in me. I have only you to thank for that.'

'But nothing could ever have taken away from your glorious hair,' he said indiscreetly. 'I have never seen a colour like it.'

Mrs Jacquetta Fortune looked down at the table and said nothing.

Sixteen

As soon as John set foot in the flying coach the picture that Rose had painted so vividly came back to haunt him. He saw before his closed eyes a ghastly old woman dressed all in brown, a big bonnet concealing most of her face, what he could see of it bearing such a look of menace that he drew a breath of fear. Rose's voice came back to him. 'When you see her, lie flat.' None of it, neither description nor words, made any sense, and yet he knew a great deal better than to ignore the prediction of his incredible daughter who was gifted in so many ways.

A great deal of time had been passed in London and it was June before he returned to Devon, firstly to see Elizabeth and his twin boys and secondly to attend the wedding of Miranda Tremayne and the Earl of St Austell. Not that he particularly wanted to witness the joining of such a pair, but out of respect for Lady Sidmouth, in whose house his sons had been born, he felt duty-bound to attend.

He had worked hard during the intervening weeks, bottling the water in the new bottles which had arrived from the manufacturer, dividing his time between his business and his shop in Shug Lane. Of Jacquetta he had deliberately seen little, telling himself that it was foolish of him to feel attracted to her when she was obviously more interested in Gideon than himself. And who was he to query the gap in years that lay between her and his apprentice when his own relationship was with a far older woman? And a woman who meant more to him than any other?

John opened his eyes and surveyed the other three passengers. They consisted of a stocky middle-aged couple and their loutish, spotty son who was carefully picking his teeth, which were spaced very widely apart, with a silver toothpick. The boy, feeling John's gaze upon him, gave the Apothecary a dirty look and turned his attention to the passing scenery. John wished momentarily that he had chosen Irish Tom to bring him down rather than leave him at Mrs Fortune's disposal. But in fairness the poor woman had appointments all over town whereas he was merely seeking pleasure.

'Good day, Sir,' he said, addressing the youth, who looked put out.

'Good day,' the boy mumbled back.

'Eh?' said John, cupping his ear.

'I said good day,' thundered the other, waking his mother up, who regained consciousness with a scream of alarm.

John looked at her earnestly. 'Oh, my dear Madam, are you quite well? Such a cry you let forth I thought the Devil himself might have attacked you.'

'No, I'm perfectly well, Sir. I was just a little alarmed.'

'Eh?' said John, and cupped his ear again.

'He's deaf,' the boy whispered to his mother.

She repeated the remark at full volume.

John looked testy and said, 'All right, all right. I can hear you.'

The poor woman looked highly embarrassed. 'Do forgive my son, Sir. He's only doing his best.' She turned on John a weary look which spoke of years of martyrdom at the hands of the horrid youth.

Suddenly John felt terribly sorry for her. 'What do you call him?' he asked, as if the boy were not there.

'Herman, Sir. My father's name.'

She smiled, quite kindly, and John instantly regretted his earlier behaviour.

'A very good name.' He turned to its owner. 'And are you a very good boy?'

Herman, who was probably about sixteen and was wearing a white wig which had clearly been handed down from his father, flushed.

'Yes, I suppose so.'

John was tempted to make a witty remark but thought better of it because at that moment the father, who had been snoring gently, woke himself up with a tremendous trumpet.

'Ha, ha,' he said, 'have I missed something?'

'No, dear,' replied his poor wife, 'this gentleman was just asking Herman's name.'

'Ah, it's introduction time is it? Well, how dee do, Sir. I am
Cecil Cushen. Pleased to make your acquaintance.'

'And I yours, Sir. John Rawlings is the name.'

'Rawlings? Rawlings? You're no relation to Fanny Rawlings
of Islington, are you?'

'I regret not, Sir. Tell me, are you travelling all the way to
Exeter?'

'Indeed I am. My wife's late cousin's wife is there. She is
much distressed by the recent loss of her husband and we are
going down to comfort her.'

A look of deep gloom settled over Herman's features and
John felt a certain pity for the youth, bored to the gappy teeth
as he was destined to be.

'I am sorry to hear that,' he said. 'So where do you live in
town?'

'Islington, Sir. A quaint and pretty little village. And you?'

'In Piccadilly. My business is also there.'

'Let me guess what you do,' said Mr Cushen jovially. 'I'll
swear you are a lawyer, Sir.'

'Nothing so fancy. I am an apothecary by trade and I have
a shop in Shug Lane.'

He had opened the flood gates. Mr Cushen spent the next
quarter of an hour talking about his digestive problems
together with Herman's spots, while his wife, not to be
outdone, described in graphic detail her terrible pain when
she had fallen and fractured her leg whilst visiting Scotland.
John endured it all with a brave smile and the occasional
exclamation of horror as he had done so many times in the
past.

He had found through bitter experience that it was better
by far not to mention what he did for a living. Though in
this particular case he had had little option but to do so.
Therefore he knew with a feeling of doom that the rest of
the journey was going to be punctuated with remarks and
questions about the family illnesses and, indeed, so it transpired
until, at last, the horses feet clattered over the cobbles of
Exeter.

'It has been a truly splendid experience, Sir,' said the head
of the household jovially.

'Indeed, Sir, it has,' echoed his wife. 'Quite remarkable.'

'Thank you,' John answered weakly.

Only Herman remained silent and the Apothecary guessed that it was the public discussion of his spots which had proved too much for him. As he got out of the coach John bowed to the boy.

'Goodbye, Master Cushen. Perhaps we shall meet again some day.'

Herman bared his teeth in what John supposed was a smile. 'I expect we will if you patronize the taverns of Exeter at all.'

'Well I do occasionally.'

'I do most of the time. Got to know 'em during our not infrequent visits. Picked up a few cronies as well. In fact, I enjoy it here.'

'You prefer it to Islington?'

'In a way, yes.'

'Perhaps one day you'll move to Devon.'

'You may be right at that, Sir.'

John was relieved to see the family get into a waiting carriage and be on their way. He turned to find that Elizabeth had paid him the same compliment. A conveyance from the Big House had been sent to meet the flying coach. Realizing how difficult this must have been to time, the Apothecary felt doubly grateful as he climbed into its comforting depths.

The house was unnervingly quiet when the footman showed him into the echoing Great Hall. Looking up John saw that Britannia, complete with spear, still guarded the premises, only this evening she seemed to be wearing a less belligerent expression.

Perhaps she's getting to like me, he thought.

Making his way up the grand staircase John proceeded to the nursery, looking for his sons. But to his surprise the room was empty. Somewhat perturbed he went down again and out through the French doors into the gardens beyond. And there, lying beneath one of the magnificent elm trees getting the last of the sunshine were the two little mites playing with their nannies. In typical fashion Elizabeth had them stripped to their napkins, and they were lying on a large rug with plenty of noisy toys within grabbing distance. John stood quietly and surveyed the scene.

For the millionth time his heart plummeted as the awfulness of his situation hit him yet again. His longing to lead a settled family life with everyone in their correct place, the twins growing up alongside their sister, seemed at that moment to be his primary objective. But then he knew quite certainly that if that was his criterion he had fallen in love with the wrong woman. Yet who could resist her with her dark, haunting, ugly beauty; her vivid and enigmatic personality; her complete rejection of social mores and conventions?

As if his thoughts had conjured her up he heard the distant thudding of hooves and she came riding into his line of vision, straight and tall in the side saddle, her long skirt skimming the grass, her hair swept up beneath her hat.

'John!' she called out, and quite literally jumped to the ground and flung herself into his arms.

Standing there, like that, John knew that leaving her would be almost impossible for him. Her dark hair filled his nostrils with its delicate fragrance, her skin was wholesome, like a freshly cooked sweetmeat. Elizabeth was all he had ever wanted in a woman – and yet . . . John knew at that moment that he was indeed getting older. His values were changing. The wild spirit that he had always possessed was still there, still guided him, but was being diverted into different channels.

On the spur of the moment he said, 'Elizabeth, my darling, let me take the boys back to London with me. Just for a visit. It would please my father and Rose so much.'

She drew back, staring at him with a chilly glance. 'You don't understand, do you? The twins mean everything to me. They have replaced my lost son. I could never part with them, not even for a month.'

'Then why don't you come as well? It would fill us all with so much joy.'

She turned on her heel. 'I will give it some consideration.'

John would have felt triumphant had it not been for her tone of voice which was hard and unyielding. Instead he felt like a beggar at a feast. Why should he, who had, in his own particular way, achieved quite a bit, have to implore her to visit him? Even worse, plead for access to his own sons? Feeling decidedly put out, the Apothecary walked downhill towards the Exe without looking back.

Two days later they went to the wedding. The ceremony was held in the small Saxon church nearest to Sidmouth House. Located close to the village of Sidmouth, it stood at the bottom of the hill from the top of which the Great House had its commanding position of both land and sea. Obviously for such an important society marriage the church was packed to the doors, and John, to his great surprise, saw that as well as Sir Clovelly Lovell – who was squeezed into a pew with a formidable dame of menacing mien – there were several people whom he recognized. Cuthbert Simms, whom he had met while investigating the strange death of the hawk-featured Mr Gorringe, had been called back to organize the dances, or so John imagined. The gossipy woman from Exeter, Lettice James, eyes darting round like a hen's, was present, as were also Mr and Mrs Cushen whom he had met recently whilst travelling to Exeter. Their gappy-toothed son, Herman, was thankfully not present.

This day Elizabeth seemed exquisite. Tall and lean – her normal figure having restored itself since the birth – she was clad in a deep, sulky red, its cut more towards the back than the sides. With this captivating look she wore a veiled hat, a large and lovely creation over which some poor little milliner had clearly slaved for hours. John, not to be outdone, wore his moire silk ensemble in crushed hyacinth, the double-breasted waistcoat of deep purple dazzling the eyes in the morning sunshine.

As well as the local people there were, of course, all the relatives and friends of the bridegroom's. John saw that the three grandchildren were present. Lady Imogen, desperately trying to conceal her pregnancy by wearing a strange robe-like garment; Lord George, looking more dashing and handsome than was decent in a fine suit of rich blue, heavily embroidered with a myriad of sparkling winkers; the absent-minded Viscount

Falmouth, wearing dark colours and appearing to be lost in thought behind his misty spectacles. Freddy Warwick was also present, staying as close as he could to Miss Cordelia Clarke, who was there with her chaperone, Lady Bournemouth.

It was at this point that the bridegroom turned and ran his frightening blue gaze over the congregation. Just for a moment his eyes met those of the Apothecary and John had to restrain himself from shuddering. He was looking into pools of ice in the depths of which were madness and depravity. He feared for Miranda Tremayne, who had been acting so demurely of late, and then it occurred to him that she actually was a willing participant in the excesses of Lord St Austell, and that her wedding night would come as no surprise to her.

As if his thoughts had conjured her up there was a flutter in the doorway as the merry organ – a surprisingly mellow and fine sound – leapt into life and the bridal party began their progress down the aisle. Miranda, a fragrant vision in taffeta and lace, was on the arm of Lady Sidmouth's son, whom John recognized with astonishment as the amazingly effeminate Robin Sidmouth, he of the pouting lips and very high heels. Robin had aged, there was no denying that, but he still presented the same bustling figure as he hurried Miranda up to the altar, far more quickly that she would have liked.

So she stood beside the Earl and they exchanged a glance. John wished that he could have been a mind reader because he would have been glad to know their thoughts. However, he had no time for that. The couple made their vows in subdued voices and then with a flamboyant gesture St Austell picked up her hand and placed a gold ring on it. Miranda had achieved her ambition and was now a Countess, but John, watching as the newly married pair made their way from the church, could not help but wonder what dark and terrible secrets they were about to share.

Outside, a group of fisher folk cheered loudly, the illusion of perfection somewhat ruined by the fact that someone threw a dead fish at Robin and shouted out, 'Light heels!'

The strain of the wedding now over, John became hysterical

and laughed audibly, a fact which annoyed the bridegroom who shot him a dark look. So it was in this atmosphere that the assembled company got into their waiting conveyances and started up the hill to Sidmouth House and the feast which awaited them.

Seventeen

It had always amazed the Apothecary that such a peculiar little woman as Lady Sidmouth should have such great artistry in the matter of interior decoration. He had thought that her ball had reached the heights of splendour but on this occasion the wedding feast excelled it. The Grand Saloon, in which the reception was to be held, was without doubt the most stunning room in the entire house as well as being the largest. From the pillars surrounding the doorway to the huge French doors giving a full view of the gardens and lawns sweeping down to the sea, everything was in perfect proportion. Not only that, the room had a harmony most pleasing to the eye and the senses. Decorated throughout in a pale shade of yellow it caught the sun's beams and reflected them, like the heart of a primrose.

For the feast Lady Sidmouth had stripped out a great deal of the furniture and instead had set up long tables covered in elegant white cloths, all laid with the most exquisite silver and glassware. She had also filled the room with late spring hyacinths which added their strange heady scent to the air and added a dark shade of blue to the decorations. Entering the Saloon in a long line, being greeted first by the Earl and the new Countess, together with Lady Sidmouth as hostess and Robin, her son, as host, John came face to face with his old acquaintance.

'My dear Lord Sidmouth,' he said, giving a small bow, 'do you remember me?'

The cherubic face which had been quite becoming in his youth had now run to fat and represented a florid faun rather than anything angelic.

Robin peered closely. 'Well, damme! Ain't you Rawlings? A friend of Orlando's?'

'Yes, we met in Bath if you recall.'

'So we did and had a merry time of it. But what a tragic

end Orlando had. I would have thought him the very last to commit suicide.'

John's face did not move a muscle as he replied, 'Quite so.'

Robin leant closer and there was a puff of hot, rather smelly breath. 'Would like to talk to you more but duty calls. Do seek out my wife. Name of Maud. That's her over there in the mauve gown.'

He gestured and John turned his head to look, his eye alighting on a listless woman with a pained expression.

'We shall be delighted to do so,' said the Marchesa rapidly, taking John under the elbow and steering him towards the Earl and his new wife.

The pair stood slightly apart and John had a second or two to look at them before he arrived before them. St Austell seemed almost rejuvenated by the recent ceremony, his long white hair glinting in the sunshine, tied back with his usual scarlet ribbon. Beside him the bride looked like a vixen who had just killed a chicken and was waiting to devour it. They were one of the nastiest wedded couples that the Apothecary had ever clapped his eyes on.

Lord St Austell spoke. 'May I say how damned fine you look, Madam.'

This remark was addressed to the Marchesa, who dropped a small curtsey in response.

'But not as fine as your bride, my Lord.'

The Earl made no answer but seized Miranda roughly round the waist and pulled her towards him in a gesture so familiar that John knew they had already been to bed together.

'No, nobody could be as lovely as my Countess.'

He said this with such an air of satisfaction that John wanted to hit him. Elizabeth, sensing his tension, complimented Miranda on her appearance and hurried John into the wedding feast proper.

The meal began with schooners of sherry, dry as a bone and much to the Apothecary's taste. Then when everybody was seated in their appointed place, the food was served by Lady Sidmouth's staff with extra people brought in so that there should be no slacking.

John found himself between Elizabeth and Lettice James,

once again minus a husband whom John was beginning to suspect was a figment of her imagination. She had outdone herself as regards her ensemble and had topped the whole thing with an enormous hat, representing a ship in full sail, the mast of which threatened to prise John's eye out whenever she bent forward.

'My oh my, what a noble company, is it not, Mr Rawlings? I feel quite elevated by being amongst them, so I do.'

John dodged the mast and got slapped by a spinnaker instead.

'Your husband is not with you today, Mrs James?'

'No, poor dear, he suffers terribly with a personal complaint and is laid low with it I fear.'

John hesitated to ask in case she told him, but Elizabeth entered the conversation.

'I'm sorry to hear that. What form does his illness take?'

Lettice lowered her voice to a hoarse whisper. 'Flatulence.'

'Indeed. Is there no cure?'

The Apothecary felt it coming before the words had formed.

'I wondered if Mr Rawlings would have a look at him and might indeed prescribe something. Many local doctors have washed their hands of the case.'

John winced. 'Gladly, Madam. One of these days I will call in.'

'Could you not be a little more specific, Sir?'

'Alright. I'll come next week.'

'Oh thank you, thank you,' gushed Lettice and hit John with a mainsail for a reward.

The meal progressed and the sunlight slowly moved round until it was coming in across the sea. Cuthbert Simms appeared and informed them that the orchestra was setting up in the Great Hall and, indeed, strains of music could be heard.

'My Lords, Ladies and Gentlemen,' he announced importantly, 'the dancing will be led by the bridal couple.'

The Earl of St Austell rose to his full height and his cruel mouth forced itself into a smile. 'Come, Miranda,' he said, 'let us show the young folk how it should be done.'

The company rose as he led his bride outward and then followed him in a mass, drunk with wine and with the general atmosphere of high excitement. John led Elizabeth out, taking her by the hand, noticing the way the folds of her gown gleamed in the dusky light. How could he ever let her go? he wondered.

They stood round the room in a vast circle watching the Earl and Countess perform an old-fashioned minuet. It should have been charming, a delight to see, but John felt quite repelled by the expressions on their faces. St Austell's smile seemed cruel and rapacious; Miranda's was so demure that it could not be believed. Their dance ended to polite applause and then the whole room began to form into sets as Cuthbert shouted out the names of the dances, then participated himself, his partner being the listless Maud. Robin Sidmouth meanwhile whirled about with a lovely local lass – though his smiles were reserved for her brother, John could not help but notice.

The dancing was eventually broken up by the bride being taken upstairs to her chamber, her attendant females giggling girlishly. Somehow or other Miranda managed to manufacture a deep blush which she made sure the assembled company could see. The bridegroom, attended by a motley selection of elderly rakes, followed shortly afterwards. John turned to Elizabeth, having no wish to see the grand bedding.

'I feel like another drink. What about you, my dear?'

'An excellent plan indeed.'

They wandered back into the Grand Saloon, where many of the other guests had already foregathered, the orchestra taking a well-earned break. The sun was beginning to set over the sea and the very first candles were being lit in the room, giving it a soft and glowing and highly atmospheric feel. Leaving Elizabeth talking John went over to the long doors and looked out at the dying day, gazing out towards the sea as was his habit. And then he saw her. Just for a split second he could have sworn that an old woman in a poke bonnet stepped out from behind a tree and stared towards him, then in the blink of an eye was gone.

The thrill of horror that the Apothecary experienced was indescribable. The creature he had glimpsed had been exactly as Rose had described. He stood stock still, chilled to his soul with fear. Elizabeth came to join him.

'John, what's the matter? You look as if you've seen a ghost.'

'I think I just have.'

But further conversation was impossible for, with a great whoop of triumph, carried shoulder high by his ancient cronies, the bridegroom re-entered the room. John realized that quite a time must have passed because the Earl was now arrayed in a scarlet robe with a matching turban placed upon his head.

'Well?' called Lord George, his grandson.

'Very well indeed,' called back the disgusting old man. 'Miranda has just parted with her most precious gift.'

There was a roar of truly raucous laughter in which the Apothecary did not join, and the Earl of St Austell was placed in the bridegroom's chair by his cheering supporters.

'Here's to your health, Sir,' somebody shouted, and the company raised their glasses.

At a nudge from Elizabeth John did likewise, and then his eyes were drawn to the windows once more. For there, etched against the dying sun, stood that terrible figure he had seen before. He was paralysed with fear, and then in his head he heard Rose's voice: 'Lie flat.'

Pulling Elizabeth down with him, he headed for the floor.

'What . . .' she began.

But he silenced her by putting his hand over her mouth. All around them they could hear the cheers of the wedding guests at the bridegroom's triumph and then they heard a woman's voice turn from a laugh to a terrible scream. This was followed by the sound of shots, two at a time, several of them. And then there was an unnatural quiet.

Very slowly, the Apothecary peered over the edge of the tablecloth. He took in several things at once. First of all there were two old women, both of their faces hidden by those hideous bonnets. They were firing double-barrelled pistols and as one reloaded the other fired. The guests were falling slowly, like leaves, and he could only guess at the number of dead and wounded. Sensing a movement at his end of the table, one of the crones turned and fired straight at him. Momentarily the bonnet tipped back and John had the impression of a face, a face that gave him the feeling he had seen it somewhere before. But like a dream the memory was gone as quickly as it had come. John feigned death as the bullet whistled straight past his ear and into the floor. He felt Elizabeth do the same and they both lay still as corpses until eventually the firing stopped.

'Happy wedding day, my Lord,' one of them shrieked in eldritch tones, then there was the sound of the French doors being thrown open and running feet.

Nobody stirred. There was absolute stillness. It was just as if the two old women had murdered everyone in the room. And then there came a little sound from the doorway. John cautiously opened one eye and without turning his head peered in the direction from which the noise came. All he could see was a pair of men's shoes, extremely high heeled. So Robin Sidmouth had at least escaped.

Very gingerly John eased himself upwards and was relieved to see that other people were doing so as well. At least half of the gathered guests had escaped unscathed, it would seem. From the doorway came a series of high-pitched shrieks and the sound of a heavy weight crashing to the floor. It would appear that the Earl of Sidmouth had been quite overcome.

But it was not to him that John's attention was drawn, for a far more dramatic sight met his gaze as he heaved himself upright. The Earl of St Austell lay slumped forward on the table, his turban half shielding his face, his scarlet robe darker in the middle where a mass of crimson dyed it a deeper red. Someone – the Apothecary did not know who – gingerly approached him and tapped him on the shoulder. The body fell forward a fraction but other than that did not stir. But the movement dislodged the turban which slipped even further to one side. If John had not been a trained apothecary he could easily have vomited. Because the Earl's face had been shot away and what lay in its place was a dripping red mass of brains and eyeballs. For the first and only time John pitied him.

Elizabeth, who by now was also standing upright, followed John's gaze. 'Oh God's mercy,' she said softly.

John turned to her and seated her back in her chair, pouring a brandy from a nearby decanter.

'Here, drink this,' he said, and handed her the glass. She took it and sipped and John thought he had never seen her so pale in all the years he had known her. 'Now you must excuse me,' he said. Raising his voice he shouted, 'Is there a physician present?'

'Yes, Sir, I'm a surgeon,' called a man of no more than thirty, a man with carrot-coloured hair whom John had noticed amongst the dancers and who was just rising to his feet. 'Are you similar?'

'I am an apothecary. For God's sake let us assess the damage.'

They both crossed to the most obvious victim of the shooting. Mr Perkins, as he briefly introduced himself, with more courage than had the Apothecary, put out a hand and removed the turban entirely. The ooze underneath, that had minutes earlier been the head of a man, trickled into the tablecloth.

'God almighty,' said the surgeon, 'whoever did this certainly had no respect for the Earl of St Austell.'

'Clearly not,' John answered, as a thought occurred to him. 'He's been shot at least four times.'

And it was true enough. Their brief examination of the body revealed four different wounds. Two in the back, one in the knees – which meant his assailant must have bent down to attack him – and the face once, close-up and with both barrels.

'There's nothing we can do for him,' said Perkins, shaking his head. 'It is the wounded who should be our primary concern.'

Strangely there were not as many of these as the noise and confusion had first suggested. Lord George Beauvoir had a shoulder injury, Lady Imogen had been shot in the leg – and from the whimpering she was making John presumed that she was shortly going to miscarry the child she bore. A whisper to Elizabeth had her being escorted upstairs to one of the many spare bedrooms. Poor little Cuthbert Simms had received a graze from a passing bullet and was bearing it manfully, despite the fact that he was trembling like a blancmange. The only other tragedies were Lettice James, who had been shot dead, a wound straight to her heart, and a young man whom John did not know, had been killed.

In the doorway Lady Sidmouth could be heard remonstrating with her son.

'Oh do get up Robin, do. You're like a girl, so you are,

fainting at the sight of blood. Go to poor Maud. She looks fit to die.'

Maud was indeed very ashen-faced but only because she had been sitting near the Earl of St Austell and some of his blood had spattered on her. To make matters worse it was starting to dry and it wasn't until Mr Perkins set to with a damp cloth that she showed any signs of revival. Meanwhile Viscount Falmouth rushed in from outside and quite literally screamed when he saw his grandfather's body, still in its chair but sprawled out on the tablecloth before it. He approached it running, but when he saw what was left of his kinsman's head he turned away, clutching his guts.

But at that moment there came a voice from the doorway, calling out merrily. People picking themselves up, the wounded being tended to, the dead being covered by fresh white table-cloths brought in by the ever-sensible Lady Sidmouth, all but the eternally silenced turned their heads.

Miranda stood in the entrance, dressed in a gorgeous night-gown and nothing else. Barefoot and without any kind of robe on the top, John felt she represented some old Norse goddess come to earth to bring summer. She stood immobile, staring from one to the other. Then she saw what lay there, cried out, 'Montague,' and rushed towards the heap that Lady Sidmouth was just covering.

She stopped short. 'Is the naughty man in his cups?'

Lady Sidmouth gazed at her gently. 'No, my dear, it is a little worse than that.'

Miranda looked roguish. 'He has lost consciousness. Oh la, that is a fine way to spend a wedding night.'

She began to tug at the corner of the tablecloth. 'Oh Monty, you are a bad boy. I think it is time you came to bed.'

Viscount Falmouth straightened himself up and crossed rapidly in her direction. 'Don't do that, Miranda. It is better that you don't see.'

'You'll address me as Your Grace, in future, Maurice. Remember that I am now the Countess of St Austell.'

'Whoever you are,' he snapped at her, 'don't look under that tablecloth.'

'Oh pooh,' she answered and gave it one final tug.

The mortal remains of her husband lay before her like a piece of butchered meat and there were cries from around the room as people saw him.

Miranda clapped her hands over her mouth and her eyes widened in a most fearful manner, then with a great groan she fell unconscious to the floor.

John leapt forward but did not reach her before the Viscount, who scooped her up into his arms, then stood staring helplessly about him.

'Odds my life!' said Robin Sidmouth. 'I do believe the lady faints.'

There followed a profound silence and just for a second John closed his eyes, thinking of all the duties that lay before him. The acrid smell of blood was suddenly everywhere and mixed with it the scent of hyacinths, sweet and beautiful. It was like the two extremes of life. The cruelty of people, the beauty of spring flowers forever mixed in one overpowering perfume. The Apothecary sighed, opened his eyes, and set about the tasks that must be done.

Eighteen

It turned out that three people had died in all. As well as St Austell and Mrs James there was a third guest that nobody knew particularly well, but still a lost life for all that. Of the wounded there were many more than John had first realized. These amounted to a simple graze as a bullet had flown past to several people having been hurt. The Apothecary and the surgeon were in the middle of giving life-saving first aid when Elizabeth came from upstairs and called Mr Perkins to attend. Much as John had suspected, Imogen was miscarrying her child. Which would, no doubt, be a relief to the anxious woman he had spied in the apothecary's shop.

At last the line of hurt people was dealt with and John was just sipping a cup of coffee, which he had requested in order to steady himself, when a very pallid Felicity came to stand beside him.

'Mr Rawlings, I wonder if you would look at my arm. I think I might have a bullet in it.'

He noticed then that the shawl with which she had covered herself was bloodstained and as he pulled it away she gave a little shudder.

'I'm sorry. Did that hurt you?'

'Yes, it did rather.'

She gave him a brave smile but he saw as soon as he examined her that she had indeed a bullet lodged in her upper left arm.

'I will bandage this up for you but I daren't remove the cause of the problem. We must get the surgeon to look at you fairly soon.'

'Tonight?'

'Yes, tonight. There's no escaping that fact, young lady. Where is your mother?'

'Over there.' And Felicity pointed to where Lady Sidmouth was dispensing hot drinks and small eatables to the shocked and wounded.

'How was it that you got shot?' John asked the girl, his opinion of whom was rising by the second.

'I picked up a candelabra and threw it at one of them.'

John leant back and gave a low whistle. 'We shall have to report all this to the Constable. By the way, has he been sent for?'

'Mama thought it best to wait until tomorrow.'

'I don't know that that was entirely wise. He really might like to see the scene as it is.'

'But who is the Constable. Do you know?'

'I have no idea because the job changes annually. But Exeter seems to have a system of each citizen chosen for the unpleasant task employing a certain individual to take his place. And if that system still holds good and if the individual is the same as the one I came across when last there was a murder in Devon, then his name is Tobias Miller and he is a first-class individual.'

Felicity gave a little shiver. 'Must I go to the surgeon tonight? He seems awfully busy.'

'Yes, you must, foolish child. It will be painful but it is best the bullet comes out as soon as possible, otherwise infection might set in.'

'How do you know that it won't anyway?'

'Because I have spread on a good paste from Lady Sidmouth's store cupboard. That will look after it very well until the bullet can be removed.' John looked round him. 'Is there anybody else?'

But it seemed that there wasn't, and he decided that it was time he had a brief chat with Felicity's mother before leaving.

Lady Sidmouth had proved herself to be a woman made of steel. Her headdress had come off, she had bloodstains all over her dress but, nothing daunted, she plunged into caring for the injured and keeping up the spirits of the rest as if it were her bounden duty. Which, John considered, it probably was. She looked up as he approached.

'Well, Mr Rawlings, this is one wedding you won't forget in a hurry.'

'Indeed not, Madam. I can honestly say that it will be imprinted on my memory for ever.'

She smiled grimly. 'Lady Imogen has lost a child, by the way. I had half guessed she was pregnant. Had you?'

'Oh yes. It is better all round that that burden has been taken from her.'

'Indeed. They say it was old St Austell's by the way.'

'*What?*'

'Apparently he has been interfering with her since she was a child. If it's true then he met his nemesis today.'

'What a foul old bastard!' John said with vehemence. 'He deserved everything he got. Of course I feel sorry for Miranda . . .'

'I wouldn't do too much of that,' came the sharp reply. 'I think she knew perfectly well what she was getting into.'

The Apothecary held up his hand. 'Say no more, please. Let me have some illusions left. Now, my Lady, Felicity must see the surgeon tonight. She has a bullet in the arm which I cannot remove.'

'Young Perkins shall come as soon as he's finished with Imogen. He's a nice fellow. Lives in Exeter. As a matter of fact he is quite a friend of Felicity's. Indeed I have certain hopes. Damn this going after a title business. If he's a sound man, then let nature takes its course.'

John gathered from this somewhat convoluted statement that Mr Perkins was a possible suitor for Felicity's hand.

'Then will you get him?' he asked.

'I'll go upstairs at once,' she answered.

Having reassured himself on that point, John surveyed the scene. Lady Bournemouth was spreading her girth on to a small chaise while Cordelia and Freddy both fanned her face frantically. Mr Cushen, very grey about the gills, was escorting Mrs Cushen out to their waiting coach. Robin Sidmouth had tired of trying to comfort Maud and had whirled round the room like a bee and was presently deep in conversation with Viscount Falmouth while Maud sat alone, a miserable and solitary figure. Meanwhile a group of strong young estate workers, obviously having been called from their beds, had come into the Grand Saloon armed with planks and determined expressions. They went first to the late Earl and regardless of the blood seeping through the cloth that covered him, hefted him on to the plank, shoulder high.

'Where is he going to be put?' asked John.

'The cellar is to become a temporary mortuary. It's cool down there, and besides the Constable will no doubt want to examine the bodies,' answered Elizabeth, returned from the room above. Her voice changed. 'John, as soon as you are finished here I want to go home. I want to ride out into the night and search for those two old besoms. The fact that they got away has hurt my *amour propre.*'

'It would appear that they did the world a service in getting rid of Milord.'

'Yes, but think of those they wounded indiscriminately. Think of poor Felicity. Think of poor Mrs James – foolish, yes, but actually harmful, no. Think of the other man, a meek fellow in life and perfectly inoffensive in death. Should not they be avenged?'

'Indeed they should.'

'Then let's ride out. It will be a great adventure. In the darkness, you and I.'

Something of the excitement she felt began to penetrate his weary body. Much as he disliked riding at night, he felt himself wanting to accompany her. Besides, she was right. Those two creatures – had they been men all along? – must not be allowed to wreak such carnage and then walk clean away. They must be hunted down and tried by jury.

A thought occurred to John. Unless the couple had acted on their own volition, then there was somebody else to find, the man or woman who had masterminded the whole thing. For surely two such crazy people as the assassins appeared to be, apparently shooting at random, had really had but one target and that could only be the Earl of St Austell. The very number of his wounds was some proof of that. The rest of the volley of bullets would have been to mask the fact that he was the actual victim. The Apothecary thought more deeply and it occurred to him that Mrs James with her gossipy manner and her constantly clacking tongue might also have been on the list to be taken care of. As to the third man, a Mr Meakin, he knew nothing of him but he intended to find out.

He turned to Elizabeth. 'As long as I am no longer wanted here I'll come with you. The night air might clear my head. By the way, where is Miranda?'

'Lord Falmouth took her upstairs. She has been put to bed and Mr Perkins has given her a sleeping draught.'

'Then that's as well.'

Outside it was cold and John suddenly began to shiver, realizing that he was suffering from delayed shock. Elizabeth glanced at him in the cushioned interior of the coach.

'I think a large brandy for you, my friend.'

Once inside her house he poured himself a drink and sat by the fire, reliving every moment of the sudden and terrible attack. At that moment he longed to be with Rose, reassuring her, telling her that the old woman had come and that he had survived. And then he looked up and gasped.

Elizabeth had come downstairs, not clad as she normally was but in the guise of the woman he had met on his honeymoon, many years ago. She was dressed in men's clothes, her dark hair drawn up into a net and concealed by the hat that she wore. Her body looked long and lean and, to John's eyes, immensely attractive.

'God's teeth,' he said. 'You've turned back into her. To the vigilante.'

'Yes,' she answered. 'Now are you going to ride out with me or do you leave me to search on my own?'

'I'll come,' he said, standing up. 'Give me a second to change. But first let me kiss you. It has been a long time since I last saw you dressed like this.'

She laughed, and even that sound excited him. They clung together in a deep kiss and then she pushed him towards the stairs.

'Change to riding clothes. We're off to seek those two murderous creatures.'

'If we find them it will only be the beginning.'

'What do you mean?'

'I mean that behind tonight's shooting there lies another brain, cool and cunning and utterly ruthless.'

'I am aware of that. He must be drawn into our net slowly. But we will find him, don't you worry about that.'

'It could be a woman who was behind tonight's bloodshed,' John answered, thinking of Imogen and the child she had so fortunately aborted.

'Indeed it might,' Elizabeth said over her shoulder as she left the house and headed towards the stables.

John thought that despite all the horrors that the evening had held for him he had never felt so alert. Every sense was tuned to high pitch as he mounted his horse and set off, Elizabeth cantering beside him. She had turned in the direction of the wild moor and he, not knowing the terrain as well as she, just followed.

It was a clear, cold night; a night of mystery and illusion. The moon was tiny, a sliver held in the arms of the old moon. John felt heightened, ready to receive every signal that the night might send him. Just for once he no longer dreaded riding out, his mind concentrated on all the sounds of the impenetrable darkness. Beneath the churning of pounding hooves came the noise of other things. Of unseen creatures making their way through the undergrowth, calling out a warning. Close at hand a vixen screamed an unearthly cry. Something altogether bigger bayed a response.

Slightly in advance of him Elizabeth rode easily, her body almost seeming part of the black beast on which she was mounted. John thought how magnificent she looked in man's clothing and was vividly reminded of when he had first seen her, peering at her through the crack in a cupboard door while she undressed.

She must have read his mind because she turned and called out, 'Shall we go to the Grange?'

'I don't know that my nerves could stand it,' he answered.

'Nonsense. If those two old biddies are hiding out it is the logical place for them to go.'

'Why?'

'Because they must have had horses tethered somewhere, and the sensible thing would be to make for the Grange. No mortal person ventures near the place after dark I can assure you.'

'I can understand that perfectly.'

'Oh John, don't be lily-livered. Remember the time we went there together.'

And suddenly he did. Remembered with a certain embarrassment how he had nearly made love to her and would have done so had he not, in a great pang of guilty conscience, recalled his marriage vows and thought of Emilia, his wife.

He answered, rather shortly, 'Yes, I recall it.'

She must have guessed his feelings because she slowed down and leant across to take his horse's bridle.

'John, we needn't go there if you do not wish it. But I do feel it is worth taking a look, just in case.'

'But it would mean climbing all over that monstrous house and after my experiences earlier this evening I don't feel that I am up to it.'

'Then you shall wait outside while I go in,' she said soothingly, which was just the sort of thing to say to the Apothecary, who at once felt that he was being cowardly.

'No, I wouldn't hear of it, Elizabeth. I shall accompany you.'

But as they neared the gaunt building, its ruined towers and turrets reaching into the dark sky like clutching fingers, John's heart plummeted once more.

'Must we go?'

'Yes, we must.'

Motioning him to be silent Elizabeth dismounted in a spinney of trees and tethered the two horses to the branches. Reluctantly John also swung down and they proceeded on foot towards the ghastly edifice.

'I thought it better to arrive without prior warning,' she whispered.

John could not help but grin at her. 'You're certain they are in there,' he murmured back.

'I'm not certain of anything, but it is worth a try.'

But strangely, as they approached the building, they could see that certain alterations had been made and there were definite signs of restoration work. Windows that had hung open to the skies had now been boarded up and made secure. Scaffolding had been erected against one of the walls. Various workmen's tools were gathered neatly together in a newly built hut.

Elizabeth turned to John, her eyes wide. 'I'd heard a rumour that someone was interested in buying the place. It would appear to be true.'

'But who would want it?'

'Obviously somebody wealthy with a large family. I've no idea of his identity though. And I had put the whole thing down to local tittle-tattle.'

'Shall we try to get in nonetheless?'

Elizabeth looked at him, her eyes sparkling. 'Let us do that. It will obviously be the last time.'

Their usual mode of entry through one of the sagging windows was now barred to them, but walking cautiously round they discovered a kitchen door that had worked loose and was swinging on its hinges. Moving lithely – rather like a panther, John thought – Elizabeth made her way in.

There is nothing more soul destroying than a big, empty kitchen. The whole place smelt of rot and decay, and John gazed around at filthy sinks, greasy spits and mucky ovens. The Marchesa marched onward on silent feet and the Apothecary followed as quietly as he could. They reached the bottom of that formidable staircase and Elizabeth had started to climb before he could stop her. It was then that John thought he glimpsed the real reason why she had come to Wildtor Grange. She wanted to revisit the apartments she had once used as a hideout when she had been younger and not so honest a citizen as she was these days.

She had increased her stride so that John was forced into a half run to keep up with her. He could not for the life of him remember in which direction her apartments lay and he stood in the dark, trying to get his bearings. And then Elizabeth reappeared carrying a candle. She had stripped off all her clothes and he was terribly aware of how gorgeous she looked. In fact he could not keep his eyes off her. She smiled enigmatically.

'Do I still attract you?' she asked.

'More than I can say.'

'Then show me.'

He needed no further invitation. He allowed her to lead

him to those old rooms which still bore something of the perfume she had once worn, where he flung her down on to the bed. And then he made love to her, so many times and so beautifully, as if in so doing he could put the memories of that terrible wedding out of his head for ever.

Nineteen

John was woken by the sunlight playing on his face and stretched out an arm to reach for Elizabeth. But she was not there. He was alone in her great bed in that terrifying house, with its monstrous staircase and its long dreary suites of rooms leading one upon the other. How anyone, however wealthy and with however many children, could think of buying and restoring such a place was quite beyond him.

He sat up and looked around. Once, long ago, when the Marchesa had been a vigilante avenging the death of her only son, she had used it as a hideout and had slept alone in the great house, first having furnished an apartment to her own luxurious requirements. Now, though the curtains and cushions were faded and dusty and generally tired, the rooms still had the air about them of somewhere that had once been rather grand. He supposed that with enough money spent upon it and enough cheerful fires lit and constantly thronged with hosts of people, Wildtor Grange might again achieve something of its original potential after all.

He swung out of bed and had started to put his clothes on when the door opened and there stood Elizabeth, fully dressed and already wearing her tricorne hat. She smiled at him becomingly.

'Guess what I've just found.'

John shook his head. 'I don't know. What?'

'These.'

And she pulled from behind her back two brown shifts, of the type worn by working women, and two hideous poke bonnets.

'So they *were* here,' exclaimed John.

'They most certainly were. My reading of the situation is that they came here, changed, then went on to Exeter where they disappeared into the crowd.'

'Let me have a look at those dresses,' said John, buttoning up his shirt.

Elizabeth passed them to him.

'These have been specially made. Look at the size of them. They're too long for a woman for a start, though admittedly one is shorter than the other. But then so were the assassins.'

The Marchesa sat down on the bed. 'What else did you notice about the couple?'

'I glimpsed the face of one of them. Briefly.'

'What about their hands?'

'Their hands? Now those I did see. One had long fingers and I do believe brown spots. So he must have been quite middle-aged. The other, younger. Rather reddish hands, square.'

'And did you not see that one of them wore a bracelet of some kind?'

'No, I didn't. Which one?'

'The taller. He had something round his wrist which I only just glimpsed but thinking that he was a woman I did not pay much attention. But these dresses prove their gender. Conclusively.'

And she held one garment against her. The skirt folded at the hem leaving a good part of the dress trailing on the floor.

John took hold of the bonnets and held them up to the light.

'What are you looking for?'

'Hairs. Have you got any tweezers?'

'I'll go and look.'

She crossed to the dressing table and after searching for a few minutes came back to him with a pair.

'Thank you.'

He scooped around inside the hats and eventually gave a cry of triumph and produced a longish hair, held between the tweezers.

'There,' he said.

Elizabeth stared at it. 'It's red.'

'Indeed it is. And it belongs to one of the killers. But how to keep it, that's the problem.'

She went back to the dressing table and raked about, then returned with a small box, satin lined, that had once housed earrings.

'Will this do?'

'Perfectly,' and he carefully tucked the hair within. Vaguely, very vaguely, the colour reminded him of someone, but he could not for the life of him think who it was.

A search of the second bonnet proved less favourable. It was full of the smell of sweet pomade and John imagined that the wearer must have slicked his hair down into a net and put the bonnet on over the lot.

'Where did you find all this?'

'In a pile at the bottom of the stairs.'

'Then it must be as you thought. They could have gone on to Exeter and boarded a stagecoach and be halfway to anywhere by now.'

'John, we've got to go and see the Constable. He must get on to the case. If those two blackguards get away with this I shall be furious.'

'I didn't realize that you were that attached to the Earl of St Austell,' the Apothecary said wryly.

'He can be damned. It is the innocent victims I am concerned about.'

She was itching to be on the move, to do her part in bringing the criminals to justice. She slapped John's hat on his head and headed for the staircase without another word. He followed behind her, carrying the box with the hair in it, and, telling himself not to be afraid, began to descend that nightmarish staircase. And then his eye was caught by something. Something dropped on one of the stairs. It was a man's handkerchief and on it were smears of carmine and white as if someone had wiped it over their face to remove their make-up. It could as easily have belonged to a belle or beau of fashion, yet John's instinct told him it was a man's. He snatched it up and put it in his pocket for more careful examination later on.

They reached Exeter about forty minutes later, having gone like the wind. John, terrified by the ordeal of riding fast, had clung on for dear life, losing his hat and his stirrup at one point. The hat he gave up as a bad job, the stirrup he eventually regained. Panting, mud streaked and definitely pale, he arrived at Tobias Miller's house in the High Street, hoping that the citizens of Exeter still held on to their custom of re-appointing Toby when it was their turn to undertake the much-hated job. Elizabeth, looking cool as a cucumber and calm to boot, slid out of the saddle and knocked at the front door. A round-cheeked, jolly little woman answered, explaining that she was his sister.

'No, my Lady, Tobias has gone off to Lady Sidmouth's house. Appears there was a terrible shooting up there last night. He went off soon after dawn when one of her footmen arrived in a coach.'

The Apothecary groaned aloud and spoke forcefully.

'Elizabeth, I am going off to have breakfast. The horse is exhausted and so am I. You do as you please.'

He had not intended to sound so brusque but obviously it touched a spark with the Marchesa. She was silent for a moment or two and then she said, 'You're quite right. We must give the animals a rest. I'll join you.'

They did not speak a great deal during the meal until John covered one of Elizabeth's hands with his and said, 'Thank you for last night. It was tremendous and exciting. And worth all the riding.' He laughed then and added, 'In every sense.'

She laughed back and, pulling his face towards hers, plonked a kiss on his nose. 'I suggest we take the horses home, then change. And we'll go to Lady Sidmouth's by coach.'

'I utterly agree with you,' John said thankfully.

Tobias Miller stood in the Grand Saloon and looked about him carefully. Then he crossed to the French doors and let himself out into the garden, seeing if the villains had left any visible tracks behind them. Sure enough, there were a couple of footprints in the flower bed and Toby, after staring at them for a moment or two, took out a little ruler from his inner pocket and measured them. They were clearly not left by a woman – unless she had simply enormous feet – and the indent of the heel was larger than any left by a woman's shoe. Taking out a notebook from another hidden pocket, he made a rough pencil sketch of the footprint before stepping back into the Saloon.

Lady Sidmouth was inside, looking more than a little miserable.

'I cannot think why there should have been such an attack. And at a wedding feast. It really is too bad.'

'My Lady, may I sit down?' asked Toby politely.

'Oh there I am forgetting common courtesy. Please do, Constable Miller. Now how can I assist?'

'First of all, Madam, I would like a list of all the people present yesterday, including their addresses, if such a thing should be possible.'

'Oh yes indeed, it most certainly is. It was a wedding and we had sent invitations and listed all those who could come and those who refused. I will get a servant to fetch it for you.' She rang a little bell and when a footmen came ordered him to fetch the wedding list and also bring some refreshment for Constable Miller.

'Thank you, Ma'am, you are very kind. A cup of tea would be pleasant. And now, if you'll forgive me, I would like to speak of the events of yesterday afternoon.'

'Certainly.'

'These assassins. You say they wore brown shifts and poke bonnets, but did you conclude they were disguises, to hide their true identity?'

'Oh quite definitely. I thought they were men, in fact. You see, they had big hands and feet and quite broad shoulders. One of them definitely, though the other was smaller.'

'Um. And though they shot at everyone, would you say the target was the Earl of St Austell?'

'That really is hard to conclude. It seemed to me that they were on a mad killing spree. But that doesn't really make any sense. But then, what does?'

'Quite.'

The Constable was silenced by the arrival of his tea. When the footman had left, he asked, 'And where is the widow now?'

Lady Sidmouth stared and then said, 'Oh you mean Miranda. She is prostrate in her room, poor girl. She has stepped straight out of her wedding gown and into deepest black.'

'As you say, Madam, she is to be much pitied. Now, as you know, I have examined all three bodies and it will be my duty to send them on to the Exeter mortuary. The Coroner will release them in due course and then they may be duly buried.'

'I see. Tell me, what did you conclude from your examination?'

'I am no medical man as you know, my Lady. But judging

from their injuries I would say that the Earl was definitely the target. He was shot four times. Mrs James had one bullet wound to the heart and Mr Meakin looked as if he had been shot almost by accident.'

'I see. So what does that tell you?'

'You want my honest opinion?'

'Of course.'

'Then I would say they were hired assassins and their brief was to kill the Earl and, perhaps, Lettice James. Mr Meakin I am not so certain of.'

Lady Sidmouth went very white. 'But who could possibly have hired them?'

'That's what I'm going to find out. Did the Earl have any enemies that you know of?'

'Dozens, I should imagine.'

Tobias looked up from his notebook. 'Really? Who for example?'

'I really don't think I would care to say that.'

'That is up to you, Lady Sidmouth. But I shall find out in any case. You can be assured of it.'

'That is entirely your affair, Constable.'

'Yes, Madam, it is.'

As Tobias Miller was making his way out he ran into that most exemplary man, John Rawlings, together with that formidable female, the Marchesa di Lorenzi.

'Ah, Mr Rawlings, how are you, my dear Sir? What are you doing in this part of the world?' John opened his mouth to reply but the Constable continued, 'Let me hazard a guess. You were invited to the wedding and witnessed the happenings of yesterday afternoon.'

'Quite right. But what you didn't know was that the Lady Elizabeth and I called on you this morning to be told that you had made an early visit to Lady Sidmouth.'

The Constable lowered his voice. 'Is there anywhere we can talk privately?'

'I can only think of the cellar. Nobody will venture down there because of the bodies.'

The Marchesa spoke. 'Then I'll call on Lady Sidmouth and

keep her occupied. Meanwhile you two can have your private discussion.'

'Thank you, Madam,' said the Constable and gave her a formal bow.

Walking quietly, John and Tobias made their way round the house and in at the back door used by the servants. The steep circular staircase that it was the daily lot of the employees to climb or descend was immediately to their left. Without a word both men plunged downwards.

The atmosphere in the cellar was horrible. For no good reason John felt the hairs on his neck rise. All the old stories of ghosts and ghouls flashed through his mind. And then, quite distinctly, he heard a sound. Tobias turned to him with raised eyebrows and the Apothecary motioned him to be quiet. They crept forward to where lay the three mounds, all covered with fresh white linen.

'Don't move or I'll shoot,' said Tobias, drawing a pistol.

For answer there was silence, followed by a long, terrible, gasping sob.

Twenty

Pistol drawn and looking thoroughly menacing, Tobias strode forward to see a quivering heap clutching at the sheet covering the Earl of St Austell and letting forth a series of loud sobs.

'Stand up, Sir!' he shouted. 'Stand up and act like a man.'

Much to the Apothecary's surprise the fellow whose character he was still attempting to read, Viscount Falmouth, rose to his feet and stood noisily crying into his spectacles.

Tobias showed no mercy. 'Well, Sir, and what do you have to say for yourself?'

'He was my grandfather, for the love of God. Have you no pity?' came the reply, punctuated by sobs.

'I am sorry, your Grace, but I do not think this is a suitable place for you to be. I am here investigating a crime and I think you would be better off praying in a church.'

The Constable's form of address brought home to John the fact that the Viscount was now the new Earl of St Austell and as such should be acting with a certain dignity, however racked his emotions were. Remembering his first meeting with him, when Falmouth had come into his shop and asked him for strengthening medicine for his elderly relative and behaved with such absent-mindedness, John could hardly marry the different parts of the man's character. Looking at the sobbing wreck before him and recalling the vague young man he had first encountered, the Apothecary felt quite puzzled by the whole affair.

Falmouth slowly dried his eyes. He looked at Tobias with nothing short of loathing.

'Are you devoid of all feelings, man? This was my beloved grandfather. Have you ever lost a relative?'

'Yes, indeed I have, your Grace. When I was sixteen years old. Both of my parents died of influenza. And I was left in charge of a brood of siblings. Which, I might add, I brought up as decent and hard-working people. Every one.'

'Well, that's very commendable I'm sure. But I am newly struck by grief and I insist on paying respect to my grandfather's remains.'

And remains were about all they were, John thought, vividly remembering the fact that after the shooting the late Earl had been nothing but a mass of torn flesh and eyeballs. But further discussion was useless as from the staircase came a banging and crashing announcing the arrival of officials of some sort.

'We're from the coroner's office,' said the headman, who obviously knew Toby from years past. 'Three to take to the mortuary. That's right, isn't it?'

'They're not coffined up,' answered the Constable.

Falmouth intervened. 'Have a care there. I'll have you know that one of the bodies belongs to the late Earl of St Austell.'

The man looked unimpressed. 'Would you rather he was removed by your undertaker then, Sir?'

'Of course I would. Does he have to go to the mortuary?'

'The law is the law, Sir. Earl or churl, it's all the same in the end.'

'I've had enough of this conversation,' said Falmouth. He turned to Tobias. 'I am charging you as part of your sacred duty to see to it that my relative is treated with the respect he commanded in life. Do you hear me?'

'I certainly do, Sir,' answered Toby, and gave a little bow.

The new Earl stormed out of the cellar with John following behind him.

'Please don't be angry, your Grace,' he said in as pleasant a voice as he could muster. 'The Constable was only doing his duty.'

'Duty be damned. The man's an officious oaf.'

John was about to add that Tobias Miller was also extremely good at his job but thought better of it. In fact he maintained a stolid silence as Falmouth strode into the garden, snorting like a dragon and muttering under his breath.

'Please calm down, your Grace,' he ventured finally. 'Would you like me to fetch you a cordial?'

'No, but I'll have a brandy. And fetch one for yourself as well.'

Hardly able to come to terms with the two sides of the

Earl's character, John went into the house and immediately encountered Lady Sidmouth.

'Falmouth's in one of his strops, I see,' she said. 'I've been watching him out of the window.'

'He was down in the cellar, mourning beside the late Earl's body. He did not like being interrupted.'

'Obviously not!' she replied acidly. 'Now, go and get him to sit down and I will send one of the servants to you. What is it he requires? Brandy, I suppose.'

'You're right. Where is Elizabeth, by the way?'

'She has gone upstairs to comfort the Countess – Miranda to you and me – and then to see Lady Imogen, who has done nothing but weep uncontrollably since her miscarriage. Must run in the family.'

'Obviously. And where has Lord George skulked off to?'

'Heaven knows. He's probably getting drunk in some Exeter tavern. He roared off from here in his coach and hasn't been seen since.'

'Oh well at least he's out of harm's way. Unless he's punching Freddy Warwick, of course,' John said with a smile, and got a rather watery response from Lady Sidmouth.

The woman must have an iron constitution, he thought. To put up with the ghastly affair of the shooting at the wedding feast and then to cope with a household of uncontrolled people falling apart, must take an iron will. Without really thinking, the Apothecary put his arms round her.

She looked at him, a little startled. 'What's all this then?'

'I just wanted to say what a truly remarkable woman I think you are.'

Lady Sidmouth set her jaw. 'Oh come now, Mr Rawlings. I am only doing my duty as head of the house.'

'You're a fine woman, Madam. Now, did you know that some men have arrived from the coroner's office?'

'No. Why are they here?'

'To take the bodies to the mortuary where they are to be examined by a physician. The coroner will definitely hold an inquest because of the circumstances.'

'I see. So when will St Austell be released for burial?'

'I'm not sure. But not too long. I think the new Earl had

better get on with making the funeral arrangements. Give him something to think about.'

'It will indeed. Mr Rawlings, please tell him so.'

John went back to the gardens, but it was to find that Falmouth had wandered off somewhere and he was alone. After hunting around he decided that he would be better pursuing investigations, so he returned to the great house to find that Elizabeth had come downstairs and was ready to leave. Bidding farewell to Lady Sidmouth they got into their coach. As soon as they were seated the Marchesa positively burst into speech.

'My dear John, what a house of wailing women! First Miranda. She is clad from head to toe in deepest black and even has a veil over her face. She lies on a bed with curtains drawn, sobbing into the pillow and refuses to speak to anyone. It is one of the best acts I have ever seen.'

'You think it is pretence?'

'I'll swear it is. I mean, when one looks at the situation it was obvious she was marrying simply to get a title – and the riches thrown in, of course. I don't think she had any feelings for St Austell at all. But now she is milking her widowhood for all she is worth. Silly little cat.'

'Oh come now, don't be unkind.'

'I'm sorry but it is what I believe. And as for Imogen – well, she defeats me.'

'In what way?'

'Well, as far as rumour has it her horrible old grandfather has been interfering with her since she was a child. But the way she is carrying on makes one think that the loss of her baby was a terrible blow to her.'

'Perhaps it was fathered by someone else.'

Elizabeth was silent. 'I had not thought of that. You're probably right.' She squeezed the Apothecary's arm. 'Has this been helpful to your investigations?'

'Very,' John answered. He thought for a moment then said, 'Do you know I've a mind to call on Sir Clovelly Lovell. The poor old boy was terribly shaken by yesterday's events. I saw him leaving the feast looking pale as a wraith. Unfortunately I didn't get a chance to speak to him.'

'He was not injured, surely?'

'No, I'm glad to say he was not. But still it must have upset him terribly. Do you mind if I take the coach?'

'Not at all. Give him my love.'

'I certainly will.'

An hour later he was sitting in Sir Clovelly Lovell's parlour where an anguished figure, looking drawn and haggard, was shaking his heavy jowls from side to side and reminding John vividly of a miserable dog as he did so. He was still clad in his night shirt and gown and had a turban on his head which was fractionally too small, so that it appeared like the fez worn by a performing monkey rather than the adornment of a sultan.

'Oh John,' he was saying. 'I mean to say, my dear fellow. Pour me another glass of port if you'd be so good.' His glass refilled, he continued to speak. 'What a ghastly moment. I thought my last hour had come.'

'Do you mean to say that you were aimed at?'

'Most certainly I was. And that was the damned odd thing. The smaller of the two pointed his pistol directly at me and the taller man whispered, "No, not that one."'

'What?'

'"Not that one." At least it was something on those lines, but I was too busy ducking beneath the table to make it out completely.'

'And you were sure they were men?'

'Positive. Remember I heard them speak.'

'Of course. So how are you feeling now, old friend?'

'Terrible. I called my physician this morning. He came and charged me a small fortune for telling me to lose weight. He said the whole experience had raised my heartbeat and that I was to take things somewhat easier. Then he told me to cut down on alcohol and food. Damn killjoy.'

John nodded sympathetically, then ventured, 'Of course, when one is in a state of high alarm one should abstain from certain substances.'

Sir Clovelly's jowls positively trembled. 'Really? Is that a fact? It's not just the wretched physician trying to frighten one?'

'No Sir, it is true alas.'

Sir Clovelly hastily swigged down his port then handed the glass to the Apothecary. 'Here, you take this. And ration me to a glass an hour if you would be so good.'

'I will gladly do so, Sir.'

But all the time he was speaking John's mind was turning over what Sir Clovelly had told him. Could the assassins possibly have known the fat old fellow and realized that he was not on their list? It looked extremely like it. But then, he thought, they would had to have been local men. Unless the cold brain behind the killings had had them brought down from London. But in either event it seemed that their victims had not been chosen at random. That some kind of organized inventory had been at work.

He came back to attention as Sir Clovelly let out a great sigh. 'You promise to come and see me again, dear boy. I think all this resting is going to become monotonous.'

'May I suggest, Sir, that a little gentle exercise might help you to overcome your condition. Perhaps a turn or two round the green or a quiet stroll by the river. I think they would do you the world of good.'

'Really? Then I shall start tomorrow. Indeed I will. So I think I'll just have a final drink to toast that. If you would be so good as to fill my glass, my dear.'

Having left Sir Clovelly's house John decided, on a whim, to make his way into the cathedral, a place which to his shame he had not visited before. Immediately as he entered through the mighty doors the feeling came over him of quiet, of tremendous peace. Just for a moment John felt his cares float away as he looked around him.

Dominating the whole thing was the great East Window, parts of it medieval, a vivid flash of colour on a sombre afternoon. As John approached it a hidden organist burst forth with a voluntary, the sounds of which tore the Apothecary's heart from his body. At least that is how it felt. In a weakened state he sat down in a pew and studied the various saints portrayed in stained glass, including St Sidwell, whose waif-like looks and tumble of fair hair particularly appealed to him. With the music of the voluntary filling the entire building he got up again and wandered round, noticing the number of strange heads surrounded by foliage that were carved everywhere. He had always supposed them to be pagan, a fertility symbol most probably, but they had crept into Christian architecture and were extremely well represented in Exeter cathedral, to say the very least.

He walked down a side aisle, looking at the various tombs, realizing as he did so that the whole building was ancient in the extreme, that it dated back to Norman times and earlier. With a strange feeling of calmness he turned back to glance at the glorious East Window once more – and then he spotted a familiar figure. On her knees, crouched in a pew, eyes closed and lips mumbling silently, was Mrs Cushen. It was an opportunity too good to be missed. John silently slid into the pew behind her.

She must have sensed his presence because her head suddenly shot up and she glanced over her shoulder. For a second he had a feeling that he was looking on something raw with pain, then Mrs Cushen collected herself and grimaced at him.

'Oh gracious how you startled me. Fancy seeing you here, Mr Rawlings.'

John assumed his honest face. 'I came in to seek a little solace after yesterday's terrible happenings.'

'I too. Oh what a dreadful experience it was. My poor husband is lying in bed, suffering from shock. The whole affair has quite unhinged him.'

'I'm not surprised.'

'And I believe that the Countess has taken it very badly. Oh, it is such a sad thing.'

The familiar sentences rung round John's ears, but looking deep into Mrs Cushen's face he could see the poor woman actually was in deep distress. He wondered why. Had one of the victims meant more to her than he had previously thought?

He said, 'This is hardly a suitable environment for conversation. May I escort you to a teashop where we can talk more freely?'

She opened her eyes very wide and the Apothecary sensed her panic. 'No, no thank you. I really would prefer to remain here for a while. I am praying for those who lost their lives, you see.'

'Of course. I do beg your pardon for disturbing you.
Forgive me.'

'Naturally. Farewell, Mr Rawlings.'

And she bent her head, closed her eyes, and raised two hands
in front of her. John rose and with one final look at the East
Window – from which, or so it seemed to him, Saint Sidwell
flashed him a grin – he left the building and for a moment
or two stood uncertainly. Then, overcome with the need to
use the facilities, he hurried into The Blackamore's Head where,
holding forth loudly and as drunk as a fiddler's whore, was
Lord George Beauvoir. John hurried outside to the bog house,
and when he returned it was to see George come crashing
down towards the floor.

'Is he drunk?' he asked a fellow standing at the bar, watching
the proceedings with interest.

'Drunk?' chortled the other. 'Why, you could hang him on
a line for a week and he'd never know the difference. Why,
do you know him?'

'Never seen him before in my life,' lied John cheerfully, and
whilst ordering his pint of ale observed George being picked
up by the shoulders and feet and hurled into the street outside.

Having downed his drink, the Apothecary set forth to call
on Toby Miller who lived a short distance away. But he never
got there because he had only walked a step or two when he
saw the Constable coming towards him.

'Constable Miller,' he called.

'Good afternoon, Mr Rawlings. I was just on my way to
call on Mr James and offer him my condolences. Would you
care to join me?'

'Very much indeed.'

They made their way down to the river where some
delightful small villas had been built overlooking the great
waterway. John thought it a fine place for a gossip and a farter
to dwell, but was disappointed when they turned into a small
alleyway which backed on to the pretty houses.

Toby looked in his notebook. 'This is it. Number Three,
River Row.'

He knocked on the door which was answered by a scowling
hag. 'Yes?'

'I've come to see Mr James, if it is convenient.'

'Well it ain't,' she answered, and was about to slam the door in their faces when a faint voice called from within, 'Who is it, Gertrude?'

'Who are you?' she demanded, displaying a rotten brown tooth that hung quivering on her upper set.

'Constable Miller and Apothecary Rawlings,' replied Toby formally.

'I heard that,' called the distant voice. 'Show them in, Gertie.'

Reluctantly she opened the door a couple of inches. 'He's in,' she said, and fixed them with a beady, beastly eye as they made their way up a dark and dusty staircase.

Twenty-One

Mr James had pulled himself out of bed and into an ancient armchair by the time they entered the room. He had a rather grubby blanket wrapped round him and was almost bent in half, snuggling into it. He looked thoroughly decrepit but in fact, thought the Apothecary, peering into his face, he was probably little more than fifty and far from stupid.

Tobias Miller broke the silence. 'I am so very sorry, Sir, that your wife has been called to her Maker. The whole thing is a complete tragedy.'

Mr James straightened slightly. 'Yes, my heart is broken. Though, to be honest, she was rarely at home. Her social life, you know. Always flitting from one place to another. But she moved in good circles, I can tell you.' His eyes swivelled round to John, who noticed that they were a strange colour, a type of river grey. 'I presume that you are the apothecary that was mentioned.'

'You presume correctly, Sir. That is my profession.'

Mr James suddenly pulled the blanket up over his face and began to moan, rocking himself to and fro like a forlorn child.

Toby and John exchanged a glance of surprise before John stepped forward and gently put down a hand. 'Hush, Sir, please do. I know you are in the depths of mourning but try to brace up.'

The blanket was lowered very slightly so that the pair of eyes became visible – and what anguish in their depths. 'How can I brace up? I am in mourning for all of my life as well as that of poor Lettice, shot by some thug on a whim. Oh God, I might as well be dead myself.'

At this moment the poor fellow voided some wind with such a loud explosion that John found himself in the unfortunate position of wanting to laugh. Constable Miller however kept a straight face.

'That's as may be, Sir. But I am afraid I am here on official business and I have to ask you some questions.'

There was no reply as Mr James hid once more behind the blanket.

Tobias Miller came as near to losing control as John had ever seen him. 'Mr James,' he thundered, 'for God's sake act your age. You can't revert to babyhood unless you are a total idiot, in which case you should be committed to an asylum. Now what is your Christian name?'

The man slowly sat up straight. 'My name is Geoffrey James and I am a merchant of Exeter. Indeed I have been one for many a long year.'

'And what do you deal in?'

'Spices. I import them from the Indies and distribute them to my many customers.'

'And how can someone of your importance behave as you are doing? Wrapping yourself in a blanket and behaving like a child. For shame.'

'I think you are addressing me out of turn. I suggest you apologize,' Geoffrey answered, slowly getting out of his chair.

John decided that this was the moment to intervene. He put on his sympathetic but professional manner. 'My dear Mr James, I am actually here to offer you some help. Your late wife mentioned to me – in the strictest confidence of course – that you suffer badly with flatulence. I think I can procure a cure – forgive the pun.'

The grey eyes looked at him with bored resignation. 'I have had quacks treating me for years. All to no effect.' As if to prove the point he voided wind thunderously once more.

'What have they prescribed?'

'I don't know,' Geoffrey answered sadly. 'All sorts of things. I couldn't name them.'

'Tell me, are onions included in your diet.'

'Yes, I do like a boiled onion. I must admit I do.'

'Well, I should give that up for a start. Have you had a clyster?'

'Not in a while. I don't like the things.'

'Nobody does. But you must persevere. I am going to prescribe for you a weekly washout with the combined flowers of Melilot and Chamomile together with a half a dram of the powdered root of Lovage, taken by mouth once a day. You will find it very warming and further it actually dissolves wind.'

Mr James heaved a sigh. 'If you think it will do any good.'

'I most certainly do, Sir. I shall call on your tomorrow with an apothecary's boy to administer the purge. And now, Sir, may I suggest that you retire to bed. You are obviously worn out with sorrow. At what time would you like me to arrive?'

Somehow John managed to glance at Toby unseen and the Constable picked up his cue. 'I can see, Sir, that you are not well enough to answer questions today. I too will return tomorrow at the time you wish.'

Geoffrey nodded with affected weariness. 'That would suit me better. You can fix the times with Gertrude. But please don't come together.'

They bowed their way out and walked down the street and straight into a tavern.

'That,' said Toby Miller, 'was one of the most awkward interviews of my life.'

'I think the man is in genuine grief. He looks utterly care-worn – and as for his distressing and odorous complaint. It would be enough to try the nerves of any human being,' John answered, and drank the strong jigger of gin he had ordered.

An hour later the Apothecary got into the coach which had been waiting for him, but instead of going straight to Elizabeth's home went to see his patient, Felicity, at Sidmouth House. He found her feverish but making good progress. The surgeon from Exeter, Alexander Perkins, had removed the bullet and spent the night at Sidmouth House. Indeed he had only just returned home, and the Apothecary found Felicity dropping off to sleep when he entered her bedroom accompanied by her mother. On examining her arm he found it bandaged. Very carefully John raised the wound to his nostrils and sniffed.

'The surgeon has spread it with a different paste from the one I used.'

'Alehoof,' answered Lady Sidmouth. 'I keep a supply of it in my medicine chest. When I am running low I get a fresh batch from the apothecary in Exeter.'

'Very wise. And clever of Mr Perkins to use it.'

'I think he is a very clever young man,' said Lady Sidmouth pointedly, looking in Felicity's direction.

At that moment there was a noise downstairs and the mistress of the house was called urgently to settle some minor dispute in the kitchens. As soon as the door had closed behind her, Felicity patted the bedcover.

'Pray sit here, Mr Rawlings. There is something I want to tell you that nobody else must hear.'

John sat, agog.

'Last night you can remember the confusion and noise. Well, after you and everybody else had eventually left, my mother insisted that I go to my bedroom and lie down, awaiting Mr Perkins' arrival. But I could not sleep. My arm was throbbing and hurting so much and the room felt hot and oppressive. Anyway, to come to the point, I decided to disobey her and take a turn round the gardens. I walked to where the lawns begin, where they sweep down to the sea. And there, on the beach below – it is only visible at low tide so you may not have noticed it – I saw two distant figures. I could not recognize who they were but they were walking close together and they kissed from time to time. They must have been connected with our house because there is no other way down to the beach. I know it was probably two of the servants but nonetheless it gave me quite a start.'

'You didn't recognize them at all? Was there nothing that gave you any clue?'

'No, except that . . .'

'Yes?'

'Except that the woman had something on her head – a scarf of some kind I think – that blew out from time to time on the wind.'

'You're absolutely sure about this? It wasn't by any chance the two assassins?'

'No, these two people were shaped differently. It most certainly wasn't them.'

'I see,' said the Apothecary, and sat silently, thinking.

The sound of Lady Sidmouth returning had him leaping up again and examining Felicity's arm once more.

'Well, Mr Rawlings, and what is your prognosis?'

'In bed for a few days, then up and taking a little gentle exercise. Particularly of the arm. In short, Felicity should keep using it. But I am sure that Mr Perkins has said this to you already.'

'He certainly has. He will be calling again tomorrow.' She looked at Felicity, who went very pink.

'Then there will be no need for me to return except for a social call. I am sure Elizabeth will be visiting soon.'

John took his leave, filled with thought. He could picture the couple walking in the moonlight, dark shapes alone on that small beach that only appeared when the tide was out. They must have climbed the wooden staircase back to the house, then parted to go – where? Had they only been serv-ants as Felicity had wondered or had there been something altogether more sinister about their tryst? All the way back to Elizabeth's house he turned the matter over and over in his mind but could come to no conclusions whatsoever.

That night he dreamed such a dream. He was on a strip of sand, walking behind the couple who constantly eluded him. For however much he increased his pace they always remained at the same distance in front of him. He could hear them laughing quietly and he watched the girl's scarf blow out in the wind, taking off over her head as if she would fly away with it. The couple reached the end of the beach and turned to go back in the other direction and the Apothecary, rather than being able to see their faces, felt that he had to turn too. So now he walked in front of them and he heard them both pursuing him. He broke into a run but whichever way he went he knew that they were right behind him. In the end he was so terrified that he ran into the sea and swam out a little way. But the sea was black and cold and hateful, and the moon had gone in. Down he went, down and down into the inky depths, then he gave the most almighty scream and woke up.

He was alone in the big bedroom and the door was open. Elizabeth must have got up to see to the twins, as was her custom despite the nursery maids. Still feeling nervous because of the dream, John got out of bed and pulled on a nightrail.

He crossed to the window and looked out and suddenly he had a mental picture of Rose and Sir Gabriel. It was quite distinct. Sir Gabriel was fetching her from school and she was greeting him with radiant eyes and a glowing complexion. She was happy, John felt certain of it, yet as always when he thought of his daughter he had a longing to see her. He wondered whether to get a flying coach to London and go home for a while, leaving the investigation in the hands of Constable Miller, a most able man in John's view.

Yet there were so many things that just didn't add up. The two men dressed as women, ready to kill, yet holding back from Sir Clovelly Lovell; the thread of red hair; Mrs Cushen's strangely fearful manner in the Cathedral; sad Geoffrey James behaving like a baby; and lastly Felicity's strange sighting of two people walking on the beach below her. What did any of it mean? Were the incidents even related? Shaking his head, the Apothecary went downstairs to find something to eat and drink in a hope that this would finally get him off to sleep peacefully.

Twenty-Two

His appointment with the extremely miserable Mr James, who had given John some cause for concern in the hours of wakefulness he had had the night before, was not until two o'clock. Therefore the Apothecary decided to put the morning to some use and make a call at the home of the late Mr Meakin, the third person to die in the shooting affray.

The deceased had not lived in Exeter but in a very small village outside called Clyst St Agnes. His house, however, denoted someone of wealth, standing as it did in its own beautiful grounds and reached by a short drive with a carriage sweep in front. As the coach approached – borrowed from Elizabeth once more – John peered through its windows trying to work out the profession of the newly dead man. He concluded that he was either a lawyer or a physician.

The door was answered by a footman wearing a very solemn face. Outwardly the house had signs of deep mourning, the curtains all being drawn and the knocker swathed in black material.

'I am sorry, Sir, but Madam is not receiving anyone at all. There has been a tragedy in the family, you see.'

'Yes, I understand completely. I was just hoping for a brief word with . . .'

'Will I do?' interrupted a voice.

The door opened a little wider to reveal a wee dot of a woman, no more than four feet and a few inches, with a tiny busy face and hair scraped back off her face into a high curly bun.

John made a bow. 'Mrs Meakin?' he asked.

'Alas no. Poor Ella is lying down. She is with child, you know. I am Miss Meakin, sister of Alan.' She suddenly burst into tears like an April shower, dry one minute, rain pouring the next. And as suddenly, it was gone again. 'To whom am I speaking, if you please?'

'John Rawlings, Madam. I am here on semi-official business.'

'Are you? Are you going to solve the mystery of dear Alan's death? Then enter, pray do. Hawkins, be good enough to fetch sherry for two to the parlour.'

As he walked through the house the Apothecary could see that it was finely appointed and tastefully decorated and reckoned that the family were monied people.

'Do take a seat,' said Miss Meakin. 'Now, what can I do for you?' A pair of bright eyes were fastened on him and she added, 'Please do not think me callous in receiving you like this. It is just that I want this horrid mystery solved and if I can help in any way, I will.'

'I am very obliged to you for seeing me. I just have a few questions if you would be so good.'

'Certainly.'

At this point the sherry arrived and Miss Meakin poured them both a schooner.

John raised his glass. 'Your health, Madam. Let me just explain that I am assisting the Constable of Exeter, Tobias Miller, with his investigations.'

This was not strictly true but the Apothecary had no hesitation in telling a white lie, anxious as he was to find out if the dead man had a more intimate relationship with St Austell and his family, or had merely been acquainted through business. He guessed at the latter.

'Obviously, Miss Meakin, you have been told all the details of the terrible affair at the Earl of St Austell's wedding feast. Tell me, how well did your brother know the Earl?'

'Well, socially, he didn't. But the Earl had considerable dealings in Devon – as well as Cornwall – and Alan was a lawyer, in charge of the Earl's Devon affairs.'

'I see. Very much as I thought.'

'What else can I help you with?'

'I don't know really.' For once the Apothecary was at a loss, having failed to make any true connection between the two dead men.

'Would you like another sherry while you think?'

'Yes please.'

Miss Meakin refilled his glass and John sipped, wondering what to say.

'Alan's wife could not go with him to the wedding feast – and God be thanked for that in hindsight – because she is very near her time. My poor, poor sister-in-law. Heaven alone knows what future awaits her.'

'But surely you have enough money.'

'Yes, we do. Though Alan's salary was a goodly part of it. He was very clever you know. As I told you he handled all the Earl's affairs.'

John had a moment of inspiration. 'St Austell wasn't by chance making a new will, was he?'

'Oh yes,' replied Miss Meakin earnestly. 'Alan was much involved with it. The Earl left a personal bequest to his bride, apparently, which would see her comfortably off for the rest of her days.'

'Really? And do you know if it had been signed or not?'

She looked bewildered. 'Oh yes. It was signed shortly after they became betrothed.'

Suddenly the Apothecary saw a thread. Lord George and Viscount Falmouth must have been quite displeased about that, to say nothing of Lady Imogen. He drank his sherry rather fast and stood up. 'It really has been a pleasure to meet you, Miss Meakin. If there is anything I can do to help you or your sister-in-law please do contact me. I am staying with Lady Elizabeth di Lorenzi at her house near Exeter.'

The little dot opened her eyes wide and then wept again. 'Thank you for being so polite, Mr Rawlings,' she said in a muffled voice.

'Thank you for receiving me, Miss Meakin.' He bowed his way out, hat across his chest. 'Please give my condolences to Mrs Meakin.'

'I will, I will.'

He left her crying in full flood and stepped out and into his carriage with an entirely different view of the case.

Unfortunately he had no time to pursue his idea at present because, looking at his watch – still the one that Sir Gabriel had given him for his twenty-first birthday – he discovered that he had less than half an hour until his appointment with

Mr James. But when he panted to the front door, a minute or two late, the horrible Gertrude waved her tooth at him and shouted, 'He's out,' before slamming it shut in his face.

John stood, slightly annoyed and quite definitely nonplussed. He had made a firm arrangement to call on Geoffrey James and now the fellow had backed out. He decided that he would try to locate him and knocked on the door again.

It was opened after a minute and Gertrude thrust her unlovely face out. 'Wot is it?'

'Do you know where Mr James has gone?'

'Down to the river. Says he's going to drown hisself.'

'Oh for God's sake,' John answered impatiently, and set off at some speed.

Originally the River Exe had been tidal and navigable up to the city walls, and it had thrived as a busy port. In the 1270s, however, Isabella de Fortibus, the Countess of Devon, had built a weir across the river to power her mills. Whether this was a deliberately spiteful action no one knew but it had the effect of cutting off Exeter's thriving harbour from the sea. Twenty years later trade with the port resumed only to be cut off once more, this time by Hugh de Courtenay, Earl of Devon, Isabella's cousin. This meant that all goods had to be unloaded at Topsham – a town that John could remember clearly from the days of his honeymoon – and carried by road. The Earls, rubbing their hands in glee, collected heavy tolls to anyone using the highways,

For 250 years the city sent petitions to the King to have the port reopened, until finally in 1550 Edward VI, the boy King – Henry VIII's son by Jane Seymour – finally granted permission. In 1563, Exeter traders employed a Welshman, John Trew of Glamorgan, to build a canal to bypass the weirs and rejoin the river in the centre of the city, where a great quay would be built. In 1677 it was extended and the entrance was moved to Topsham, and in 1701 the canal was deepened and widened to allow ocean-going sailing ships right of passage.

This was how Elizabeth had met her husband, the Italian trader, the Marchese di Lorenzi, who had sailed his ship to Exeter loaded with Murano glass. And she, the daughter of an English Earl, pampered and cosseted since birth, had run off

with him and lived a wild and exciting life in Italy. Until
tragedy had intervened and she had returned to England to
bring up her son on her own.

But now, John thought, she had a lively pair of twin boys
to cope with, and just for a second came near to understanding
her possessiveness over them.

It seemed to him that as a merchant of Exeter Geoffrey
might go down to the quay, and it was to there that John made
his way. There was no sign of his quarry but for a few minutes
he stopped in open-mouthed admiration of the great ships –
sails furled, decks swarming with men – that lay at anchor
there. Then he felt a tap on his shoulder and looking round
saw the melancholy Mr James, drunk as a wheelbarrow, swaying
on his feet, and looking a ripe shade of green.

'Greetings,' said Mr James, then shambled to the water's edge
and was horribly sick into the river.

John, observing him with a seasoned eye, waited till all the
retching was done and then walked forward and dragged the
wretched man back to where two barrels offered a temporary
sitting place.

'Now,' he said, 'tell me everything.'

'I loved her, that was the trouble,' said Geoffrey incoherently.
'She was an awful wife, terrible in fact, but I couldn't help
myself. I just loved her.'

'Why was she so bad?' asked John.

'Unfaithful. Always out. Gossip. Everything that one wouldn't
desire in a woman.'

He hiccuped violently and John instinctively leaned away.

Mr James continued, his speech somewhat clearer. 'You see,
she was fascinated by what she thought of as the "best people".
She had very humble origins, you know. Born to a labouring
family. Her father heaved goods coming off the ships. But she
was very pretty at one time and had a pleasing way with her.
So pleasing that I married her. I loved her so much. Oh God's
wounds.' His voice broke on a sob. 'Anyway, she set about
cultivating society people. She would do anything to get to
know them. Anything at all.' By now he was crying openly.

John watched in silence, certain he knew what was coming
next.

'That wretch the Earl of St Austell. She became his mistress. He would bed any doxy and I am certain he took her as part of a wager. And after that, he would torment her. Send for her once a year and openly laugh in her face before seducing her. He turned her into a flip-flap. My pretty little Lettice.'

'Did you kill him? Were you one of the two shooters?'

Geoffrey looked at him in astonishment. 'No, I did not. I went out drinking that day – the day of the wedding. No, Sir, you can look elsewhere for your murderer.'

John nodded quietly, anxious not to stop the flow. 'I understand. Tell me, did Lettice share any of the Earl's secrets do you know?'

'I can't imagine it.' He was sobering up and looked at the Apothecary quite acutely. 'Why, may I ask?'

'I am just wondering if that was the reason for her murder?'

'I should think there must be at least fifty of Exeter's citizens who had a motive for killing my poor wife. She gossiped about everyone and everything. Except herself. But in a way she was quite proud of the fact that she was St Austell's whore. Made her feel that she had risen up in the world.' He sighed deeply.

'And she told you all this?'

'I charged her with the fact she was his mistress. And do you know what she replied?'

'No.'

'That I was a fumbler and no use to woman or beast.'

John said nothing, thinking of all the tragedies of life, of all the million and one hurts and cruelties that people inflict on other human beings. How nothing ever seems to go straightly from A to B. That living was punctuated by a zillion and one relentless wounds, starting, perhaps, with a child falling down and ending with the death of someone near and dear. What a treacherous path indeed.

Geoffrey stared at him soberly. 'The trouble was that she fell out of love with me. That is probably what drove her to do what she did.'

John shook his head. Even at this most dire of times, Mr James was still making excuses for Lettice. He forced a cheerful smile on to his face. 'It is a sad loss for you, Geoffrey. I may call you that? But let me hear no more nonsense about ending your life. Living is a challenge to each and every one of us, and it is up to you to do it, for better or worse.'

'The house is so empty without Lettice.'

'Nonsense. You said she was always out and about. The best thing you can do is get on with your business and make it better. Work is the greatest cure-all for everything.'

Mr James straightened his shoulders, clearly sobering up. 'You're right, of course.'

'And the other thing you might do to improve things . . .'

'Yes?'

'Is sack Gertrude.' And the Apothecary raised one of his mobile eyebrows and grinned.

When he got home it was to find a letter from Jacquetta Fortune awaiting him. It was neatly written in a long flowing hand and was so descriptive that John chuckled as he read it. Apparently Gideon was running the shop as if he were an apothecary of many years standing, while the apprentice, Robin Hazell, was turning out to be a boy of quick understanding and obvious merit. His great friend and admirer, Fred the Factotum, was proving adept with his letters and had added a post scriptum to Jacquetta's script:

I WRIT THIS WITH MINE OWN HAND.
FRED.

Slyly John slid his eyes up from where he sat opposite Elizabeth, calmly reading a newspaper with a minute pair of spectacles perched upon her nose, comparing the colour of her hair with that of Mrs Fortune. They were as unalike as any two women could be yet, he had to admit it, though he loved Elizabeth with all his heart he still had a *penchant* for Jacquetta, with her competent manner and her glowing locks.

'Interesting letter?' said Elizabeth, looking at him over her glasses.

'Yes, it's from Mrs Fortune. She says that the business is booming, that Gideon has taken over the shop as if I never existed, and that both the boys are doing well.'

'And what of Rose?'

'She says nothing.'

'Why is that?'

'Probably because she knows nothing. Remember Rose is at school now.' He sighed. 'I wish I could see her.'

'There is nothing to keep you here,' Elizabeth answered with a hint of acidity.

John knew the right thing to say. 'Yes, there is, by God. There is you, the beautiful woman who will not marry me. And there are my twin sons whom I love almost as much as I love you. And thirdly there is this wretched affair of the shooting.'

'Are you any further with the investigation?'

'Indeed I am. It seems that the Earl of St Austell had made a new will in favour of his bride, Miranda. And further that Lettice James was his fancy piece.'

Elizabeth burst out laughing. 'And to think of the face she pulled when she learned that I was giving birth to bastards! What a beastly woman. But it does not surprise me regarding Montague. He bedded with anything wearing a skirt. Tell me, did he sign the will?'

'Indeed he did. A will that could be, perhaps, overturned by his grandchildren at some later date.'

'What about Geoffrey James?'

'I think we can count him out. He may be weak, he may behave like a total idiot, but I don't think he is capable of murder.'

The Marchesa nodded. 'And what of the two assassins? Any further clues to their identities?'

'None. Nothing at all. Not a trace.'

'They're probably back in London by now.'

'I wonder,' answered the Apothecary slowly. 'I just wonder.'

Twenty-Three

By now it was high summer and an exultant day. John rose early, even before Elizabeth was awake, and going to the stables borrowed the most placid mount that she had in her collection. Then he rode through the burgeoning landscape at his own pace, taking in the beauty of his surroundings, glad to leave behind him the ugliness of recent events.

Beyond the estate lay long slopes of meadowland with, here and there, groups of tall trees. It seemed as if every bird in Christendom sat in their branches singing sweet praises to the deep blue sky. John reined in his horse and breathed deeply. The scents of lavender and sage, comfrey and wild roses filled his nostrils. There were harebells in the grass and in the shadow of the trees cattle stood at ease, munching the vegetation in solemn majesty. Looking up, he saw the sky arching above him, enormous, with tiny wisps of cloud flowing through the blue like the waves of a placid sea. John wished at that moment that he could stay like this, halfway between the earth and heaven, for ever, and be worried no more with healing the sick and investigating brutal, ugly death.

John's horse moved abruptly, shying at a rabbit that ran close to its hoofs, and slowly he returned from his idyll and knew that he must continue on through the glorious landscape which looked as if it had just been painted by the imagination of a poet. Almost reluctantly he kicked his heels into the horse's flank and headed towards the sea, whose wild seductive song soon came within earshot.

It had been his intention to call on Lady Imogen, acting in his role as an apothecary, and offer her some soothing medicaments to ease her pain. For now, since the revelation of Lord St Austell's new will, she was high on his list of suspects. But much to his surprise he spied her limping along in the gardens down towards the restless ocean. She was thin and looked pallid, devoid of animation, yet there was something of determination in the way she made her way slowly downhill despite her recent wounding.

John dismounted and secured his horse to the branch of a tree. Then he approached her silently. She had not seen him and leapt with fright when he said, 'Good morning, my Lady.'

'Oh,' she said, her hand clutched to her breast, 'I didn't see you. Have we been introduced?'

'I was at your grandfather's wedding feast but I am afraid we have not had a formal introduction.' He bowed low. 'Allow me to present myself. My name is John Rawlings and I am currently staying with the Lady Elizabeth di Lorenzi.'

She looked down her nose as only daughters of ancient lineage can do. 'Oh, I see.'

'May I converse with you for a moment?'

She hesitated, on the brink of refusing, but eventually said, 'Very well. If you insist.'

'I must offer my profound condolences on the loss of your grandfather, Madam. His death must have affected you very deeply.'

Very subtly her eyes changed, a hint of something glinting momentarily in the iris. 'It was a great tragedy.'

'Indeed. Together with the loss of your child . . .'

He hadn't anticipated the lashing sting as her hand came out and slapped him hard on the face.

He gingerly fingered his chin. 'I suppose I deserved that for being so blunt. But the fact is that I am an apothecary and therefore am more observant of these things than are most men. I humbly beg your pardon if I offended you.'

She stood silently, clearly weighing him up, then suddenly a voice called from beneath them. 'Imogen, I'm here.'

They both turned, equally surprised, to see a robust countryman with a handsome ruddy face and big square shoulders, dressed like a keeper with gaiters on his legs and the inevitable dog walking at his heels, coming towards them from the lower path which led down to the sea. He spoke before either of them could say a word.

'Oh my little love, what terrible thing has happened to thee?'

The Apothecary could have clapped his hands. For all her snobbish attitude and high-and-mighty manners, Lady Imogen

was clearly having an affair of the heart with a man who could
not have been more simple and homespun if he had tried. No
wonder she had wept at the loss of her child. It had been her
lover's and nothing to do with her horrible grandfather after all.

The man turned his honest face towards Milady. 'I am so
sorry to have disturbed you, Lady Imogen,' he said, giving an
over-formal bow. 'I had no idea you were going to meet
anyone. I shall be on my way.'

'No, Jessamy. I have much to say to you. Please stay.'

'Well, ain't you going to introduce me to your friend?'

'I don't really know the man.'

'Then I'll do so myself,' Jessamy answered with an air of
slight reproof. He held out a hand, hard with years of outdoor
living. 'How do you do, Sir. I'm Jessamy Gill.'

John bowed again. 'John Rawlings, Apothecary, of Shug
Lane, Piccadilly, London.'

Suddenly, in the face of this honest and artless man, Imogen's
possibilities as a suspect seemed lessened. She turned to the
Apothecary, her expression stricken.

'Please, Mr Rawlings, I beg you to tell no one at Lady
Sidmouth's home of my liaison with Jessamy. Nor mention it
to anyone on the St Austell estate. My brothers would make
my life intolerable if they knew.'

'I realize I am aiming above my station, Sir, but I plan to
give Imogen a good, clean life away from all the filth that her
family engendered.'

'I am sure of that. But tell me, how did you two meet?'

''Twas here at Lady Sidmouth's place. I work for her. I'm the
estate keeper. Lady Imogen was out walking one day . . . but I
am speaking out of turn. She'll tell you the tale if she wants to.'

John was amazed at the man's frankness, his lack of inhibi-
tion, his total fearlessness in the face of someone who could
be classified as the enemy. The keeper saw his look and inter-
preted it correctly.

'Provided you keep quiet about what you've just seen, Sir,
I plan to marry Imogen just as soon as she has recovered her
strength. Then let her brothers come looking for us. I'm man
enough to deal with them.'

And the Apothecary suddenly felt tremendously glad that

the Earl's granddaughter who – if rumour be true – had been brought up in degradation by a disgusting old man, had found this remarkable countryman with whom to share the rest of her days. Looking at them, he was suddenly seized by a warning premonition.

'I think you should go now before they find out. I realize that you have only just risen from your sickbed, Lady Imogen, but if I were in your shoes I would lie very low at Jessamy's cottage for a day or two before moving on.'

She spoke. 'But Lady Sidmouth is caring for me. What will she say?'

'She is a woman of the world and will accept it. Society might be shocked but surely you made that choice long ago when you decided to go away with your lover.'

'He's right, Imogen. I wouldn't put it past your brothers to kidnap you and take you back to Cornwall with them. I think you have a simple decision to make, my dear.'

'Can you leave Devon and get another position?' John asked him.

'Aye. There's a big estate in Dorset that is looking for a gamekeeper. I know 'cos my cousin wrote me about it. We could make our way there, Imogen.'

She hesitated, on the brink of changing her entire way of life. Then made her choice by laying one of her hands in Jessamy's.

'I'll go with you, if I may.'

'Well done,' said John. 'Now leave before something bad happens.'

Having said their farewells they set off down the cliff path and the Apothecary watched their departing backs. Then an idea occurred to him.

'Do you two ever walk on that tiny beach below late at night?' he called.

Jessamy turned. 'Never, Sir. It be far too dangerous. There are very tricky tides down there and you could easily get cut off and drown.'

John gave them a parting salute and they both waved, then disappeared from his view as they went round a bend in the cliffs.

So who *was* behind the murders, he thought, as he walked slowly back to where his horse was tethered and climbed, with some difficulty, into the saddle.

He rode, reasonably fast for him, straight to Exeter, heading for the house of Tobias Miller. But the Constable was out. Very thirsty by now and extremely saddle sore, John made his way to the nearest tavern and ran into that rather strange boy, Herman Cushen, who had evidently made some money gambling for he was buying drinks for everyone present which, admittedly, were fairly few.

'Ah ha, Mr Rawlings,' he said loudly. 'So we meet again. Have a drink, do.'

'Well, thank you very much. I'll have a pint of ale.'

It was duly poured and John sat down at a table opposite the unlovely youth.

'I saw your mother in the cathedral the other day. She seemed very upset by the recent slaughter at the wedding feast. I felt quite sorry for her.'

Hermann waved an airy hand. 'Oh, she takes things very hard, does my mother. I think she suffers from what you might call a nervous disposition.'

'I'm very sorry to hear that. An infusion of the leaves of the lime tree might be very helpful. Go to any apothecary and ask him to make you some up. It really should help her.'

Herman looked vague. 'I'll tell her,' he answered with singular lack of interest. 'Anyway, how have you been keeping? You were at the Earl of St Austell's wedding, weren't you?'

'Yes, I was. The only way I escaped was by playing dead.'

The young man grinned, showing his gappy teeth. 'That was very smart. How did the old women react to that?'

It occurred to John that the gossip must have spread throughout the length and breadth of the county.

'They weren't old women,' he said. 'They were in fact men dressed up.'

Herman looked thoroughly startled. 'How do you know that?'

'It was obvious. Besides, a friend of mine heard one of them speak. It was a man's voice he heard.'

Herman went slightly green about the gills, a highly unbecoming look with his carrot-coloured hair. 'Well, I am surprised. I truly am.' He sank his ale down in one draught and then looked at the Apothecary appealingly.

'Would you like another drink?'

'Yes, I would rather. Your news has come as something of a shock. I was led to believe that two old women carried out the raid.'

'No, they were definitely men, believe me.'

Herman relapsed into silence and John was left to consider how sore his behind was and how he was dreading the ride home.

'So will you be staying in Exeter for a while?' he asked the brooding young man sitting opposite him.

'I really don't know. It is all very much in the air at the moment. I might go back to London ahead of my parents. See something of the town.'

'Of course. It must get boring, particularly if you don't have many friends round here.'

'Oh I have friends,' Hermann said with a sly grin.

John, assuming that the boy frequented brothels, merely nodded and smiled.

Quarter of an hour later he took his leave, suddenly weary and tired, and he and his horse plodded back to Elizabeth's great house just as dusk was falling and the brilliant sun was lowering itself against the darkening landscape. Yet all the way there something nagged at the back of his mind, some indefinable something that he could not bring to the surface. Try as he would he could not grasp the unseen thread nor make any sense of his jumbled thoughts. But when he finally entered the house, having walked round from the stables, he realized that Elizabeth had company and had to put any such meanderings out of his head.

Twenty-Four

John rushed upstairs to change into night clothes, and put on something rather dark and fetching before going into the salon to see who had arrived. And there, draped decorously on a chaise with Freddy Warwick sitting as close to her as was decent, was Miss Cordelia Clarke. Of the redoubtable Lady Bournemouth there was no sign. Crossing over to Miss Clarke, John kissed her hand and gave a formal bow to Freddy, who had risen to his feet and returned the compliment.

'My dear,' he said, going to Elizabeth and kissing her on the cheek.

'Where have you been?' she asked, not crossly but curiously. 'You've been out since first light. What have you been up to?'

'Nothing much,' John answered, not wishing to discuss the love life of Lady Imogen in front of anyone else. 'I went into Exeter and bumped into someone I met on a coach. I just felt like riding,' he added apologetically.

'How unlike you,' Elizabeth answered with just a hint of acidity. 'Well, now that you're here, Cordelia has something to tell you.'

'Yes indeed,' echoed Freddy, gazing at her adoringly.

Cordelia gave a little shiver as she embarked on her tale. 'It happened on that terrible night of the wedding feast. Fortunately I was sitting next to Freddy . . .' They exchanged tender glances. '. . . and he pulled me to the floor when he saw what was happening. We lay very still but kept our eyes open and thus I had a fine view of everything that happened at that level. I was terrified when a pair of feet came and stood right in front of me. I thought I was going to be killed.'

'I would have protected you,' said Freddy nobly.

'Anyway, as I was watching, the crone's garter came undone and slipped right off. When he had moved away I stretched my arm out and found it, then I hid it underneath me. And here it is.'

And with a triumphant move of her hand she reached into her reticule and produced the garter.

'May I see it?' asked John.

Cordelia handed him a decorative ribbon, definitely past its best and decidedly grubby but quite clearly a man's. It had woven into it a slogan, namely 'A toast to King George'. John passed it to Elizabeth.

'Would you wear this?'

'No, I would not. It is male attire.'

John took it back and stared at it. Whoever had owned the shabby thing had murdered – or assisted therein – three people. If it could help him hunt the killer down . . . But John knew that was impossible. It would be preposterous for him to even imagine going about such a task. Nonetheless, he turned to Cordelia and said, 'May I keep this?'

'Of course. It was meant for you and the Constable.'

'I know he will be delighted to see it.'

'He called here while you were out,' Elizabeth said. 'I think he is rather anxious to see you.'

'If you have nothing planned for tomorrow, sweetheart, I shall ride into Exeter and catch up with him.'

Elizabeth's vivid gaze caught his and he saw humour flicker in the depths of her eyes. 'I have several females coming to admire the twins. I think it would be as well if you were elsewhere, my dear. But do please borrow the small coach. I could not bear to think of the pain to your posterior if you continue to ride.'

Everybody laughed, including John, though inwardly he felt somewhat slighted. He felt he had ridden well and as a town dweller had acted more like a countryman, directing his mount with a firm hand. But he suffered in silence and was glad when Freddy changed the subject.

'I have asked Cordelia to marry me, and she has been kind enough to accept my proposal.'

'Whenever did you ask?' said Elizabeth. 'I thought Lady Bournemouth had Cordelia under night-and-day protection.'

'She was somewhat *hors de combat* after the shootings and I stole a moment whilst in Lady Sidmouth's garden.'

John thought to himself that Lady Sidmouth's house seemed

to be a magnet for all kinds of emotions, whether they be for good or ill. And his mind went off at a tangent, grasping at straws, trying to form some sort of pattern yet still unable to see one.

Elizabeth rose and kissed the betrothed pair and asked all kinds of questions about where and when the wedding would be but he could barely move, so caught up in his thoughts and angry with himself that he had so many threads which refused obstinately to weave into a pattern. Vaguely he heard Freddy's voice.

'I have decided to study medicine, Madam. I am going to follow in my father's footsteps.'

John came back to earth. 'Very good. And where are you going to do this?'

'At St Bartholomew's Hospital. As you know it is one of the oldest, and my father studied there.'

'We are going to live in London and be very poor but very happy,' said Cordelia in a jolly voice.

John shook the young man's hand. 'Well done, both of you. My warmest congratulations, Sir.' He turned to Cordelia. 'And for you, young lady, a kiss on the cheek if I may be so forward.'

'You certainly may.'

Elizabeth signalled a footman and champagne was brought in and consumed with much gaiety but John could not join in wholeheartedly. Something was niggling in his mind. Something indefinable yet which he knew had already been said to him.

Later, when the guests had gone and Elizabeth had retired for the night, he sat up late and thought the whole thing through. At the wedding of Miranda Tremayne to the old rake the Earl of St Austell, two hired assassins, dressed as women, had made their way into the wedding feast and deliberately shot three people, all of whom had strong connections with the Earl. Mrs Lettice James had been his mistress but an indiscreet one. A born gossip, a woman who could keep nothing to herself but must talk about it through the town. Then there had been Mr Alan Meakin, a country solicitor who had worked closely with St Austell and had drawn up his recent will – duly signed and perfectly legal – leaving a considerable fortune to his bride.

Felicity had been wounded and John had had a bullet fly right past him. Other people had suffered minor injuries – but Sir Clovelly Lovell had heard the assassins say 'Not him', or words to that effect, which suggested some local knowledge.

So who stood to gain? Possibly the Earl's three grandchildren: Viscount Falmouth, Lord George and Lady Imogen. Mr James, if he had loved his spouse sufficiently, might have wiped out her lover. The Meakins? John could only discount them when he thought of the heavily pregnant wife. Perhaps Felicity, who might have willingly received a wound in order to cover some enormous secret. And lastly Miranda, the weeping widow, still confined to her room and refusing to eat.

A fine list of suspects indeed. But of them all the biggest question mark hung over Lady Imogen herself. Just supposing that the child she had carried *had* been fathered incestuously by her grandfather and that she was using Jessamy Gill as a means of escaping from her sordid past? What then?

For once the Apothecary felt quite ill-at-ease thinking about the whole sorry affair. He had instinctively believed Mr James and Imogen – but supposing the reaction of his gut had been incorrect? And what about Mrs Cushen, who had been nervously praying in Exeter Cathedral? Why had she been at the wedding? What connection did she have with the Earl of St Austell?

John stepped outside to get a breath of night air, wandering into the garden and gazing up at the full moon, feeling oppressed by his wretched thoughts. Yet as he did so he felt rather than heard another presence. Somebody was watching him, he felt certain of it.

'Who's there?' he called.

Nobody answered and nothing stirred but still he felt that pair of unseen eyes observing him. He was in no mood to investigate. Turning on his heel John sprinted back into the house and locked the doors behind him.

The next day he took the small coach to Exeter, leaving at an ungodly hour and for once forgoing his breakfast. He knew that the Constable rose early to start his investigations and was determined to catch him before he began his official duties.

Consequently he knocked on the door of the small house close to The Blackamore's Head at eight o'clock in the morning. A girl with a mop and pail answered and showed him into a small parlour where Toby was just finishing his breakfast. He looked up in some surprise.

'Oh, it's you, Mr Rawlings. I have a great deal to tell you.'

'And I you. Furthermore an important piece of evidence was handed to me last night and I wanted to give it into your safekeeping.'

So saying, John removed the garter from where it lay in tissue paper and handed it to Toby, who examined it and gave it back.

'And where did this come from, Sir?'

'Could I have a slice of your toast and then I'll tell you?'

'By all means, Sir. Would you like some tea?'

John nodded, his mouth already full and the girl trudged in and took the teapot away.

'Mrs Miller not here?' John asked.

'Alas, no. She died of an infection last winter. I am a widower, I fear.'

'I am very sorry to hear that. You must miss her terribly. Now, if you've no objection, I would like to tell you about that garter.'

And John proceeded to fill Toby in with absolutely everything that had taken place since they had last been together. It was a long tale and during it John managed several cups of beverage and consumed a fairly hearty breakfast. He wound up by presenting his list of suspects and his reasons for being doubtful about Geoffrey James and Lady Imogen.

Toby nodded thoughtfully. 'Well, the Coroner opened his inquest on the Earl and closed it again till a later date. Likewise with the other two. But he has released the bodies for burial so we are going to have three funerals on our hands.'

'I see. So where are the late Earl's grandsons at the moment?'

'Staying at an inn in Exeter. They plan to wait here until they can accompany their grandfather's body back to Cornwall.'

'Any news of them?'

'Well, apparently Lord George is going round getting into fights and falling fantastically drunk. The new Earl, however, having recovered from his little fit which I believe I engendered, has seen the light and is now being very solicitous of those who were injured. He has called repeatedly at Lady Sidmouth's asking to see both his grandstepmother – the weeping Miranda – and Felicity. The former won't have anything to do with him; the latter, who is allowed up to sit in a chair, has received him on several occasions. The last time he asked to see his sister and was told she was out. He did not like that at all.'

'Has he discovered that she has gone?'

'Not yet, I believe. Lady Sidmouth is either being very tactful or very clever. I know she has set in train her own enquiries but the fact that her estate manager has also disappeared is a powerful piece of evidence.'

'Does she realize they have gone off together?'

'Yes, and I think she secretly thinks good luck to them.'

'Do you feel as I do that Lady Imogen was not behind the crime?' John asked.

'Funnily enough, her choice of husband has swayed me in her favour. You see, I know Jessamy Gill. He used to come into Exeter every so often and he is the salt of the earth, as the saying goes. If he thought she was mixed up in anything like a murder plot he would have turned his back on her for ever.'

'And what about Geoffrey James?'

'Him I am not so certain of. I'll take your word that he's mad with grief but I would need a little more convincing than that.'

'I forgot to tell you that someone was in the garden last night, silently watching me.'

A gleam shone in Toby's eyes. 'Who was it? Do you know?'

'No, I saw nobody, but I was just aware of his – or her – presence.'

'Perhaps it was your imagination.'

'Perhaps,' answered John.

They formulated a plan that they would divide the suspects between them. John would take Miranda, the ex Viscount – now the new Earl, Lord George and Mrs Cushen. Constable Miller would take Geoffrey James, Lady Imogen and Felicity.

'What if Imogen has already left for Dorset?'

'Then I'll follow her there, Sir. I am very thorough, you can believe me.'

'And the owner of that soiled and grubby garter?'

'He'll have gone back to whichever rathole he emerged from long since.'

'Perhaps not. Perhaps he was an Exeter man.'

'In that case, his days are numbered.'

John had started the day so early that it was only eleven o'clock when he emerged from his conference with the Constable. Feeling that the net must be tightening around who actually masterminded the killings, he decided that time was of the essence and ordered the coachman to go first to the apothecary's shop in the main thoroughfare then on to Sidmouth House. An hour later he bowed his way into Lady Sidmouth's receiving room and asked if he might visit Miranda as he had several healing medicaments he wanted to give her.

'She won't see you, John. She allows no one near her.'

'Then what does she do with herself all day?'

'She lies on her bed of grief and weeps.'

'Well that's not going to do her a lot of good. I mean she'll have to come out for the funeral.'

'And she'll have to journey to Cornwall for it. I mean sooner or later she will have to take up residence in her new home. Perhaps you will be able to persuade her.'

'I can only try.'

But a gentle knocking on the door of Miranda's bedroom only elicited a shout of, 'Go away. Have you no pity?'

John disguised his voice, speaking falsetto and trying desperately to sound like a maid. 'The apothecary has called with various medicines for you, Milady. They will strengthen you for your journey to Cornwall.'

There was an audible sigh and then Miranda said, 'Oh very well.'

A second or two later a key turned in the lock and there she stood.

To say that she looked ghastly was an understatement; in fact she looked fit to die herself. Her skin had the fearful pallor of death, her eyes were like black stones set shockingly in a casing of marble, her blonde hair stuck on end and was unbrushed and uncared for. She wore a soiled and grubby nightdress. Beneath her eyes were streaks where tears had poured down her unwashed cheeks. They widened now as she took in who was standing before her.

'What are you doing here?' she asked in an indignant tone.

'I am an apothecary and I have brought you some of my simples,' he said, his face ingenuous, his manner sweet.

'Oh, very well, come in. Shall I call a maid for chaperone?'

He affected a slightly offended air. 'There will be no need for that. I merely wish to administer my potions.'

'I'm sorry, I did not mean to offend you. My grief is so great that I do not always know what I am saying.'

She turned away from him and disconsolately walked towards the bed on which she threw herself and indulged in a fresh bout of weeping. John hastily gave her his handkerchief, removing the other – completely sodden.

'I would like a little light if you have no objection,' he said, and before she could say a word crossed to the two large windows and pulled back the curtains.

The glare of daylight fell on Miranda's ravaged features and John swiftly unpacked the parcel that the apothecary in High Street, Exeter, had prepared for him. There was autumn Gentian for debility, together with white Dittany for hysteria. To restore Miranda's ailing appetite the apothecary had also added an infusion of Polypody sweetened with honey.

'Well, here we are then,' said John in a jolly tone.

Miranda looked up from the pillow and a deep sob raked her body. 'What are they?'

'Physics to make you better. Try some, there's a good girl. Remember that you will have to get up soon and journey to your new home. You won't want the servants to see you looking worn out with weeping, will you?'

'No,' she said a little reluctantly.

'Then drink these down please, Countess St Austell. I promise they will restore you to full health.'

Miranda perked up at that, saying in a wistful voice, 'Yes, I am the Countess. Not even dear Montague's terrible death can take that away from me.'

'It most certainly can't,' John answered.

He looked at her, assuming his honest citizen face. 'Tell me, Miranda, did you truly love your husband?'

A beatific smile lit her saddened features. 'Oh, Mr Rawlings, I loved him with all my heart.'

Twenty-Five

Unable to visit Felicity who was out in the garden with Mr Perkins, the surgeon who had removed the bullet from her arm, John decided to go for a solitary stroll and see if he could sort out his thoughts. Almost without knowing it his feet were leading him away from the formal gardens and downhill to the bottom of the cliff where he could just see a small strip of sand appearing. He waited, perched on rather an uncomfortable rock until slowly the beach became visible, then he ventured downwards.

Removing his shoes and stockings and putting them into his pocket, he walked on the strand barefoot, feeling the sand rising between his toes and squirming his feet in the dampness beneath him. The beach was no more than a quarter of a mile long but was quite endearing, being a pretty shape, lying beneath one of those marvellous red cliffs that abound in Devon but which, John believed, could fall at any time giving no more notice than a distant rumble. With its rapidly running tides leaving interesting rock pools, and its white wavelets beating on the shore, John thought it delightful, suitable indeed for lovers to walk upon – until he recalled Jessamy's warning that it wasn't safe and one could easily get cut off.

Remembering this he turned to go, but as he did so his eye was caught by some netting high up on the cliff face, snagged on a promontory that was sticking out. Reaching up, he pulled it down and immediately a lump of the cliff fell at his feet and sent a cloud of powdery dust straight into his eyes. Reaching into his pocket he pulled out an extremely moist handkerchief and rubbed it over his face. But it did little good and the Apothecary, choking and with very poor vision, struggled along to the man-made path that led away and climbed a small distance up. Then he turned and looked down.

A floating cloud of red dust was still making its way along the shoreline and he could see that some more rocks had fallen.

He thought then that it was just not the swift tides that made the beach a potential death trap. It was the red rock above. So attractive to look at, but a potential killer if it were to fall in any great amount.

Suddenly tired and with his eyes still stinging, the Apothecary plodded his way to the top and went straight to the small coach that Elizabeth had lent him for the day. And it wasn't until he was ten minutes into the journey that his vision recovered and he was able to look at the piece of netting that had caused all the problems.

It was much finer that he had thought, made of a delicate lace, and though rendered somewhat the worse for being exposed to the elements for some time, it could still be seen as ebony in shade. John's mind immediately leapt to the couple that Felicity had seen, walking on the beach in the moonlight, the woman's scarf blowing up and up. He felt that if he knew who they were he would somehow come closer to finding the murderers and the ruthless mind lying behind them.

'Where are we going, Sir?' asked the coachman, on seeing John recover himself somewhat.

'To Lady Elizabeth's house, please, Samuel. I have something to discuss with her.'

'Very good, Sir.'

And they trotted off in the direction of Withycombe House.

But a quiet chat with the Marchesa was not to be his fate that day. He arrived home to find that not only had she gone out but that she had taken the twins and nursery maids with her. Other than for the servants the house was empty. John wandered restlessly from room to room, his mind buzzing with thought, unable to settle. And then, almost like an answer to a prayer, the knocker on the front door banged impatiently. The Apothecary immediately settled himself in the Blue Drawing Room, crossed one negligent leg over the other, and picked up a copy of *The Gentleman's Magazine*. A footman came in importantly.

'The Earl of St Austell and Lord George Beauvoir have called, Mr Rawlings.'

'Then show them in. And Harper, bring in some sherry if you would be so good.'

For once Lord George was completely sober and walked in

looking immaculate, his clothes, though black, fitting him like
a glove, showing off his broad shoulders and small waist, his
trousers tight and quite the latest fashion. His dark hair was
tied in a queue, his eyes audacious and bright. The new Earl,
by contrast, was dressed in sombre hues and looked slightly
vacant behind his spectacles, reminding John vividly of how
he had appeared when he had walked into his shop all that
time ago.

The Apothecary stood up and made a bow. 'Gentlemen,
how may I help you?'

They bowed back, the Earl's quite courteous, George's as if
he couldn't care a fig.

'We wondered if you had any idea as to the whereabouts
of our sister. Seems she walked out of Lady Sidmouth's house
and hasn't been seen since.'

If there was one thing in which the Apothecary excelled,
it was lying. He immediately assumed his concerned face.
'Good heavens! When was this?'

'Yesterday, apparently. We wondered if she had come here
to talk to Lady Elizabeth.'

'Not that I know of. We spent a quiet night at home last
evening and nobody called. Unless she came this morning but,
if so, she would have found everybody out.'

At that moment the sherry arrived and John asked the servant
to send in the head footman, who came hurrying in a short
while later.

'You wished to see me, Sir?'

'Yes, Miller, has the Lady Imogen Beauvoir called at the
house in the last twenty-four hours?'

'No, Sir. I have not seen sight nor sound of her.'

'Thank you.'

John turned to the two men and spread his hands helplessly.
'I'm sorry. I can't help you.'

'Fact is,' said George, downing his sherry in one and holding
out his glass for a refill, 'that she's in an odd state of mind.
Apparently she miscarried after that ghastly shooting debacle.
If I could find the father I'd string the bastard up,' he added
under his breath. 'And now she's wandered off with a wound
in her leg. Frankly we're afraid she might do something silly.'

'I see,' said John, fingering his chin. 'Have you informed the Constable?'

'God's wounds,' answered George, flinging himself to his feet. 'Do you think we'd advertise the fact that our sister has been behaving like some common slut?'

What an arrant hypocrite, the Apothecary thought. George had sired more bastards than there were ships in the navy – well, almost – and if they had known that their grandfather was abusing the poor wretched girl they should both have been shot. Which set him to wonder why they hadn't been.

He looked helpless, an expression which he had virtually mastered. 'I would suggest that in my professional opinion she has had a complete mental collapse and gone back to the only home she knows, your estate in Cornwall. In fact, the more I think about it the more certain I become. That is where you will find Lady Imogen, gentlemen.'

The two young noblemen looked at one another.

'What do you think, Maurice?' George asked.

'It's a reasonable conclusion.'

'Do you want me to go down ahead and have a look?'

'May as well. I've got to accompany Father's coffin back for the funeral.'

'So have I. But I'm sure that I can get to Cornwall and back by the day after tomorrow.'

John adopted a long face. 'Is that when the obsequies are being held?'

'Yes. You and Lady Elizabeth are both invited to attend, of course.'

'Thank you,' he answered with much solemnity.

After they had left the room John collapsed back in a comfortable chair and thought about what a fantastic liar he had become. He had kept up his performance in front of the brothers with not even a flicker in the eyes to tell them that he sincerely hoped that Imogen and Jessamy had left the county and were safely in Dorset and starting a new life together.

The sound of the carriage wheels starting up lifted him out of his thoughts and he crossed to the window to watch them go. The coach was just turning in the sweep and he noticed that it had the coat of arms of the St Austells emblazoned on the door. He studied the design with interest, noticing the spread black eagle, its red tongue protruding from its beak, its glaring eye staring fiercely, the words *Loyal A Mort* written above. He thought about the brothers who had just left him and wondered whether either of them could live up to the family motto. He very much doubted it.

Going upstairs to change, John carefully laid the piece of black lace he had found on the bed for Elizabeth to see. Then fishing deeper in his pocket he found the handkerchief he had used to wipe his eyes after a piece of the red cliff had fallen. It was absolutely sodden and had gone a rusty colour, so badly in fact that John threw it in a bowl of water which he had used to wash himself before he changed. Then he set about putting on night clothes, this time a rich damson shade. From the window he heard a carriage coming up the drive and saw Elizabeth's dark head, a little bundle seated on each knee, her arms tightly round them, protecting and loving them. He knew in that moment that he could never separate the Marchesa from her sons. That she would fight like a tigress to keep them by her side and that he would have to settle for that. A thought that made him sad and melancholy. But he put those feelings away as he descended the stairs to greet her.

After the twins had been bathed and put to bed – a ritual which John enjoyed very much – he and Elizabeth dined informally at a small table in the parlour. Over the meal he proceeded to tell her of the day's events. She listened attentively and eventually said, 'There is something there of interest but I can't for the life of me tell you what. I shall sleep on it and hope it comes to me.'

'I can't tell you how frightening it was when the cliff began to crumble.'

Elizabeth looked thoughtful. 'Some of the red cliffs round here can be very dangerous indeed.'

But John could tell by the way that she spoke that her mind was on something else. He knew to question her would not be productive. That she must think whatever it was through and tell him when she had assimilated her ideas. He put his hand over hers.

'I love you, you know that.'

'Yes I do. And I love you, you strange little apothecary.'

The meal finished, they went for a stroll in the gardens.

'The new Earl and brother George called here today.'

'Oh? What did they want?'

'To know if either of us knew the whereabouts of their sister.'

'And?'

'I lied magnificently. Said she had probably become deranged and gone back to Cornwall.'

'And all the time she is safely in her lover's arms.'

'Let it be hoped that they have packed up and gone.' John turned to look at her. 'I am fairly certain that Lady Sidmouth has guessed the truth.'

'She will never breathe a word, I can assure you of that. She is one of the strangest looking yet kindest people I know. And that is why I have asked her to be godmother to the twins.'

'They are to be christened?'

'As soon as this monstrous murder is cleared up.'

'And who will you have as the other godmother?'

'Why,' said Elizabeth, 'your daughter Rose of course.'

Twenty-Six

The Marchesa had gone for an early morning ride and John ate his breakfast alone, thinking that there was one person left on the list of people he had promised to see, and that was Mrs Cushen. When he had last met Tobias Miller the Constable had informed him of her address – or rather that of the distant relation whom she had come to Exeter to comfort – and the Apothecary was just wondering whether his hindquarters could put up with another day in the saddle, when Elizabeth walked in.

She was fresh from her morning ride, her skin glowing, her eyes clear, smelling of the sweet countryside. John knew with a lurch of his heart that whatever happened in the future he would never forget this moment of seeing her like a goddess of spring, of loving her, of knowing that unless the situation changed he must one day inevitably part from her.

She smiled at him. 'You are looking wistful. Why?'

'I was just wondering if my behind could take another ride to Exeter.'

'You want to borrow the coach again? Well, you can. I intend to stay at home today and mull over all the things you have told me and come to some sort of conclusion. Because there is a thread there and I am determined to find it.'

'Sweetheart, I could not manage without you.'

'I think you could do so perfectly well. Remember that you are now running a successful company as well as having your own shop. I think you are a highly competent young man.'

'Mrs Fortune is in charge of the business. She is the one you should call competent.'

'And is she beautiful as well as clever?'

'Not beautiful exactly but certainly very attractive.'

'Ah ha,' answered the Marchesa, and would say no more.

An hour later the coach set off for Exeter and proceeded at a fine pace towards the city. Somewhat to the Apothecary's

surprise it stopped at a small house immediately opposite the
great cathedral and the coachman called down, 'This is the place,
Sir.'

Thinking that the lady would not have far to go to pray,
John climbed out and knocked at the door, then waited. There
was no reply and he was just about to turn away when he
heard the shuffle of feet and the bolts being drawn back. The
door opened an inch or two and there stood Mr Cushen,
looking bleary and still in his night attire.

'Oh forgive me, Sir,' the Apothecary said pleasantly. 'I just
came to call to see how you were. But I can tell this is an
inconvenient time so I shall leave you in peace.'

The door opened wider and Mr Cushen answered, 'Oh no,
come in, I beg you. You are an apothecary are you not? My
wife has fallen into an hysterical fit and I have been awake all
night trying to calm her. Please see if you can do anything.
Anything at all.'

John turned to the coachman and said, 'If you don't mind
hurrying to the herbalist's shop on High Street and getting
him to give you an infusion of Black Horehound. Then when
you come back, knock at the front door and I will answer.'

The carriage rattled away and John followed Mr Cushen up
the stairs and into a dark and rather smelly bedroom where
Mrs Cushen lay twisting and moaning on a narrow bed.

'My dear Madam,' said John, crouching down beside her.
'What is the matter? How can I help you?'

'You can find Herman for me,' she said, then suddenly started
to cry, throwing herself at John and weeping all over his shirt.

'Millicent, hush dear,' said Mr Cushen from the doorway, a
strange urgency in his tone.

John glanced at him and saw how white the poor man was.
Indeed he looked the very image of a being in an agony of
spirit.

'Why, where has he gone?' he asked.

'Oh, he's drinking in some low tavern with his equally low
associates. But he has been away several days now.'

A tremendous flash of inspiration came to the Apothecary
as he recalled the red hair he had gathered in Wildtor Grange.
He produced from his pocket the awful shabby garter that

Cordelia had picked up at the wedding feast and which Toby Miller had decided it would be better if John kept.

'I came to return him this,' he said, opening his palm to display it.

The parents stared at it, then Mr Cushen said, 'Yes, that's his. He lost it somewhere or other. Where did you find it?'

As quick as a lightning flash the whole picture came into focus. Herman's sudden wealth in the inn the other day, his fondness for the Exeter low-life. Surely one of them had been hired by the person behind the killings and had asked Herman to help him execute the plan. Into John's pictorial memory he flashed a picture of the two old women who had come in to kill the company and, sure enough, the shorter of the two had been the same build as young Mr Cushen.

'It was found at the wedding feast,' he said in a calm voice. 'It was dropped by one of the murderers.'

His father looked at John blearily. 'No, he . . .'

'The truth will always come out,' said the Apothecary, cutting across him, not unkindly. 'And I think you half-guessed it already. Didn't you?'

'What will happen to him?' whispered his mother.

'I don't know,' answered John.

But he did. Herman would be tried by judge and jury and the sentence of death would be passed on him. And that would be the end of his wretched life. But behind him would be left two people who would grieve for the rest of their days on earth and who did not deserve to endure such a terrible punishment.

There was a knocking at the door and the coachman returned with the physick. John administered both poor wretches with a strong measure and finally left the house when they began to calm down. Then he went into the cathedral and offered up a prayer for the salvation of Herman's soul and for some sort of peace to be granted to his parents. Then he went in search of the Constable.

Tobias Miller was at home, sitting at his desk, going through a sheaf of papers. He removed his pair of little glasses, perched on the bridge of his nose, and listened quietly while John recounted the scene at the house where the hysterical Mrs Cushen was residing. The he sprang to his feet.

'So that's who the killer is. Well, we'll find him. He's bound to be in one of the alehouses drinking his brains into a pulp.'

He rapidly made a list of all the inns of Exeter and divided it in half.

'Here you are, Sir. You can start at The Dragon by the East Gate and work your way through.'

'What shall I do if I see him?'

'Nothing. Engage him in conversation, keep him talking. If I don't find him first I'll follow in your footsteps. In any event we meet in The Blackamore's Head in an hour's time. Better still, bring him with you if you possibly can. He strikes me as a rather solitary young man from what you've said. I think he'll be glad of a companion to drink with.'

The Dragon revealed nobody and so turned out the rest of John's perambulations through the drinking houses of town. Eventually he turned up at The Blackamore's Head, slightly weary, and glad to see that the Constable had got there before him.

'Did you find him?' John asked.

'Yes, I found him alright.'

'What happened?'

'I arrested him on the spot and he threw a punch at me that caught me completely unawares and felled me to the ground. Then he and his companion – a long, lanky fellow who was probably the other old lady that you saw – took off at a rate of knots. I ran after them, I raised a hue and cry, other people joined in, but the villains were too fast for any of us. They completely vanished in one of the many alleyways. I have failed in my duty, Mr Rawlings, and to prove it I've got an eye that will shine like a shitten barn door tomorrow.'

John leaned forward and saw that the Constable's eye was indeed turning a dramatic shade of black. 'Come on. We'll go to the apothecary in High Street. He can put some leaves on that that will greatly reduce the swelling.'

'But what about our two runaways?'

'Leave them for the time being. We can put up posters and somebody will turn them in, you may depend on it.'

John had never been more glad in his life than to have a coach at his disposal. He took the ailing Tobias to the apothecary, saw his wound dressed, escorted him home and then set off to join Elizabeth who was waiting for him, sitting thoughtfully in the Blue Room and staring into space. She jumped up as soon as she heard him come in and said, 'There is much I need to discuss with you, my dear.'

'Sweetheart, can we talk over dinner? I have had nothing to eat since breakfast.'

'It will have to be supper. I dined at four with Lady Sidmouth.'

'Did you now? And did she have much of interest to say?'

'Very much so. I promise to tell you all about it as soon as we are seated.'

John hurried upstairs to change and on the way looked into the nursery. In two cots on either side of the room his sons lay sleeping peacefully. First he leant over James, noticing the details of his face which seemed to be changing. The Apothecary wondered then when exactly it was that babies grow. Every day you saw them and they looked the same, but all the time they were doing that miraculous thing – getting bigger.

He crossed over to Jasper, identical in every way to his brother. How sweet he was, a flicker of light coming through a gap in the drawn curtains illuminating the sweep of dark lashes against the creamy skin. The hair, curly like the Apothecary's but midnight black like Elizabeth's, was already growing thickly on his head. John tiptoed back to James and saw that he, too, had a good dark thatch. His eyes filled with tears and he wished for the millionth time that everything could have been different and that Elizabeth had been a woman who wished for a settled life. But then would he have loved her as much and as powerfully as he did? He knew the answer as he left the room, shutting the door quietly behind him.

She was playing with the piece of veiling and looking thoughtful as he came downstairs ten minutes later. She smiled up at him.

'Would you like some sherry?' she asked.

'Indeed I would.'

He sat down opposite her and told her, quite quietly, that Herman Cushen had been one of the two assassins and that though the Constable had given chase he had lost him in the back streets of Exeter.

'But why him?' Elizabeth said. 'What grudge could he possibly bear against the people he shot?'

'None whatsoever. It was done for money, pure and simple. He probably fell in with some of the rough element of local society and one of them was hired by the murderer to go and do the dirty deed at the wedding breakfast. That is my reading of the situation.'

'So who is the murderer?'

'At the moment your guess is as good as mine. Tell me, what did Lady Sidmouth have to say?'

'She is extremely worried about the sick women in her house. Mostly she is concerned about Felicity, who is recovering somewhat slowly from the bullet wound she received. The surgeon from town calls every day to tend to her.'

John pulled an amused face and one of his mobile brows was raised.

'Exactly what I was thinking,' Elizabeth continued with a laugh. 'She is slightly less concerned about Miranda, however, who has started to eat again, but very little. The Countess insists on keeping to her room and cries at least once an hour. Very loudly.'

'What a bore! Did she have anything else to say?'

'Only that Felicity feels that she is in some sort of danger but cannot explain why. Her high fever has made her delusional and prone to strange fears.'

'I see,' said John, and put his chin on his fingers. 'I should like to go and visit her tomorrow.'

'I don't see why you shouldn't. After all, you can call in a professional capacity.'

'I should not like to interfere with Mr Perkins,' he said, grinning once more.

'I am sure that Mr Perkins can take care of himself,' Elizabeth answered innocently.

Twenty-Seven

All night long the thought that Felicity believed herself in danger came back to haunt him. Was it merely that she had a high fever and was suffering from delusions or was it something more sinister? Whatever the problem, John slept little and rose early and made his way to the stables as soon as he had eaten. There he once more borrowed the good-natured horse – as good natured as any horse can be, that is – and heaved himself into the saddle. Then he set off for Sidmouth House as quickly as it was possible for him to go.

He had taken the precaution of packing a small bag with medicaments for fever and ague: Cinquefoil, for he had been taught in his training that one leaf cures a quotidian, three a tertian and four a quartan ague; Angelica, otherwise known as Tansies or Heart's Ease, and a pleasant plant to use; and Centaury, which when boiled and rubbed into the skin was a sure-fire cure for everything from sciatica to voiding the dead birth.

Halfway to Lady Sidmouth's residence it started to rain, heavily, with large drops that penetrated his clothes and soaked him to the underwear. Cursing his luck, the Apothecary rode gamely on but eventually drew to a halt beneath a large tree, to give the animal a rest as much as anything. Dismounting, he drew the horse into the deep shade and there waited for a quarter of an hour.

While he stood in silence he saw a horseman go by. Admiring the man's easy athleticism, John stared with envy as he passed close to them. He did not have a full glimpse of the face for the man had his collar turned up and his hat pulled down, but he could have sworn it was Lord George. So he was back from Cornwall empty handed. In the excitement of yesterday John had forgotten to ask Tobias Miller if he had any news of the whereabouts of Imogen, and now he found himself truly hoping that she had made her escape from that rotten family.

John's thoughts turned to Maurice, the new Earl. He was

certainly a strange character, not exactly unlikeable but nebu-
lous. He seemed to have a different skin for every occasion,
rather like a chameleon. The Apothecary was in the unusual
position of still being uncertain as to what the man was really
about. He wondered then if Maurice had something of a yen
for Felicity, but discounted that idea in favour of George. The
handsome rake would have married anyone who could have
brought him a good dowry and he had certainly had his
eye roving around at the wedding feast. But that had been
before the two assassins came in and killed three people.

The rain had eased off and John remounted again with some
difficulty and continued on his journey. A quarter of an hour
later the splendid house came into view and John walked the
horse round to the stables so that he might arrive on foot.
Feeling like a tatterdemalion, his hat slopping water, a bag in
his hand like a salesman, his coat drenched through, the
Apothecary rang the bell.

A footman answered and looked at him in some surprise.
'Mr Rawlings, isn't it?'

'Yes, I have called to see Miss Felicity.'

'If you would wait in the small receiving room, Sir, I shall
send for Lady Sidmouth.'

John handed the footman his damp coat and hat and waited
in silence for a moment or two before the door was flung
open and Lady Sidmouth stood there. To say she was much
changed would have been too great an exaggeration, but she
was most certainly haggard and looked on the point of collapse.
So much so that the Apothecary hurried forward and helped
her into a chair.

'My dear Lady Sidmouth,' he said, 'sit down, do. You look
quite weary.'

'I am wrung out, my friend. I am so worried about my
daughter. She seems to be getting weaker by the minute, despite
the ministrations of Mr Perkins. He cannot understand it. The
wound is healing up but in her body she is deteriorating. Oh
dear.'

And she flung the apron she always wore over her face so
that John could not see her tears. He waited a moment then
said, 'Would you like me to have a look at her?'

The apron lowered. 'Indeed I would, Sir.'

'Tell me, is she eating?'

'All she will have is a little vegetable soup. She spends most of her time sleeping.'

'But a few days ago she was in the garden with Mr Perkins.'

'That is the strangeness of her complaint. It is as if some awful thing is attacking her. But heaven alone knows what when she is tucked safely in her room night and day.'

'And how is Miranda coping with life?'

'Oh, she's calming down a little. After all, she has to follow her husband's coffin to Cornwall tomorrow. The funeral is to be held there in two days' time.'

'And Lady Imogen will not be present, I take it.'

She shot him a look and in her eyes he read everything. Lady Sidmouth knew exactly what had happened and, indeed, condoned it.

'No, Sir, she will not be there. She has eloped with my estate manager and they have both gone to Dorset to start a new life. By now I believe they will be man and wife and there is nothing anybody can do to her any more.'

'May I ask you a straight question?'

'Of course.'

'Was she abused by her grandfather?'

'Most certainly. In a way those masquerading old women did her an enormous favour.'

'Do you think she was behind the killings?'

Lady Sidmouth gave him a startled look. 'Good gracious, no. She was desperately unhappy but she would never have stooped that low.'

'Then who was it? Do you know?'

She shook her head. 'No, Mr Rawlings, I don't. It has puzzled me ever since. Who would want to see the Earl dead other than Imogen? And she is quite definitely innocent.'

John ran his mind over the other two victims but would have sworn an oath that neither of them had a family that could have done such a thing as murder.

He looked at Lady Sidmouth with a great deal of sympathy. 'Let me talk to Felicity. Perhaps I will be able to glean something of what this mysterious ailment is.'

He found her lying in a great bed with the curtains drawn darkly round it. As John pulled them back she let out a little mew and put her hand over her eyes. He turned back to Lady Sidmouth.

'Would you mind leaving us alone for a few minutes? She will be perfectly safe with me.'

'I know that. Just find out what ails her, John. I am begging you to do so.'

'Don't worry. I shall do my absolute best.'

Sitting on the bed he leant closely to Felicity who was whispering something in a tired, small voice.

'John?'

'Yes, I'm here. Tell me what is happening. Why do you feel threatened?'

'I saw them again.'

'Who?'

'The couple on the beach. And they saw me, I know it. They both looked up and they noticed me gazing at them from the top of the cliff. And after that my condition got worse and worse. Oh John, I think I am dying.'

'Nonsense. Once I've found out what is going wrong I shall have you up and about in no time. Now, tell me. When was it you last saw them?'

'Three nights ago. Mr Perkins had called that evening and I felt neither too ill nor too tired to sleep after he had gone. So I wandered the length of the garden to where the grasses sweep down to the sea and then I stopped in my tracks. Because there on the beach below they were walking in the twilight, arms around each other, her scarf blowing up in the wind.'

'Did you recognize them?'

'No, not really.'

'What does that mean?'

'I would hate to name the wrong person and get them into trouble.'

John decided to leave that for the moment and asked instead, 'What have you been eating?'

'Only a mouthful or two of soup. And a little sip of wine.'

'Who brings it to you?'

'The maids. It comes from the kitchen.'

'I see. Promise me you will let nothing pass your lips until I return. I need to talk to your mother urgently.'

Felicity brought her mouth close to his ear. 'Is someone trying to poison me?'

'I don't know yet but I am about to find out.'

So saying he pulled the curtains back round her bed and hastened downstairs to where Lady Sidmouth stood anxiously waiting.

'What is the matter with her? Were you able to discover anything?'

'I think someone is giving her poison. If you take my advice, Lady Sidmouth, I would bundle her into a nightrail and several shawls and send her in a carriage to Lady Elizabeth's. There we can be absolutely sure of the food that is given her and she can recuperate in peace.'

The heavy-lidded eyes of the little woman opened wide. 'Poisoned, you say? But who could be doing such a thing? The staff are all devoted to her.'

He looked at her very seriously. 'I cannot say at this stage and, besides, I would prefer not to do so until I am absolutely sure. But please take my advice and get her away as soon as possible.'

'You are certain Elizabeth will not object?'

'She most certainly will do as I ask when I tell her how urgent the matter is.'

Just as Lady Sidmouth was going upstairs Miranda was coming down, escorted by her personal maid to whose arm the Countess clung for dear life. She was skeletally thin and her little-girl face had now slimmed down to one of high cheekbones and beauteous curves. Her eyes were dry but were red-rimmed through many hours of weeping. She was dressed entirely in black, her widow's weeds hanging round her face. She jumped when she saw John below, watching her.

'Oh, Mr Rawlings, how you startled me. This is my first time downstairs since that terrible tragedy. I am awaiting the arrival of my grandstepsons who will escort me back to Cornwall and my new life.' She wrung her hands. 'But what life could there possibly be after the death of him I loved most?'

She gazed downwards as she negotiated the last few steps and John noticed that tears threatened to spring up once more.

'Madam, calm yourself, I beg you,' he said. 'You must make a resolve to act with an iron will in the presence of all the servants and relatives who will, no doubt, be examining you with a mixture of love and envy. Chin up, I implore you.'

She turned on him a look which contained a myriad of emotions. 'It is easy for you to speak, Sir. You live comfortably with your mistress and your little bastards, but I have to carry my sorrow with me to the grave.'

'You forget that it is only a temporary home for me. I must leave for London soon and then what of my mistress and my bastards, as you choose to call them? I shall miss them as cruelly as if they had died, believe me.'

She softened. 'I am sorry that I said that. You speak the truth indeed. We all have problems to bear in one way or another.'

But John did not answer. Instead he was looking out of the window to where Maurice – who had presumably met George on the way – was greeting his brother. 'I think your grand-stepsons have arrived for you now. My, how handsome they are in their black.'

The new Earl and, or so he supposed, the new Viscount Falmouth, formerly Lord George, were alighting from their horses and making their way to the front door, hats clutched firmly in hands.

As they came into the hall the Apothecary gave them a respectful bow. 'Good day, your Lordships.'

'Good day, Mr Rawlings,' answered Maurice. 'Have you anything to keep up the spirits with you? We have a long journey to Cornwall ahead of us and are quite in the dumps at the thought of it.'

Miranda spoke. 'It is all very well for you to talk, my Lord. It is I who bear the greatest burden of grief.'

They rushed to her side, making sounds of sympathy, leading her away to a nearby room where they seated her on a sofa and rang the bell for brandy. John kept an eye on them through the partially open door which he gently closed shut as he saw Felicity being carried in the arms of a stout-hearted footman towards the front entrance. Outside a carriage was drawn up, presumably summoned by Lady Sidmouth.

'I'll follow in ten minutes,' he whispered to the fragile girl. 'Don't worry. Elizabeth will look after you.'

She opened her eyes, nodded, then closed them again. Lady Sidmouth let out a subdued sob and John put his arm round her shoulders. And at that moment George opened the door and walked into the hall.

'Well, stap me, if it isn't Felicity. Where are you going to my pretty maid?'

John gave a disarming smile. 'She is going to stay with Lady Elizabeth for a few days. Recuperation and all that.'

'Good heavens. I didn't realize she was that ill. I'll go and tell the others. They'll want to bid her farewell.'

'I'd rather you didn't do that, my Lord. It is imperative that the patient is kept absolutely quiet. If you would be so good.'

The new Viscount stood nonplussed, his handsome face suddenly rather silly and slack-jawed.

'Thank you so much, my Lord,' John continued airily.

Lady Sidmouth picked up the theme and said, 'Thank you, George. I knew you would understand.'

And his lordship could do nothing but stand there and gape as the others swept out through the front door into the dreary afternoon.

Twenty-Eight

As soon as John had seen Felicity into the coach and given instructions to the driver, he hurried round to Lady Sidmouth's kitchens where he gave great attention to a pile of unpeeled parsnips. Having sniffed and gingerly tasted the end of one of them he seemed satisfied, and without saying farewell to anyone he left by the kitchen door and rode home.

He passed the coach bearing Felicity on the way back and rode as hard as he was able to get to Elizabeth before the sick girl. He made it with about ten minutes to spare, and during that time blurted out his suspicions about poisoning and his findings in Lady Sidmouth's kitchen.

'And are you certain?' demanded the Marchesa.

'Positive. It was common Water Hemlock lying innocently amongst the parsnips, which it closely resembles.'

'But anyone could have eaten it.'

'Precisely. I think we are dealing with an evil and diseased mind here. Now please look after Felicity. I would advise you to sleep in the same room in case anyone tries to get at her in the night. I realize that it might sound melodramatic but there is a cruel poisoner at work.'

Elizabeth gave him a direct look. 'Is this the same person who organized the killings at the wedding feast?'

'Very probably, yes.'

'Then I shall arm myself accordingly.'

Even in these dire circumstances the Apothecary could not help but smile. The Marchesa might be one of the most beautiful, most seductive women ever born, but she was also one of the toughest and strongest street fighters he had come across in his entire life. He knew that she had personally practically annihilated the gang of dross who called themselves The Angels. They had based their doings on The Mohocks of London and had terrorized the poor people of Exeter who hardly dared leave their homes after dark. And they had also killed her son by making him an opium addict. The Marchesa's revenge had been swift and terrible but just. The Society of Angels no longer existed.

'Thank you,' he said. 'And now I've one more favour to ask.'

Before he could say another word she smiled and said, 'Can you borrow the coach tonight?'

'The words saddle-sore were invented for me alone, I fear.'

'You are nothing but a wretched Londoner, my good man.'

'Nonsense, Madam, many people in town are fine riders. I just do not happen to be one of them.'

She laughed and threw her arms around him and he was surrounded by the heady smell of lilac and woodruff and all the wonderful scents of her.

'I shall always love you, you know that.'

'Yes, I know,' she answered.

And they were just about to exchange a longed-for embrace when the sounds of the carriage approaching came from outside and broke their wonderful moment.

The day cleared of rain and began to fade gently. Tiny white clouds that looked as if they had been puffed out by putti bounced across the sky and the moon rose in a thin sliver. The air was gentle after the earlier rain, soft as a cat's fur, and all the birds in the world began to sing their hymn to the coming night. John had always loved this time of day; dusk, twilight, eventide. He had loved it in all seasons: when the ground beneath his feet had been hard and crisp with snow and the night had been lit by a thousand crystal stars; when warm summer breezes had wooed his senses with the smell of flowers and somewhere in the distance a nightingale had started to sing; in autumn when he had kicked around the crisp, colourful leaves and had felt the first chill of coldness in the air; in the spring, that outrageous season, that despite the cool weather allowed the camellia to come into bud and delighted the eye with the first glimpse of snowdrops and crocuses.

And now, as the carriage passed through the countryside and he saw that the evening was still light and early summer was lying over the land, his thoughts flew away for a moment and he forgot the reason for his secret journey back to Sidmouth

House. But they came back to him with a jolt as he knocked on the ceiling with his stick and called to the coachman to pull up.

They had stopped short of the property in the woods that centuries before had been partially cleared by labourers so that a fine house and glorious gardens could be built. The house had now been replaced and the gardens modernized, but, though thinned out, the woods still stood, and it was through the depths of these that the Apothecary silently made his way until the song of the sea sounded softly in his ears and he knew that he was going in the right direction.

No one knew of this evening visit except John, who was determined to take a look at the beach and see if the lovers who walked on it would reappear, because he now had an opinion as to who they might be. Silently he proceeded through the hushed atmosphere of the trees until at last he emerged on to the open cliffland where the gardens of Sidmouth House went down to the lawns that, in turn, swept down to the sea.

Twilight had come while he had been walking amongst the shady trees, and what he saw now was a small beach far below him lit by the crescent moon and the first stars. The sun was just spreading its last rays to the west, adding a warmth to the scene, and showing him that the beach was empty.

John paused, turning his head slightly. It seemed to him that there was a slight noise behind him as if somebody – or something – was following in his footsteps. But when he swivelled round there was nobody to be seen and he thought he had imagined it. Silently, he began to descend the tiny path that led down to the shore. And then the two figures appeared out of nowhere, giving John a fright, though he realized immediately afterwards that they must have been in a cave and had just stepped out. They were walking away from him, entwined round each other, clearly very much in love.

Quiet as a stalking cat John made his way down the path until it died away and he had to scramble over a couple of small rocks to reach the sand below. The couple were still walking away from him but he could see them clearly, their outlines etched blackly against the white of the waves and the glow of the sand. He knew who they were even before they turned

around. He had suspected her, in particular, for some time. Of
the identity of the man he had not been so certain. They turned
at the beach's end and John sank down behind a rock. Yet again
he thought he heard a noise behind him but was in no position
to wheel round and look. Very distantly he could hear snatches
of the couple's conversation.

'. . . you have borne it all well, my love.'

'. . . the thought of you . . .'

'. . . you have earned that fortune . . .'

'. . . lecherous old beast. Indeed I earned it!'

From somewhere above a pebble fell to the ground, hitting
a rock as it landed and making a definite noise. The couple
froze, as did John.

'What was that?' said the woman, looking up towards the cliff.

'I don't know,' the man answered. 'We'd better be going.
We must look suitably pious for the journey to Cornwall.'

'I am dreading it. I shall hate people staring at me and then
acting as I shall have to do.'

They had walked forward as they spoke and John could now
see their faces distinctly. He decided that the element of surprise
would be best and reared up from behind his rock in an
alarming manner. So much so that the woman gave an hysterical
scream.

'You bastard . . .' said the man.

But he never got any further. From somewhere above all
their heads a person unseen fired what sounded like a blunderbuss straight into the cliff wall. There was a great stirring
as if the whole mighty cliff was going to come down, and as
John scrambled for the path a vast chunk of it fell. The
Apothecary stood frozen to the spot, staring at the place where
a moment before the lovers had walked. Now all was still
except for the choking cloud of dust that was spreading over
the beach and being carried ever onwards by the west wind.

For a moment he literally could not move, his muscles
seized by a type of catalepsy. Then he sprinted up the path
as fast as was possible, aware all the time that there was someone
running ahead of him, scurrying for all they were worth. But
catching them was not his objective. Instead he wanted to
raise men from the Big House. He ran on, aware that the

sound in front of him had ceased, that whoever it was had gone off by some other route.

It was the time of day when all the candles were being lit and John stopped for a moment, panting like a dog, and thought yet again what a truly beautiful house it was. Enchanting, indeed. Even the fact that there had been a terrible murder within its walls could do nothing to defile its loveliness.

Knocking on the front door he explained breathlessly that there had been an accident on the beach below and that he needed men to help him shift the rockfall. Lady Sidmouth had retired for the night with a bad megrim so was not on hand to organize anything – but still they came. Footmen without their jackets and wigs, kitchen boys, gardeners, even the young lad whose sole duty was to clean the boots and shoes. But when they reached the top of the cliff and gazed downwards they saw to their horror that there was no beach. That most capricious of tides had suddenly changed and covered every bit of sand. The red cliff loomed silently, a scar on its face the only sign that there had been a rockfall at all.

The Apothecary looked downwards and knew that justice had been done by that oldest and most unpredictable element of all – the relentless ocean.

Twenty-Nine

They retrieved the bodies from the sea, brought in by the fishermen and landed on the beach at the small fishing village of Sidmouth. They lay side-by-side on the sand, the Countess of St Austell and her grandstepson Maurice, the Earl, before they were pitched on to a cart and driven off for identification. That was before they began to swell up and were almost impossible to identify by even their nearest and dearest. It was Lord George who was finally called in and, to his shame, he was forced to rush outside and lean against a wall gasping in great mouthfuls of air to stop himself from being sick. It was said, afterwards, that at that moment he grew up for the first time. For he was now the Earl of St Austell, and with the title went the responsibility of a great estate in Cornwall and the care of all the people who worked on and for it. Strangely, he became a responsible citizen and a much-respected man. But the last grim act he performed was to lay his grandfather and brother in the family crypt alone. For Miranda Tremayne, the new Countess, was placed in a solitary grave at the very edge of the churchyard and was never visited, being left desolate and friendless for time immemorial.

The principal players in the drama that had taken place at the wedding feast had foregathered in the home of Tobias Miller, by his express invitation. Nearly all of them were present: John and Elizabeth, Freddy Warwick, Felicity, accompanied by the large and amiable Mr Perkins, Geoffrey James and rather surprisingly the small and perky Miss Melissa Meakin who had stopped crying and was smiling a greeting at all the new company. To round off the people present – in every sense of the word – was dear old Sir Clovelly Lovell.

The Constable was in high humour, having started on the liquid refreshment some time before his guests arrived. And once the entire assemblage had foregathered and were standing somewhat tightly in his small reception room, glasses in hand, a definitely festive atmosphere could be sensed. Eventually, though, he called for them to be seated and pointed out that some of the gentlemen would have to sit on the floor as there were insufficient chairs to go round. Sir Clovelly, however, was offered a spacious chair to himself which he took with much joviality.

Tobias Miller cleared his throat.

'Ladies and gentlemen, good evening to you all and I thank you for coming to hear the resolution of the mystery. First let me say that the two killers, one Herman Cushen and his assistant – an unknown thug alas – have escaped custody and are still free. Reward posters have been printed and circulated but so far with little response. But the minds behind the hiring of the assassins have been identified.'

'Well who, jolly well, was it?' demanded Sir Clovelly, nibbling a savoury with much relish.

'It was a heinous crime because it was the Earl of St Austell's elder grandson and heir, Viscount Falmouth.'

John interrupted. 'I think I must say in the poor creature's defence that he was probably put up to the idea by a scheming woman.'

'That's as may be, but it is still a terrible thing to commit patricide,' answered Felicity, while affable Mr Perkins said, 'Hear, hear.'

'Whatever your views, with which I heartily concur, I would like to ask Mr Rawlings to tell us how he got on to it. How he solved the crime.'

John stood up, wishing he had something less ephemeral to say to them.

'It was a combination of things really. First of all Felicity told me the strange story of the couple she had seen from the cliff top. They were walking on the beach, a man and a woman, and the woman's scarf was blowing up in the wind. Some time later I went down to the beach and found a piece of black veiling snagged on a rock. It had obviously been torn from the garment that the woman had worn. I felt fairly certain that it belonged to Miranda. It set me thinking,' John continued. 'In the first instance I felt she was marrying the elderly Earl for the money and position. But quite honestly it never occurred to me that she wanted it all. That she wanted a young and attractive lover into the bargain.'

'I suppose,' said Miss Meakin reflectively, 'that she and the Viscount must have met and fallen in love and the plot must have grown out of their relationship. But why kill my poor brother? What had he done wrong?'

Tobias Miller spoke up. 'I have thought and thought about the murder of him and Mrs James, and do you know I think that their deaths were accidental.'

There was a stunned silence. 'What do you mean?' somebody asked.

'That to cover up the fact that they had one target and one target alone, the assassins shot a few people at random.'

'I concur with that,' said Sir Clovelly from the depths of his chair. 'I heard one of the killers mutter to the other not to shoot me. I suppose they must have known me from somewhere.'

'I agree they were firing at random,' put in John. 'They aimed at me all right, but I played dead and the bullet whistled past my ear.'

The volatile Miss Meakin burst into tears and Geoffrey James lent her his handkerchief.

'I too lost someone dear. My wife. She was a gossip and a fiercesome flirt, but she could be good company when she chose.'

John looked at him, relieved beyond measure that he had cured the poor man of his terrible problem and that his flatulence was now under control.

'But what about the attempt to poison me?' asked Felicity. 'Why did they do that?'

The Apothecary replied. 'Did you tell your mother about the couple you saw on the beach?'

'Yes, I did.'

'Then I can only presume that Miranda overheard you and decided she must silence you. How she got hold of the Water Hemlock I do not know. She presumably went out one evening before her midnight tryst and gathered some. It is the easiest poison in the world to use. It grows everywhere and it is just a question of recognizing it. When you pull it up its root is almost identical to a parsnip. Which is where I found four of them, mixed with the vegetables in the kitchens of Sidmouth House.'

'But Mama could have eaten some! Or the servants!'

'I can only think by that time Miranda had become a little crazed.'

'If she was not crazed from the start,' said Elizabeth. 'I thought she was just a gushing little fool but I did not realize that that act hid a scheming and devious personality.'

'But she was my cousin,' poor Felicity cried out miserably.

Nobody answered, but Mr Perkins put his arm round her and comforted her in such a cheerful way that everybody felt much better for seeing them.

'May I refill anyone's glass?' asked Tobias Miller.

There was a general chorus of affirmative replies, during which Sir Clovelly beckoned John to his side.

'There's one thing I can't understand, and that is the attitude of Maurice. I always thought of him as a regular chap, a good-hearted soul. Can you throw any light on it? Do you think it was him who watched you in the darkness of your garden?'

John shook his head. 'More probably George. He seemed to be the one to do the dirty work. As for Maurice, he always struck me as something of a cipher, a nonentity. I think that deep-down he would have been quite happy studying his books but then that state of mind came upon him which compelled him – like all mankind – to go to any lengths to achieve his objective. In other words, he fell in love.'

'Ah ha, *cherchez la femme*, eh?'

'Precisely, *cherchez la femme.*'

'Even to the extent of killing his own grandfather?'

'Yes. But what an evil creature the Earl was. Corrupt, dissolute, depraved. Miranda probably incited Maurice by describing St Austell's sexual proclivities.'

'Perish the thought. And what about that handkerchief you found in Wildtor Grange?'

John shook his head. 'I don't know. It seemed to me that it bore theatrical make-up of some kind.'

But there was no time for further conversation because Toby was clearing his throat importantly.

'There is one additional mystery of which I am about to tell you. If anyone can throw light on it I would appreciate it if you spoke up. It's just that on the night of the cliff fall which killed the Earl and the Countess, Mr Rawlings said there was somebody following him. And that is not all. A shot was fired over his head and into the cliff face thus causing the fatal occurrence. Now, do any of you know who this might have been?'

There was a stunned silence as – other than for Elizabeth – this was the first that anyone had heard of such a thing. Toby looked from face to face.

'I see that it means nothing to any of you. And I take it you can all account for yourselves on that evening? To remind you, it was the night before the bodies were washed up. Mr James?'

'I was with friends and we played cards till midnight. They can vouch for me.'

'Miss Meakin?'

'I was at home with poor Alan's widow and babe. Besides, Clyst St Agnes is quite a good way away from Lady Sidmouth's house. I would not risk prowling about at night on my own.'

'I can speak for Felicity and myself. I sat beside her bed all night, occasionally dozing. But the slightest sound would have awakened me.'

Mr Perkins flushed crimson and announced, 'I'm afraid that I was alone so nobody can verify my story. But I can assure you that the last thing I would have contemplated would be wandering along the cliff top in the late evening. I could have tripped and fallen below, you see.'

John spoke up. 'I am sure, Toby, that it was nothing more than a common poacher. I think he fired at the cliffs to put me off the scent.'

Tobias was silent for a long moment, then said, 'What you are saying makes total sense, of course. But still there is a question in my mind.'

John adopted his sincere look. 'Well, that's your line of business, Constable. To question everything.'

'Yes, I suppose you are right.' He turned to his assembled guests. 'And that, ladies and gentlemen, concludes my business.

May you all have a safe journey home. And to those of you that live in Exeter I hope to see you again soon. On a purely social occasion, let me hasten to assure you.'

They all trooped out into the night and waited while carriages and chairs were sent for. Tobias drew John to one side.

'Lady Imogen is well.'

'You have seen her?

'Yes, I tracked them down. She is a happily married woman.'

'Thank God for that,' said John, and really meant every word he said.

The first carriages arrived and the guests parted company, all as merry as if they had been at a wedding feast and thankful that the whole wretched affair could finally be put behind them.

However, later that night, it being about nine of the clock, John slipped out of the house and took a carriage to Sidmouth House where, fortunately, he caught Milady just preparing to go upstairs to her bedroom.

'Madam, I apologize for calling so late and so unexpectedly, but tomorrow I leave for London and I have something to give to you before I go.'

Lady Sidmouth peered at him. 'Oh, and what might that be?'

'This.'

And the Apothecary fished from his pocket a dried-out handkerchief which he handed to her. It was the one he had retrieved covered with tears and red dust and thrown into a basin of water, the one he had taken from Miranda. She looked at it.

'I am afraid I don't quite understand.'

'Miranda gave it me. Well, not exactly gave. I lent her one of my own and she passed me this one in its place. I thought you might like to have it.'

'Why?'

'Because she was your ward and your cousin.'

'Miranda has thankfully gone to her grave and has slipped into my memory. I want nothing further to remind me of her.'

'I understand,' John answered.

'Do you?'

'Perfectly. Do you ever walk on the cliffs in the evening?'

She caught his eye, hers heavy lidded and secretive, his bright blue, and they regarded one another silently for a moment or two. 'Sometimes,' she said eventually.

'Then you will know how dangerous it is to stroll on the tiny beach below.'

'I would never dream of going there,' she said. 'You see there could be a rockfall at any time.'

'The slightest noise could trigger one off,' said John, still staring at her.

'Indeed it could.' She sighed and stood up. 'And now, Mr Rawlings, you will have to forgive me. I really am very tired and I was on my way to bed when you called.'

She turned and threw the handkerchief on to the fire and John watched as the St Austell insignia went up in flames.

'Goodbye,' said Lady Sidmouth, but whether she was talking to him or to Miranda he was never afterwards sure.

'Goodnight, Madam,' he answered, and bowed his way out.

The last piece of the puzzle had just slipped into place. The Apothecary closed his eyes and let the carriage take him home.

Thirty

He rose early the next morning and went to say farewell to his twin sons. Jasper and James smiled and made happy sounds as he walked into the nursery and it came home to him in all its bitterness how evil a crime it was for a grandson to strike down his own grandparent. For that which had given life to be struck down by the very life it had helped to create. At that moment the Apothecary felt that he was tasting a bitter gall and had to hold back tears, not only for himself but for all who had been so terribly affected by the deaths at the wedding feast.

His trunk had been taken to the carriage as day broke and now there was nothing left for him to do but say goodbye to Elizabeth. But she slept deeply, as heavily as if she had been drugged, and did not stir when he kissed her and murmured his parting words. A madness came upon him then and he walked away from her, down the stairs and out of the front door with never a backward glance. And it wasn't until he was on the flying coach fast bound for London that he realized he had treated her as badly as Maurice Beauvoir had his grand-father, the Earl of St Austell.

A mood of terrible introspection came upon him then, and did not leave him until he was dropped at the Gloucester Coffee House and felt the cobbles of the capital beneath his feet once more. There some of his confidence returned and he decided that somehow he would be able to persuade Elizabeth to give up their boys for at least part of the year. For despite all his adventures and all his passion for investigating criminal misdeeds, John Rawlings was at heart a family man who liked nothing better than having his children around him in a comfortable dwelling.

His house at Number Two, Nassau Street was quiet when he entered it and he called out, 'Is anybody home?'

In answer he heard a door upstairs open, and looking up he saw a young lady descending at a dignified pace to greet him. He could not believe his eyes. The school had certainly done all that was required of it. His daughter Rose had an elegance and grace he would not have believed possible. Then her eyes widened and she spoilt the illusion by jumping the last few stairs and straight into his arms.

'Pappy, oh my dear Papa. You have come back at last.'

'Back to my own best girl.' He paused. 'Why are you not at school?'

'I am on holiday, Sir, and Grandfather and I thought we would come to town to pursue cultural events.'

John's spirits were rising by the minute.

'And where is the redoubtable gentleman?'

'Here, my son, here.'

And with a snatch of powder and a whiff of scent that most famous of all the beaux in London came slowly into the hall from the library.

'Damme, but it's good to see you, John.'

'And damn me, Sir, if it isn't good to be back.'

And with that the trio kissed one another and made their way into the garden.

Historical Note

As my regular readers and visitors to my website – www.derynlake. com – will know, John Rawlings, Apothecary, really lived. He was born circa 1731, though his actual parentage has been difficult to trace. He was made Free of the Worshipful Society of Apothecaries on 13 March, 1755, giving his address as 2, Nassau Street, Soho. This links him with H.D. Rawlings Ltd. who were based at the same address over a hundred years later. Rawlings were spruce and ginger beer manufacturers and in later years made soda and tonic waters. Their ancient soda syphons can still be found, these days usually in antique shops.

Sir John Fielding was another real life person. He was the half-brother of Henry Fielding, author and magistrate, who created the colourful character of Tom Jones and also set in motion what was later to become the Metropolitan Police Force, referred to in Henry and John's day as the Beak Runners, beak being the cant word for magistrate. Approximately one hundred years later they became known as the Bow Street Runners. And that is how it all began.

Lightning Source UK Ltd.
Milton Keynes UK
UKOW03f1900290517

302257UK00001B/23/P